Randall Bush

WELCOME TO SPECTARA...

...an iridescent Shade world created by currents of light flowing through a river bed of thick darkness. When Asdin, the Sacred Star of Frozen Light, is stolen, ancient evils and a series of catastrophic horrors are unleashed on the Shade inhabitants of Zil-Kenøth. A hostile political takeover and merciless executions follow.

Forced to flee his homeland, Sindle begins an adventure filled with peril, marvelous discovery, and the prospect of true love. But hope for personal fulfillment is frustrated when Sindle learns that he and his companions must run a desperate race against time to save Spectara from growing sinister forces that threaten its total annihilation.

Art Work and Cover Design by
Chris Bush
and Chris Berry

THE QUEST FOR ASDIN

BY

RANDALL BUSH

Pristine Publishers Inc. U.S.A.

Library of Congress Control Number 2003110557

Bush, Randall, date 1953-
The Quest for Asdin

ISBN 0-9716633-2-7

Published by Pristine Publishers Inc. USA

Printed in the USA

Dedicated to
David G. Parnell

A Companion of
the Quest

Acknowledgments

This fantasy fiction novel is the culmination of about twenty-five years of ideas and creative efforts that would have been impossible apart from the many friends and family members that have patiently read my manuscripts through the years. David Parnell, to whom this book is dedicated, is a longtime friend who was part of a fantasy-writing group that we began back in 1978. At that time, J. R. R. Tolkien's, *The Lord of the Rings*, had made a comeback, and we were inspired to write in that genre. Later, I did graduate work in the field of symbolism and myth and soon was directed by Professors Bert Dominy and John Kiwiet at Southwestern Seminary to examine the work of the late F. W. Dillistone, Canon Emeritus of Liverpool Cathedral and Fellow Emeritus of Oriel College, Oxford. Through him, I came to know the work of such notable authorities on the subject of symbolism as Carl Jung, Ernst Cassirer, Suzanne Langer, Paul Ricoeur, and Mircea Eliade. Echoes of their ideas abound in this work. But it was Dillistone's thought that would ultimately provide the world view in which this novel and its characters would develop and take shape.

Of the many friends who have read this novel in its earlier stages, I would mention a former colleague, Wallace Roark, who called it "the most color-conscious book" he had ever read. My wife, Cynthia; my late grandmother, Earlene Myers; my mother, Iris Morris; her friends, Peggy Johnson and Sandy Muphree; my sisters, Susan McMillian and Donna Vandries; my sister-in-law, Loyce Walker; a former administrative assistant, Brenda O'Dell; and a former Oxford friend, Duerdra Green, provided criticisms and suggestions that through the years have helped with details of character development and story line. My talented son, Chris Bush, and Mr. Chris Berry provided the basis of the cover art. More recently, my daughter, Laura Bush; my colleague, Hal Poe; and my students, Alaina Kraus and Spencer Lowery have helped with editing. Spencer, an avid fan of the fantasy genre, gave me valuable suggestions regarding how one should calculate time in Spectara. I thank Spencer for generously giving me an A- on the draft of the novel he read, and I hope that my efforts to incorporate his suggestions will help bring my grade up. To all the aforementioned individuals, I offer my heartfelt thanks.

Contents

PROLOGUE

In a time before the present universe came to be, there was a world flowing through space and time much like a river running through its bed. The water of this river was light, and its bed was darkness. This world did not orbit a star as planets normally do. Although in one sense it could be said to have "revolved" around a star, it did not do so according to laws of motion as our world understands them. Rather, the force that propelled this world forward was a pure source of eternal and uncreated light, and the force that held this world in its orbit–if it could be called an orbit– was a belief about a star known as Asdin. Indeed, it is this belief that also holds in its orbit the story to be told through the pages of this book.

To describe this world is nigh impossible, for though the river of light just described carried particles of darkness along its current as water carries sediment, it did at the same time continually separate out into every color of the spectrum. It was, in fact, this peculiarity that was partly responsible for the name given to this iridescent world, the name *Spectara*.

However, the world in which this story unfolds was also called Spectara because a species of specter beings known as Shades inhabited its lands. Unlike human beings, Shades did not possess physical bodies as such. They possessed instead shadow shells– not hard, but soft–animated by souls known as *scintillas*. Scintillas could best be described as living entities of fluid light that possessed intelligence, will, and emotion.

Though Shades, like humans, could distinguish between light and darkness, their world had neither sun nor moon, nor day nor night. Yet the Shades did have a daily rhythm of life, called a *lumen*, by which they measured time. Lumen-flow was their way of referring to the period of time in which light increased, while lumen-ebb described the period in which light decreased. Thus, early lumen-flow referred to dawn; mid-lumen-flow, to mid-morning;

high lumen-flow, to noon; early lumen-ebb, to mid-afternoon; mid-lumen-ebb, to evening; low lumen-ebb, to night; and so forth. However, daytime was never as bright as our day, nor night, quite as dark as our night. Low lumen-ebb was an extended period of twilight, the dimmest part of which was reserved for sleep. Ten lumens made a lumnus-week; fifty lumens, a lumnus-month; and five-hundred lumens, a lumnus-year. The seasons in Spectara–if they could be called seasons–were places instead of times, so one in fact had to travel to reach autumn or spring. These were the ways the Shades measured time. The main standard for measuring space was called a shadow-span, its distance being equal to two hand-lengths.

Shades, like human beings, were free to choose between good and evil. They could experience feelings such as hope and fear, joy and sorrow, love and hatred. They were capable of a wide range of beliefs and opinions. Because they lived in a shadow realm where light and darkness were mixed in varying degrees, they were often confused by shades of gray. Living in a world separated into distinct colors explains, on the other hand, why they, by nature, resisted change and tended to be somewhat set in their ways. Though resistant to change, however, they were not altogether lackluster. On the contrary, they could, on occasion, express excitement and even exhibit fervor. Such was the case, to be sure, on the day on which this tale takes its start.

The story that follows begins on the dark edge of Spectara, in the city of Zil, where the Shades of a gray land called Kenøth were gathering for the millennial celebration of a ritual begun long before by Zil Magnus, their ancestor and the founder of their civilization. This was none other than the ritual of Asdin, a sacred star composed of indestructible frozen light. Because the empire Zil Magnus had founded had lasted a thousand lumnus-years, the Shades of Zil-Kenøth had good reason to be excited. Indeed, this excitement only increased as they gathered to remember the ancient event that in their mind had once and for all established order out of chaos and had guaranteed with absolute certainty the eternal security of their world.

CHAPTER 1
ASDIN

A tall, slender, light-haired young Shade named Sindle stood on the edge of a cliff overlooking the city of Zil. Crowds were already gathering below in the streets of this colorless city located in the land of Kenøth, a gray netherworld situated on Spectara's dark edge. Sindle stood still, silent, his glowing eyes transfixed on the swelling tide of Shades. The Ritual of the Sacred Star his people called Asdin would soon be taking place, but Sindle was growing anxious because he knew all was not well. Time was running out, and his grandfather, Wizdor, had not yet arrived. This could mean only one thing. The whereabouts of Prince Neblas, son of the High Guardian of Asdin, was still unknown. Early that lumen-flow, the High Guardian had issued an order, "Prince Neblas must wield the sword of spectral light! A thousand lumnus-years of tradition cannot be altered! Find him!"

The High Guardian, emperor of all the land of Kenøth, was an immense, imposing figure feared by everyone except his son, the Prince, a young man Sindle's age who was cocky, hardheaded, and rebellious. Though Sindle admired Neblas, he was quite the Prince's opposite. Sindle was unsure of himself and somewhat shy. He had many questions about life that had not been answered to his satisfaction, and though he agonized over their answers, he kept his questions to himself largely out of fear that he might be scorned or rejected by his superiors whom he was very eager to please.

Sindle watched the dim streets of the city of Zil as throngs of ghostly forms, like puddles, fed muddy rivulets that repeatedly divided and merged as they meandered around anemic buildings made of frozen light. After coalescing into a single, sluggish river, Shades from every region of Zil-Kenøth reached the Temple court, giving it the appearance of a stagnant swamp at midnight.

Above this swamp of Shades rose the luminous Star Tower of Zil-Kenøth's Temple, a rather plain building of straight design made of frozen light and featuring a central Star Tower that rose many shadow-spans above six surrounding towers of equal height.

The Star Tower, which normally had the appearance of a lighthouse, now appeared bleak, for early that lumen-flow, Asdin, the Sacred Star made of indestructible frozen light, had been removed prior to the Star Ritual in keeping with ancient custom. Now Shades from all quarters of the land gathered in their sacred city to watch the High Guardian of Asdin perform the ancient rite and return the Star to the safety of the Star Tower where it was usually housed. As the Shades crept through the streets of Zil, their eyes glowed and flickered like eyes of night creatures. Sindle had almost fallen under their hypnotic influence when a voice, coming from behind, jolted him back to reality.

"Sorry I am late."

Sindle turned and saw the face of his grandfather, Wizdor, pointing up at him from a hunched-over frame. Sindle loved and respected the wise, old man with every fiber of his being. In Sindle's mind, all the lumens of his own life had ebbed and flowed around Wizdor's sage advice. The old Shade's long, thick, silver hair always appeared to Sindle like an angelic halo, and Wizdor's bright eyes, which burned amid the maze of wrinkles on his age-worn face, were lamps of truth that thus far had guided Sindle through the labyrinth of his short life.

As Wizdor looked at his grandson, his brow became furrowed and his eyes dimmed. "Prince Neblas has not yet been found, Sindle, and the High Guardian is in a rage. Someone will have to perform the ceremony of the Zarafat of Zil." The Zarafat was the ancient sword of spectral light wielded in ancient times by the founder, Zil Magnus. "It may fall to you, my dear lad, to do the ritual."

Sindle's eyes grew bright and his face beamed. He was an unassuming young man and so had never been given the chance to "shine." Now he was thrilled that his chance had finally come.

"When was Prince Neblas last seen?" Sindle asked, trying

to hide his excitement. Because he had been chosen to stand in for Neblas, he was truly hoping that the Prince would not show at the last minute.

"He was last seen early this lumen-flow, near the Light-Freezers Craft Houses," Wizdor replied. "Rumor has it that he and his uncle had a terrible argument. It could explain why he has gone missing. You know how difficult Neblas can be at times. It goes without saying that his uncle has an impossible job in his role as Advisor to Prince Neblas. Still, he should not have gotten the Prince so riled. Now we *are* in a mess."

Below in the Temple courts, a lake of shadows settled in what seemed the crater of a bloodless moonscape. Wizdor squinted. "Really, the Prince should know better. I know you would never do such a thing, Sindle."

Sindle smiled. "I would never want to disappoint you, Grandfather."

Beyond the Star Tower of the Temple, the impermanent outlines of the Light-Freezers Craft Houses etched themselves into Sindle's and Wizdor's vision. The buildings struggled not to be erased by the churning Sea of Darkness beyond. Against its heaving canvas of chaos, the city of Zil seemed as a fragile ghost ship disappearing into wisps of black fog.

"The sea grows restless," Sindle remarked.

Wizdor's eyes were kindled with fascination. "Why art Thou so troubled, Thou Ocean of darkest night, Thou Artificer of frozen light?"

Just then, a distant shout reached their ears, and they turned. The Temple Warden, Zil-Kenøth's magistrate in charge of the upkeep and security of the Temple buildings, came loping toward them, his thin, disheveled hair blowing in the wind. The Warden was a caustic, dour, and impatient man who had not smiled in many a lumnus-year. Indeed, he likely could not smile as his face had hardened into a permanent frown. As the Warden approached, his bushy eyebrows knitted themselves together beneath impatient wrinkles that smoothed out into a bulging forehead. Veins in his neck pulsated, and his panting made his cheeks look like bellows hard at work to ignite some fire.

When the Warden reached Wizdor and Sindle, he was breathless. "You have, no doubt, heard." He bent over, hands on knees, trying to catch his breath. "The Prince is still missing. The decision has been made. Sindle will wield the Zarafat of Zil. Do you think he is capable?"

Sindle hung his head, clearly dejected that the Warden had such little confidence in him.

"Sindle can be trusted to perform the ritual of the sword well," replied Wizdor coming to his grandson's defense. A shy smile crept over Sindle's face, and his spirits lifted a bit.

The Warden's impatient gaze fell upon the scene below. "The Temple precincts have been secured and the guards are stationed. We can delay no longer. The other magistrates await."

After hurrying from the cliffs overlooking Zil down a path and through the city's streets to the assembly place, they arrived to find the High Guardian of Asdin yelling at his brother-in-law, Lord Dargad. Dargad, a proud, pompous, and pushy man was also Advisor to the Guardian's son, Prince Neblas. Because of his prominent position in the royal family, he kowtowed to no one save the High Guardian.

Lord Dargad's bulldog face stood firm until the tirade spewing from the craggy mouth of his immense brother-in-law ceased. "He would not listen to reason," Dargad then responded. Beneath the fragile crust of calm in his voice, anger threatened to erupt at any moment. "We argued early this lumen-flow. All I tried to do was to cram an ounce of sense into that thick head of his! Then he bolted! What was I to do?"

"It must be about the Prince," Wizdor whispered to the Temple Warden. The tall, bony magistrate's eyes rolled and his bushy eyebrows writhed in an exasperated response.

Just then, the High Guardian's eye caught hold of Wizdor. "So, you have arrived at last, Lord Protector!" Then he asked the Temple Warden, "Does Sindle know what to do?"

When Sindle heard these words, his confidence fled and a lump of fear formed in the pit of his stomach. The Warden, who was clearly put out with the whole ordeal, replied, "He does, indeed, Your Excellency." The Warden's tone of voice did little to make Sindle's lump of fear subside.

"And the Starkeeper? What is keeping him?" About that time, Wizdor spotted him. "Here he comes now." The Starkeeper, who was Zil-Kenøth's magistrate directly in charge of protecting the Sacred Star Asdin, was a nervous, overwrought little man who always seemed just on the verge of hysteria. With pudgy arms, he now was treading air like water as he waddled toward them, a roll of fat bouncing up and down from his belly and almost swallowing his legs.

"Did you bring the Zarafat of Zil?" the Guardian asked.

With some difficulty, the Starkeeper's round body rocked back and forth on its stumpy legs until he had managed to turn around. Sticking out a chubby arm, he motioned to an attendant.

"Bring it to Sindle," the High Guardian commanded. The Starkeeper, who had no neck to speak of, nodded his round, bald head. The attendant handed Sindle the ancient sword of spectral light. As Sindle held it, he gazed at it with awe. The very act of holding it made him feel inadequate and out of place. Then he heard the Guardian say to him, "You had better not mess up, do you hear?" Then the Guardian turned to the Starkeeper. "I hope your people remembered Asdin, too." The expression on the Starkeeper's face revealed he did not comprehend. "The *Star*, dull wit!"

"Oh," he squeaked. "The treasury guards are bringing it." The Starkeeper seemed preoccupied with the difficult task of arranging the strange paraphernalia on his head.

Just then, the Grand Inquisitor of the Holy Task, the magistrate in charge of the purity of Zil-Kenøth's light-freezing dogmas, approached the High Guardian. "The Dark Circle is ready, Your Highness." The Grand Inquisitor was tall, handsome, charming, and always wore the black velvet cape that was the sign of his office. Of all Zil's magistrates, he was best liked with the exception, perhaps, of Wizdor.

The Guardian watched as the Grand Inquisitor's people brought forth the Dark Circle, a large hoop, approximately seven shade-lengths in diameter, covered with black velvet like that of the Inquisitor's cape. "Good," the Guardian said. "At least one of you is capable of exhibiting a modicum of responsibility." The Guardian, who towered over Wizdor, looked down at him. "Lord Protector, it is time."

Wizdor moved his hunched-over body ahead of the other magistrates and called them to order, but the Starkeeper had not yet returned. Wizdor called for him. "Over here!" came a high-pitched voice. The rotund little man waddled toward them carrying a black box. The Starkeeper set the box before the High Guardian who knelt on both knees and opened it with care. Light, splendid and brilliant, burst out, and everyone shielded his eyes. The High Guardian gently removed the Sacred Star of Frozen Light and towered to his feet. The Starkeeper closed the box, handed it to an attendant, and took his place beside the Temple Warden. Wizdor joined Prince Neblas's Advisor, Lord Dargad, directly behind the High Guardian. Then the High Guardian nodded, and the procession began.

CHAPTER 2
RITUALS

Guards pushed through the thick crowd of Shades, yelling, "The High Guardian approaches! Clear the way!" Heralds blurted random notes from coiled, serpent-shaped Ophis horns. Whiii...whiii...whaaa...whaaa...ink...ink. The odd sounds flew over the Shades like a flock of honking geese. Notes bent flat and sharp in the thick air like thin nails hammered recklessly through hard wood.

When the wheezing and coughing of the Ophis horns ceased, a crescendo of joy escalated from the crowd. The High Guardian of Asdin proceeded, and the Shades parted so that he and his entourage could pass. He wore the best gray robes that Zil's cloth merchants could weave, yet the apparel appeared to wilt into drabness when touched by Asdin's splendor.

The towering figure of the High Guardian drifted through the crowd of Shades with Asdin lifted high. Shielding their eyes, they tried to glimpse the Star through small slits they had carefully opened between their fingers. Asdin's splendor bathed the dull assembly, seeped through the shadow-flesh of their faces, and branded its image into their feeble minds. Its white fire swept away the dirt of darkness that had settled thick over Zil-Kenøth, and it beamed as a beacon of hope to a city drifting like a ghost ship on the hostile abyss they called the Sea of Darkness.

As the High Guardian pressed forward, the mouths of the Shades hung open and drooled. Asdin's magnetic power hypnotized them, drawing their thoughts toward it like insects to a lantern at evening. They longed to touch the Star, but to do so would mean certain death. Still, resisting its sway was nigh impossible. Sindle marched next to his silver-haired grandfather as the entourage proceeded through the assembly. "Why do they look at Asdin so?" he whispered to Wizdor. "Will it be safe?"

Wizdor looked up at him, his eyes aglow with seriousness. "Remember, the curse of Zil Magnus protects it, Sindle," he uttered.

When the procession halted, there was silence, and every eye became transfixed on the High Guardian. With a dramatic gesture, he thrust Asdin above his head. The sleeves of his robe cascaded down his arms, and the Star's light penetrated his flabby flesh like a beacon ray through thick clouds. All eyes glowed and swirled with awe, and stark, zombie faces sucked up Asdin's light. The Shades were again reminded that their netherworld was as a fleeting fog. The High Guardian of Asdin opened his mouth, and the ancient curse of his ancestor, Zil Magnus, uncoiled from his tongue.

"*Ophis cogert Trogzar crugar!*"

In accord, the Shades responded, "*Latrat pogsnif shalarun soogar,*" daring not to alter the pronunciation from its ancient form even by a syllable. Sindle gripped the handle of the Zarafat of Zil with his trembling right hand. Perspiration beaded on his brow.

Lowering the Star, the High Guardian handed it over to Lord Protector Wizdor who cradled it in his arms like a babe. Ophis horns proceeded to whine again with slow and somber tones. Four magistrates held the Dark Circle each quarter of the way around. Sindle's fist tightened and sweated upon the handle of the sword of spectral light. His breathing was hard; his knees weak.

The High Guardian bowed in each of the four directions. Then his hand, like a dull knife, cut a spiral gesture upward into the thick atmosphere. Sindle, who was about to pass out from nervousness, drew the Zarafat from its sheath. Holding its handle with both hands, he raised it toward heaven and lowered it in the direction of the Sea of Darkness seven times in accordance with ancient custom. All eyes were on him, making him feel very awkward.

The High Guardian shed his outer garments, and Wizdor handed him the Star. As Sindle held the sword over the Dark Circle, its weight sucked pain through his arms.

Tension sharpened in every eye, and the Shades shivered like ten-thousand dry leaves struck by a sudden wind. A lengthy silence ensued, and Sindle felt a kind of paralysis creep through his limbs. Then he heard Wizdor prompting him, "The curse, Sindle." Embarrassment flushed through Sindle's scalp. He glanced at the High Guardian and saw a frightful scowl looming on his craggy face. Sindle quickly uttered the words.

"Ophis cogert Trogzar crugar!"

The Shades chanted their response, *"Latrat pogsnif shalarun soogar,"* and Sindle's arm, propelled more by gravity than by strength, relaxed, causing the Zarafat of Zil to plummet through the center of the Dark Circle. But the hole it tore was so small, the High Guardian had trouble stuffing his enormous body through it. Sindle now wished he could somehow disappear. He glanced again as the Guardian stomped from the center of the Dark Circle that now rested on the ground. Arrows of scorn shot from the towering Shade's evil eye. Sindle's attention shifted to the crowd. Gratefully, they were not watching him but were preoccupied with the High Guardian's actions. Still, he felt that he had ruined the ritual, and he wanted to kick himself. When the Guardian had emerged from the Dark Circle, the Shades cheered. He then proceeded with the Star toward the Temple steps, and Sindle was all too glad to return the Zarafat of Zil to the Grand Inquisitor of the Holy Task who appeared tall, strong, and regal in his black velvet cape.

"Don't be upset, Sindle," the Inquisitor whispered, noticing his distress. "Neblas is to blame, not you. You performed the ceremony quite well, considering." His reassuring words brought a smile of relief to Sindle's face.

With the Sacred Star in hand, the High Guardian climbed the steps of the Temple. As Ophis horns droned with a beat scarcely detectable, the Shades, led by a chorus, started reciting the Light-Freezers Chant.

"Light frozen deep shall long endure.
Shall long retain its luster pure.

Plunged shallow, it shall soft remain,
Yet melt like tallow near a flame.

Zil's secret craft shall but increase
Until the Hell of Light shall cease
And liquid light, from lands afar,
Descends to Darkness like the Star."

Sindle now tried to get his mind off the fiasco he had made of the ritual. His memory wandered back to the time that his grandfather had taught him the words of the Light-Freezers Chant. Sindle hated and feared the Sea of Darkness because his father had died in a terrible light-freezing accident when Sindle was only three. Since his mother also had died giving him life, he was left an orphan and so was reared by his grandfather, Wizdor. Though he did not remember his father, Sindle had long tried to avoid the science of light-freezing because of the gruesome story of his father's death. But eventually, he was forced to study the dangerous craft in school, and it fell to his grandfather to tutor him. In time, Sindle became curious about the subject. He once asked Wizdor if liquid light could be plunged so deeply in the Sea of Darkness that it would remain forever frozen.

"None save the light of Asdin," Wizdor replied. "To it no frozen light compares."

"Is that why the Star never dims or melts?"

"Indeed, it is. No one has managed since the time it was forged to freeze light in those depths. The feat is thought impossible."

"If that is true, then how was it first done?"

"Considering the dangers of light-freezing, I, too, have often asked that question. I suppose one would have to lower the forms filled with liquid light to the very heart of darkness to do it. But no Light-Freezing Houses have been built that extend far enough over the Sea to make it possible. And no cables have been made that are long enough or strong enough to lower the forms to those depths. Not even Zil Magnus managed to accomplish such a feat. He knew not how Asdin came to be but simply found it one lumen lying on the shore beside the Sea of Darkness. Still, he devised the equations that proved Asdin was the key to the law of light-freezing–the calculus of *lex lucidia* on which all light-freezing is based. He also postulated that the Star was Shield and Protector against the Hell of Light, and this became the dogma that all Shades now accept as the one absolute truth of our world."

The Hell of Light... The thought of it burned in Sindle's memory. He imagined Shades shriveling there like paper thrown into a furnace. "Is the Hell of Light a place?" he remembered asking Wizdor.

"It could well be," Wizdor replied. "But long ago I concluded that it is best not to speculate about such matters. All good Shades frown on those who question the light-freezing beliefs that Zil Magnus handed down. That's why I've learned to keep silent and keep my questions to myself."

"Has anyone ever seen the Hell of Light?" Sindle probed.

"Not as far as I know," Wizdor replied.

"Then how do we know it is real? Could Zil Magnus have made a story up just to scare Shades into obeying his wishes?"

"Sindle! Your question is dangerous and foolish!" Wizdor scolded. "The security and prosperity of all Zil-Kenøth depends on the work of its light-freezers, and the work of its light-freezers depends on *all* the dogmas taught us by the Founder. Do you want to be called heretic? Be shunned? Even be put to death? You had best tell no one we've discussed such things at all. Am I clear?"

Wizdor's words stuck like darts in the flesh of Sindle's conscience. Was his grandfather feigning truth by maintaining silence? Should a dogma be used as a whip to enforce mental slavery? No wonder the Shades refused to question their beliefs. They feared change, feared what lay beyond the cliffs of Dismar that overlooked their city, feared the Sea of Darkness, and feared the Hell of Light. Fear's poison percolated through every pore of their existence explaining why so few of Zil-Kenøth's inhabitants had ever dared venture into other regions of Spectara. If anyone did leave, it was only in order to secure the liquid light needed to supply the Light-Freezers Craft Houses, and this was done only by the light-freezing elite who, upon pain of death, carried out their activities in utmost secrecy. Most Shades were content to hang upside down like blind bats in the cave of their traditions, satisfied to follow without question and never to deviate in the least from any dogma handed down by Zil Magnus.

While Sindle stood in the Temple courts preoccupied with his questions about light-freezing, impatience had started heating up the crowd like fire beneath a kettle of water. Murmuring from the Shades started forming like small bubbles and then escaping until the crowd's reaction came to a full, rolling boil. This jolted Sindle back to reality. He glanced up at the Star Tower. With its eye of hope missing, it resembled a skull. What was detaining the High Guardian? Sindle glanced over at Wizdor. The acid of worry had etched lines into his face. The other magistrates also appeared nervous. "Something has happened," Wizdor whispered to them. "The Guardian should have appeared in the Star Tower by now."

"Go, Lord Protector," the Temple Warden urged. "Find out what has happened to him."

"We will remain behind for now," said the Grand Inquisitor. "We don't want to cause panic in the crowd."

"Very well," Wizdor agreed. "Come, Sindle. I will need your help in case something has gone awry."

Like a dull knife ripping through thick cloth, gasps arose from the throng as Wizdor and Sindle cut their way through it. As they struggled up the Temple's mountain of steps, their hearts were pounding.

"Hurry on ahead, Sindle!" Wizdor directed. "Try to locate the High Guardian! I'll catch up with you."

CHAPTER 3
THE SEARCH

Sindle hurried up steps and was halted by the commander of the Temple guards. "You cannot pass."

Sindle mustered confidence. "I am the son of the Lord Protector of the High Guardian. Are you aware that the High Guardian has not yet appeared in the Star Tower?"

"Sorry, my Lord, no."

Sindle was relieved at the guard's response. "Then let me pass."

"Shall I send guards to assist you, my Lord?"

"Not without the Grand Inquisitor's approval. Lord Protector Wizdor is coming now to investigate. If the need arises, you will be called."

The commander saw Wizdor's frail frame struggling up the stairs. "Very well, my Lord," he said and then shouted to the guards, "Let him through!"

"Only the magistrates may enter. Is that clear?" asked Sindle.

"Yes, my Lord," replied the Commander, bringing a clenched fist to his heart in salute.

Sindle, heady over his success in gaining entry, passed between the rows of guards and through the Temple's immense doors. Once inside the Great Hall, he crept on cat's feet, calling out several times for the High Guardian. Each time, the echo from his voice would smooth out into dead silence. Confidence soon gave way to trepidation. He tiptoed across sinister shadows that slumbered in corners like crocodiles. Into corridors radiating from the Great Hall, he kept calling out for the High Guardian, but only the haunting echo of his nervous voice returned to him. He hurried back toward the Temple portals, but about midway, he collided with someone. A shiver of terror bolted through his spine, and he cried out.

"Sindle?" came a voice.

He was relieved that it was Wizdor's. "Grandfather! You *scared* me half to death!" he said, quivering.

"Sorry, dear boy. Any sign of the High Guardian?"

"None. Should we send for the Grand Inquisitor?"

"He will call the guards, and that may not be wise. I suggest we investigate first."

Wizdor called out for the Guardian several times but there was no response. "Come. We must search the Star Chamber." The staircase leading there spiraled upward, trailing off into a thin thread.

"Go ahead and see if you can find him," said Wizdor. "I will join you momentarily." Sindle rushed up the stairs and entered the Star Chamber. "Guardian?" he called out. The silence made a chill of dread course through his veins, but the chill turned to ice when Sindle stumbled. "Wizdor! Hurry!" he shouted.

When Wizdor entered the Star Chamber, his eyes filled with horror. The High Guardian lay sprawled on the floor with Sindle kneeling beside him. A look of terror shot from Wizdor's face. The Guardian's head was drenched with gray blood. Wizdor hurried over and started checking for a pulse.

"Is he alive?" Sindle felt helpless and scared.

"Barely," Wizdor replied. He fumbled through his robes, removed a small Ophis horn, and handed it to Sindle. "Three short blasts will alert the magistrates. Go!"

Sindle rushed through an archway to the outer balcony. His head whirled as he looked down. Distant rumbling rose from the crowd. Sindle took a deep breath and blew the Ophis horn thrice. This action threw the crowd into a panic. He watched guards surround the magistrates and start leading them through the chaos. "They're coming now!" he informed Wizdor.

Wizdor cradled the head of the Guardian. "Help will be here soon, Your Majesty. Don't die."

Sindle hurried back and knelt beside his grandfather.

"Guardian? Guardian!" Wizdor shook the body. It was limp and breathless.

"Grandfather, will he be all right?"

Wizdor knelt in silence for a moment. Then he stood up and uttered in a sorrowful tone, "The High Guardian is dead. Long live the High Guardian."

As Sindle stared at the lifeless body, his eyes welled with tears. What Wizdor said was true. The Guardian's eyes had grown dark, his scintilla—his soul—was extinguished. As bone-chilling darkness penetrated the Star Chamber, Wizdor buried his head in his hands and wept. A short time later, shouting could be heard coming from the stairs.

As Lord Dargad entered and saw Wizdor kneeling beside the High Guardian's corpse, his bulldog features froze in a state of terror. Frantic, he rushed over, fell upon the body, and shook it.

"His scintilla is become as the flame of a candle whose wick has been cut short," cried Wizdor. "The fire of life can never be rekindled."

Lord Dargad's eyes, like two stones thrown into a lake, spread ripples of shock across his face, and he muttered with quivering lips, "My poor sister...my dear nephew, Neblas...I must get word to them."

The Temple Warden and the Starkeeper merely stared in disbelief. Soon the Grand Inquisitor of the Holy Task marched in trailed by about twenty Temple guards.

"Command them to remain below for now!" ordered Wizdor, and the Inquisitor obeyed.

A few moments later, the Grand Inquisitor swaggered back into the chamber, brandishing his black velvet cape. "What has happened!"

"The High Guardian is dead," Wizdor sobbed. "All that remains now is his shadow-shell."

Lord Dargad, who had been kneeling beside his brother-in-law's corpse, composed himself and stood. "Prince Neblas is now High Guardian. Long live Neblas! Long live the High Guardian!"

"Long live Neblas. Long live the High Guardian," the others mumbled, for they were too shocked to comprehend the full meaning of what they were saying.

Then Lord Dargad urged, "My nephew must be found without delay and put under the protection of Lord Wizdor."

The Grand Inquisitor of the Holy Task spoke up, "I will organize a search at once. We shall begin by interrogating the guards. No one but the High Guardian should have been allowed access to the Temple precincts. I promise we shall find the culprit who committed this dreadful crime."

"What if something terrible has happened to Neblas as well?" asked the Temple Warden, showing very little emotion. His words made Lord Dargad cringe. "I hate to think such a thing is possible," the Warden continued as the heavy eyebrows on his nervous face started twitching. "It could, however, explain his absence."

"He is right. We can't rule it out," said the Grand Inquisitor. His countenance became grave, and he set his jaw. "We will go into this investigation expecting the worst. There could be a conspiracy behind this."

"Perish the thought," Wizdor responded, shivering.

"The search for Neblas must begin at once," returned the Grand Inquisitor. "Leave matters to me. If there is information to be had, I'll find it."

"Shouldn't we assist you?" asked Lord Dargad. "We may find Neblas quicker that way." It was typical of Dargad to try to interfere.

At that moment, the Starkeeper, who was responsible for the safety of Asdin, cried out in his high voice, "The Star! *Where is the Star?*" He was searching the chamber as fast as his stumpy legs could propel his pudgy body.

Fear coiled around Wizdor's vocal chords. "In all the confusion, I didn't even think..."

"The Grand Inquisitor is right," blurted the Starkeeper, dabbing perspiration from his brow. "The situation may be worse than we first thought! *Asdin is missing!*"

"This goes to motive," said the Grand Inquisitor. "It could explain why the High Guardian has met this untimely end. Asdin, no doubt, was stolen by the same person who inflicted these wounds."

Wizdor was almost speechless. "Who would dare?"

"Indeed, who would dare breech the perimeter of this Sacred House?" stated the Temple Warden in a deep, foreboding tone. The security of the Temple was under his purview, and he was infuriated that it had been compromised. The wrinkles on his long face became more prominent. "Finding the Star must be a priority. It is just as important as finding the Prince. Let the Grand Inquisitor organize his search for Neblas. I suggest that the rest of us assist in looking for the culprit who took the Star so it can be returned to the safety of the Star Chamber. We should begin by searching the Temple precincts. I, for one, would like to know how the murderous thief gained entrance."

The magistrates agreed.

"Then I will start the search for Neblas at once," stated the Grand Inquisitor.

"Very well," Wizdor agreed. "But I suggest you remove the guards from the Temple. Imagine the chaos that could befall Zil-Kenøth if it were to become public knowledge that Asdin has gone missing?"

"You are right, of course, Wizdor," said the Grand Inquisitor. "We should take extreme precautions to keep this secret."

"Then I shall return to my lodgings in Stargazer Street as soon as possible," Wizdor told him. "If, or *when,* you find Neblas, report to me there."

"Agreed," the Inquisitor responded. Wizdor and the other magistrates descended the stairs into the Great Hall and waited until he had departed with the guards. Then Wizdor said to the Warden and the Starkeeper, "Search the three towers that face the cliffs of Dismar." He turned next to Lord Dargad and Sindle. "Cover the three towers facing the Sea. Look carefully through every room, compartment, and corner. I will return to search the Great Hall."

They proceeded to investigate the six towers while Wizdor focused his attention on the Great Hall and its compartments. Some time later, the Warden and the Starkeeper met Wizdor again.

"We've turned up nothing," reported the Starkeeper, panting and dripping with perspiration.

Soon Lord Dargad and Sindle appeared.

"Any luck?" asked Wizdor.

"None," Lord Dargad replied. Then a brow raised on his bulldog face, and he said, "But I've been thinking. Asdin is protected by the curse of Zil Magnus, is it not? Could our worries be premature? If the Star *has* been stolen, we shall know soon enough. Doom will befall the scoundrel who took it! The culprit will be unable to hold on to the Star, I tell you. We should forget the Star for now and join the Grand Inquisitor in his search for Prince Neblas."

"Dargad, I know what great responsibility you must feel for your nephew," Wizdor replied, "but the Grand Inquisitor may not wish us to interfere. To do so may raise suspicions among the people and cause more harm than good."

"Wizdor is no doubt right," said the Warden, stroking his long chin.

"Then are we to do nothing about the Star?" asked the Starkeeper, dabbing the sweat from his face.

"The two trails will no doubt connect if we are but patient," replied Wizdor. "Meanwhile, we must not spark curiosity by acting in unusual ways. I suggest that we return to our homes and await news from the Grand Inquisitor. As soon as we hear word from him, Sindle will find you."

Suddenly, cries filtered through the Temple portals along with the sound of fists pounding on the doors.

"They are growing impatient," said the Warden, the nervous wrinkles twisting on his bulging forehead. "We can no longer delay."

"Leave the matter to me," said Wizdor. "I shall think of something to tell them."

"Shouldn't we have our story straight in case we're questioned?" asked the Warden.

"You're right, of course," agreed Wizdor. "If anyone asks, say only that the High Guardian is dead, but mention nothing of murder, or kidnapping, or the missing Star. We must do all we can to avoid panic. Take care that you all leave the Temple by the secret passage to avoid detection. If anyone does question you, repeat only the facts I've given you. Agreed?"

After conceding, the magistrates departed, leaving Wizdor to relay the sad news of the High Guardian's death to the people. Wizdor and Sindle again climbed the stairs to the Star Tower. When they reached the Chamber of Asdin, their eyes fell again on the High Guardian's corpse. The knife of pain twisted in Wizdor's heart. Sindle, seeing his distress, took his grandfather's arm, and Wizdor responded by embracing him. "We must arrange to have the Guardian's body removed in secret," he said. Wizdor began again to weep. "What a terrible, terrible thing this is." When he had composed himself, he walked onto the balcony and began his speech. "Citizens!" He raised his hands to signal quiet. "Citizens! Please listen!" Their clamoring died down. "I bear you grave news." He paused for a moment and wiped his forehead with his sleeve.

"Your High Guardian has met with an unfortunate accident and has died."

Wizdor's words spread panic over them like fire over withered grass, and it was all he could do to continue. "Citizens! Quiet and calm, please! Prince Neblas is now High Guardian. Long live Neblas! Long live the High Guardian!" His voice cracked as he said these words.

An obscure reply returned from the crowd. Wizdor's eyes darkened with pain, and Sindle felt helplessness flood his soul. Wizdor again raised his hands. "Citizens! We are trying now to ascertain the cause of the High Guardian's death. Meanwhile, the Star Ritual must be postponed until further notice."

The crowd rumbled, and Wizdor again raised his hands in an effort to bring calm. "The Star Ritual will be rescheduled during the coronation of Prince Neblas as our new High Guardian.

Now please return to your homes so that we can begin the period of mourning for our dearly departed friend and leader."

Wizdor turned away from the balcony and looked at Sindle. "We have done all we can for now. Let's go home." The light in Wizdor's eyes grew dim, and he seemed on the verge of collapse. Sindle was concerned, for he had never before seen Wizdor so distraught. Fear of impending doom was tightening its grip on them.

CHAPTER 4
TROGZARS

Wizdor and Sindle exited through the secret passage of the Temple only to find that the weather had taken a turn for the worse. Cold wind from the Sea of Darkness, like icy needles, blasted their faces and pierced their flesh. Wizdor gathered up his robes and wound them tight around his frail body. When they reached the street, they heard something that both alarmed and frightened them. A voice sputtered and crackled amid the shadows like burning leaves. "You want to know about the Star? I know who has it."

Wizdor spun around and laid eyes on a woman. "Who are you?"

She panicked and fled.

"Stop her, Sindle!" Wizdor's cry cracked through the frigid air.

Sindle sprang into action, his dark form trailing her through the streets. Her frightened cries mixed in his ears with the sound of his own panting. The gap between them closed. Sindle lunged, caught hold of her cloak, grabbed her arm, and wrestled her to the ground.

"Let me go!" she shrieked.

Feeling awkward and trembling, Sindle tried to appear forceful. "Who are you? How do you know about the Star?"

"I cannot say! They will kill me."

"Who will kill you?"

"Please let me go!"

"Tell us what you know or you'll be tried as a traitor!"

She whispered in his ear. "The Trogzars took the Star. It's part of their conspiracy."

Sindle's eyes glassed over. "Trogzars?"

"Quiet!" she whimpered. "Their ears are everywhere."

"What else do you know?"

"Nothing!" The woman tried to pull free. Her snaky body was as strong as wire. Sindle kept her pinned to the ground.

"Did the Trogzars murder the High Guardian?"

"Do not ask me that."

"What of Prince Neblas? Is he in danger?"

Nervous laughter escaped like steam from her mouth.

"Why do you laugh?"

"I cannot tell you."

Sindle twisted her arm. "You must!"

"Stop hurting me!"

"I will stop when you tell me what you know!"

"All right," she relented. "The Prince is in on their conspiracy."

As her words bolted through his mind like electricity, he relaxed his grip. "What?" Seizing the opportunity to break free, she sprung up and sped away. Sindle merely stared into space. Shock at her words had turned him to stone. What she had told him was unthinkable. Moments later, Wizdor approached. "Did you catch her?"

He could not respond at first.

"Sindle?"

He turned. "I cannot believe what she said. She claims there is a Trogzar conspiracy. Trogzars are behind the stealing of the Star. What's more, she claims Neblas is party to it!"

Wizdor found his grandson's news incredible. "Could she be lying?"

"If she were, how could she have known Asdin was missing?"

Wizdor turned pale and stared into the darkness. "Someone might be trying to frame the Prince. The woman could have been a plant." Darkness cast a pallor upon Wizdor's face. "Trogzars... The Warden mentioned them early this lumen-flow, shortly after Lord Dargad had argued with Prince Neblas. What do you know of them?"

"I've seen them beside the Sea of Darkness, chanting and playing strange music on their Ophis horns. They try to play in unison with the voice of the Sea. They call the Sea *Finsterna*."

Wizdor's eyes seemed far away. *"Finsterna...* That is an ancient name." His voice had a ring of mystery. "I've not heard the Sea called that in many a lumnus-year."

"What does it mean?"

His eyes sharpened. *"Dark Fire.* But why, I don't know."

Finsterna... The name sank its fangs into Sindle's mind.

"What else did you learn from her?" Wizdor asked.

"She was afraid Trogzars would kill her if they found out she gave up their secret plan."

"Strange. If she had been a plant, why would she be so afraid? It couldn't be an act."

"That is what makes me want to believe her," said Sindle.

"Did the woman say what the Trogzars might want with the Star?"

"She escaped before I could learn more."

"Conspiracy or no conspiracy, we would be wise to prepare for the worst," said Wizdor. "If there is a conspiracy brewing, then we may face a more serious threat than we first suspected. Sindle, we've got to alert the magistrates about this news. Go to Lord Dargad first, then to the Warden and the Starkeeper. The Grand Inquisitor may be harder to find, but search for him until you do. Of all the magistrates, we will need his expertise most. When you find them, say nothing of a conspiracy. Only say that I have important news regarding the Star. Tell them to waste no time in coming to our lodgings on Stargazer Street. Meanwhile, I must return there. I need to read up on these Trogzars."

Sindle sprinted away, and Wizdor hurried home. When he arrived, he went straight to his library and pulled an ancient book from a shelf. He thumbed through the index and then sat in his chair. His finger slid quickly over the letters. Troglodyte, Trogzar. He turned to the "Trogzar" reference and skimmed over these paragraphs:

No ancient sect was more devoted to the contemplation of the Sea of Darkness than were the Trogzars. The word harks back to the Pyrathan mysteries, but its origins and meaning remain obscure. Some have thought the name is a shortened form of the word "*Troglozarafat*," which is the compound of *Troglo* (cave) and *zarafat* (spectral sword). Such corruptions were common before the written language became fixed.

Evidence supporting the *Trogloszarafat* hypothesis is not lacking. For instance, the emblem of the Trogzars was originally a sword of light penetrating a black sphere. The black sphere has traditionally been interpreted as a symbol of the Sea of Darkness, and the sword as a symbol of the light-freezers who submerged light into the Sea in order to freeze it.

Wizdor glanced up from the book. He knew the light-sword piercing the dark circle had served as the emblem of the Light-Freezers Craft Houses for centuries. His grandson had carried out the ritual of the Sword and the Dark Circle that very lumen. Wizdor's eyes returned to the page.

This symbol of the sword of light penetrating the dark circle was abandoned by the Trogzars, however, after they adopted beliefs that influenced them to oppose light-freezing. In protest, they changed the original emblem to a black sword piercing a white circle. The sect was soon suppressed after some of its more radical adherents attempted to assassinate the High Guardian in the lumnus-year of Zil Magnus 501, and to overthrow the light-freezing craft.

Wizdor again looked up from the book. What beliefs would cause them to oppose light-freezing? He continued reading.

Although their attempts were thwarted when the plot was discovered, and the leaders of the coup executed, the original symbol of the Trogzars—the white sword piercing the dark circle—survived, ironically, when the Ancient Houses of Light-Freezers adopted it as their official trademark one-hundred lumnus years later.

Wizdor returned to the shelves and thumbed through several more volumes, but he could find no further information on the elusive Trogzars. It was as though all references to their beliefs had been deliberately erased. He kept flipping through pages until he heard knocking at the door. "Coming! I'm coming!" He tucked the old volume under his arm, went to the door, and opened it. Outside stood Lord Dargad and the Temple Warden.

"Sindle tells us you have learned something about the Star," stated the Warden. The nerves beneath his heavy eyebrows twitched.

"Come in." Wizdor led them through the corridor into the library and had them sit around his table.

Suddenly, Sindle burst into the room with the Starkeeper waddling after him. "I shall go now to find the Grand Inquisitor!" Sindle said, panting.

"What have you learned, Wizdor?" asked the Starkeeper in a high, nervous voice as he wiped his round head with a handkerchief.

Meanwhile, Sindle rushed outside. As he ran through the streets, cold wind bit his ears and burned his eyes. His heart beat so hard his chest ached. He hurried past the Temple with its blind Star Tower. Soon he reached the Grand Inquisitor's lodgings and pounded on the door, shouting for him. He kept knocking and calling out, but the windows were dark.

As he paced in front of the doorway, he suddenly heard a noise that gave him pause. It was coming from an alcove that led around the side to the back of the Inquisitor's lodgings. Fear froze solid in his veins as he went to investigate. At the end of the alcove, he found the woman he had interrogated earlier amid the shadows, huddling in a quivering, frightened mass. When she saw Sindle, she let out a fearful yelp.

"Why are you here?" he asked her.

She became hysterical. "The Trogzars know! They know I told of their conspiracy!" She started sobbing.

He stared into her frightened, tearful face. "You have nothing to fear from me." He put a hand on her shoulder to try to comfort her. "I'm sure the Grand Inquisitor will arrive soon. He will protect you. You were wise to come here. I'm looking for him now. I'll wait here until he arrives so that no harm will come to you. Now tell me more about this Trogzar conspiracy."

"My son is one of them. I overheard him discussing plans." She could not stop sobbing. "Since he joined them, he cares about nothing else. He would not hesitate to kill me if I got in their way." The woman broke down, and Sindle tried to help her gain composure. "Their hold over their followers is absolute," she continued. "Even Prince Neblas has fallen under their influence."

Just then, Sindle perked up. "Shhh," he said, interrupting her. "I think someone is coming. That may be the Grand Inquisitor. I am sure your worries will be over." He helped the woman up, and they started through the alcove. But what they saw next struck their hearts with terror. Two Trogzar thugs were rushing in their direction.

"I'll try to fend them off," said Sindle, trembling. "Now try to get away."

As the thugs hurried toward him, he positioned himself.

"Oh, no. He's going to hurt us," one of them taunted. The other one laughed.

"Look how many muscles he has," teased the laughing one. "I'm so scared." He contorted his face, trembled, and laughed again.

"Go, catch the informer,"the first one said. "I'll take care of this little wimp," and the other one sped off.

As the thug who remained approached, Sindle's heart tried to jump out of his chest. The thug's eyes were cold, hard. He rushed in Sindle's direction, and Sindle took the first swing, hitting him in the jaw. Pain throbbed in Sindle's knuckles.

"You little idiot! You shouldn't have done that!" The thug rammed his elbow into Sindle's ribs and back, causing pain to explode in his body. A fist in his face and a thud on his head sent fire burning through his scalp. He reeled and fell backwards. Then a final kick came, and he blacked out.

CHAPTER 5
MEETINGS

While Sindle searched for the Grand Inquisitor, Wizdor told the magistrates sitting in his library what he had learned. "The news I have to tell you is dreadful. As Sindle and I were leaving the Temple, a woman leapt from the shadows, claiming she knew who took the Star. She fled, but Sindle caught her and forced her to talk. It seems the Grand Inquisitor's suspicions were correct. The woman told Sindle that Trogzars conspired to steal the Star and overthrow the government."

"Trogzars? Who was this woman?" Lord Dargad's bulldog face stiffened as he awaited Wizdor's answer.

"She escaped before we could get further information."

"What would the Trogzars want with the Star?" asked the Starkeeper, resting his pudgy arms on his belly.

"I do not know," replied Wizdor. Then he paused and looked directly at Lord Dargad. "I'm afraid there's even more distressing news." His eyes dimmed. "The woman has implicated Prince Neblas in the conspiracy."

Dargad sprung up. "Why that's preposterous!" he stammered. "Surely you don't believe my nephew could be involved!"

"I don't want to believe it," Wizdor replied. "Has Neblas had any contact with the Trogzars?"

Dargad hesitated. "Well...yes, but."

Wizdor handed him the book with the passage about the Trogzars. "Read this."

After he finished the passage, Dargad glared at Wizdor. "What are you suggesting?" The tone of his voice was filled with disdain. Then he erupted with a shout. "Are you suggesting that Neblas could be party to such a scheme?"

"Let me see that," the Warden demanded, grabbing the book from Lord Dargad and scanning the page. After managing with some difficulty to pry his rotund body from his chair, the Starkeeper waddled over and read across the Warden's shoulder. The Warden's nervous brow furrowed and his heavy eyebrows twitched as he read. "I knew something was strange about those Trogzars," he said in a low, nervous voice. "If a conspiracy is afoot, we must stop it."

"That may already be too late," responded Wizdor. "If the woman's words are true—and I'm inclined to believe they are—then this time a Trogzar conspiracy may have succeeded."

"Incredible," remarked Lord Dargad, squinting his eyes. Then he added in a haughty tone. "Surely, Wizdor, you are overreacting."

"I hope I am." Wizdor walked to the window and peered out. "I wish Sindle would hurry and arrive with the Grand Inquisitor. He may have the information we need."

"Forget about the Grand Inquisitor," countered Lord Dargad. "Have you forgotten the other possibility? If Trogzars murdered the High Guardian, they just as easily could have abducted my nephew and concocted this whole story of his involvement with the conspiracy as a smoke screen."

"Possibly," admitted Wizdor.

The Warden's long face became grave. "Forgive my saying it, Dargad," he said. "But Neblas may be part of the conspiracy, just as the woman suggested."

Dargad's piggish eyes threw daggers at the Warden.

"It at least warrants investigation," the Warden added.

"I agree," the Starkeeper piped.

Lord Dargad's drooping jowls appeared to froth as he grew more furious. "How dare you even think Neblas is involved? The Prince has his faults, yes, but..." Dargad pounded his fist on the table and shot to his feet. "This talk is absurd. The woman had to be lying. There can be no other explanation." As Dargad glared at each of the magistrates, they merely stared at him. "You believe her lies?" His eyes burned against Wizdor.

"This is your fault, Lord Protector. You were responsible for the High Guardian's safety, you know."

"The Prince's alleged involvement with the Trogzars is beside the point..."

"Beside the point?" Lord Dargad yelled. "I've had all of this I can stand!"

"The Trogzars, however, are another matter..."Wizdor continued as Dargad stormed out.

"Forget him," said the Warden, frowning more deeply than usual. "He is too close to the Prince to be impartial."

The magistrates discussed for some time what course of action to take. Eventually the discussion returned to the subject of Lord Dargad.

"I don't understand Dargad's attitude," the Warden remarked. "He knows Neblas better than any of us. Surely he realizes..." The Warden suddenly became silent. A sound of rumbling began and increased in loudness until it ripped through the gut of the earth. The house shook, and books fell from shelves. An explosion followed, and the magistrates fell to the floor, covering their heads with their hands. Windows shattered, and a foul-smelling, icy gale blasted through the room. "Take cover!" Wizdor shouted. They threw chairs aside and crawled beneath the table for protection. Huddling together, they waited for the catastrophe to pass.

* * *

While the magistrates met in Wizdor's library, Trogzars flocked beside the Sea of Darkness. As they gathered in front of the light-freezing docks, black clouds from what seemed an approaching storm boiled above them, and gusts of cold wind from the Sea swept across their faces. The Trogzars, calm, but trancelike, sat chanting words in a strange tongue as others played Ophis horns in unison with the howling sea winds. Soon, their leader appeared—a tall figure clad in black. As he approached, they rose and bowed to him.

"Our plans are in jeopardy," he told them. The manner of his speech was grave, and his words were tinged with hate. "The magistrates suspect the Prince is with us, though they do not yet know the full extent of his involvement. We wanted to bring about our changes as secretly and as quickly as possible, but now that they know, we must take measures to insure our success. The future of Zil-Kenøth is at stake."

The figure clothed in black turned and issued a command to his men. "Bring her forth!"

They had in custody the woman who had informed Wizdor and Sindle of the Trogzar plot. In futile desperation, she fought to break free.

"You have committed a serious crime," he howled. The woman felt his words send the icy chill of terror through her body. "Do you not understand that what we do is in the best interest of the people of Zil-Kenøth? We cannot risk your kind of interference." Then with cold and cruel resolve, he commanded the men who held her: "Make her one with Finsterna."

At once the woman broke loose and fled toward the Sea of Darkness. As she ran, she stumbled, pulled herself up, and then struggled on.

"Stop her!" the figure in black ordered. The obedient throng pursued her as she ran down the shoreline. The Sea of Darkness now appeared to be a huge, dark, frothing mouth.

The woman eventually was cornered by the Trogzar mob. With nowhere to turn, she climbed onto one of the light-freezing docks and ran toward the end of it. Trogzars pursued her. There was no escape. As she backed away from their advance, waves of terror undulated across her face. They pressed in on her and started shouting, "Jump, jump, jump!" The woman covered her ears as they continued chanting. Then she screamed, lost her balance, and plunged headlong into the Sea. Its immense mouth welcomed her, and its lips gladly folded over her. The Trogzars cheered. Then they returned to the dark figure.

"The fates of the eternal wheel of darkness are against the magistrates of Zil-Kenøth. They cannot prevail! They will try to thwart our plans, but they will not succeed!"

Trogzars waved Ophis horns in the air and chanted. The figure clothed in black lifted his hands to quiet them. "We must now beseech Finsterna, Great Queen of the Depths, to hasten the eternal lumen-ebb of our liberation."

As Trogzars prostrated themselves before the Sea of Darkness, the air crackled with her dark electricity. It seemed to flow through every mind and control every will.

The figure in black beckoned with arms outstretched, his fingers, like dead tree branches, silhouetted against the churning black gulf. "O Finsterna, Queen of Shades, we long to lose all sensation in Thine abysmal depths. We yearn for an end to the ruler of the menace of the Hell of Light—he whose name we dare not speak in Thy presence. O, that we might soon be absorbed into Thine ocean of eternal darkness! We long for the sweetness of Thy rest, O Finsterna, Queen of Shades, Great Mother of our netherworld!"

The Trogzars chanted in unison with the howling winds from the Sea. The thought of being one with Finsterna made them euphoric.

"O Queen of Shades," the dark figure begged. "We long to find true contentment by losing ourselves in Thee! We ask Thee now for a sign, O Queen of the Deep! Answer us, that the faith of all here gathered may be sustained."

At these words, the Sea of Darkness seethed like a cauldron. The limbs of every Trogzar tingled with the thrill of expectation. They could feel in their bones the approach of Finsterna's eternal lumen-ebb. From the depths of the sea, a huge black hand, its fingers whirling like tornadoes, towered to the sky. Excitement welled in the Trogzars' faces as they watched. Then the hand propelled its whirling fingers into the Star Tower of the Temple where Asdin had been housed. The Temple dissolved like a sand castle swept away by a wave. But the Queen of Shades was not finished with her judgment upon the city of Zil. Her hand dug deep into their world, wiping away the Light-Freezers Craft Houses, the only means of their land's economic survival.

The Trogzars, with hand-covered heads, dotted the shore like flotsam. Spared from the mighty wrath of their beloved Queen of Shades, they believed she had at last vindicated herself and her devotees, and had chosen the Trogzars for her great purpose. When the terror passed, the prophet of Finsterna, undaunted by the catastrophe, towered to his feet, his face set with determination to follow the plan to the end.

"We have received a sign," he said. "Judgment time has come for many, but for us it is a time of victory. We now know what we must do. We must sacrifice to the Queen of the Deep all who oppose our plan so that Zil-Kenøth may be delivered from her fury and may find acceptance in her eyes!"

The prophet drew his black hood over his head, turned, and marched away, with the Trogzars falling in line behind.

* * *

Meanwhile, the magistrates were huddled beneath the table in Wizdor's library until the deafening, terrifying roar stopped. In the silence that followed, they could hear only the fearful drumming of their hearts.

Wizdor crawled from under the table like a snail from its shell and pulled himself to his feet. He and the other magistrates rushed from the library and threw open the front door. Outside, panic and chaos swept the city. Shades scrambled through streets trying to escape Finsterna's wrath. Screams clattered against sides of buildings and crashed into streets below. The magistrates stood watching, huddled at the door.

"What are they saying?" bellowed the Temple Warden, glaring at those scurrying past. The wrinkles on his bulging forehead were squirming in pain.

Wizdor lifted his eyes. "No! It cannot be!" His body trembled. He saw only empty space where the Star Tower once had stood. The magistrates stared in consternation and disbelief. Wizdor, followed by the others, ran into the street and looked in the direction of the Temple. More Shades ran past screaming. "What has happened?" he kept asking the passersby.

Finally a Shade paused long enough to tell him: "The Temple was destroyed by a wave from the Sea. The Light-Freezers Craft Houses are gone too."

A look of horror shot from Wizdor's face.

"It can't be true!" the Warden wailed. Keeping the Temple secure had been his life, but in one fatal moment it had been forever erased from their world. The magistrates at once started off in the direction of the empty space where the Star Tower had stood. They were almost at the site when Wizdor remembered, "I told Sindle I would wait for him," and he urged the Warden and the Starkeeper to go on ahead, that he would join them later.

On the way back to Stargazer Street, Wizdor saw a frantic Lord Dargad running toward him. "The Temple has been destroyed," Dargad shrieked. "I've seen Trogzars. They're marching this way."

"We must get back to Stargazer Street," said Wizdor. "Maybe Sindle has returned."

Suddenly, they were distracted by the distant clacking of marching feet. The clacking grew louder and louder. Trogzars were indeed coming. Wizdor's heart seemed to pound with a volume equal to the clacking, and Lord Dargad's floppy bulldog face turned to stone. "I've changed my mind," he told Wizdor when they reached Stargazer Street. "The Guardian's palace will no doubt be safer. Farewell, Lord Protector." He tried to leave but was prevented as a squad of Trogzars rounded the corner. He tried running the opposite way, but more Trogzars were marching from the other end of Stargazer Street. Escape was now impossible. Fear stabbed Wizdor's heart as they closed in, and he tried to hide his bleeding wounds of panic beneath thin garments of self-control.

CHAPTER 6
THE STONE

When Sindle regained consciousness, there was no sign of his assailants, the woman, or the Grand Inquisitor. Objects moved about in his vision like marbles in a pan. He stood, bracing himself against the Inquisitor's house, and then staggered to the street. Buildings bulged in and out in rhythm with his pounding head. He kept looking for the Star Tower, trying to get his bearings. People were jostling through the streets, screaming.

When he rounded the corner, he stopped dead in his tracks, and the blood drained from his face. What looked like a mountain of crushed ice lay where the Temple once had stood. He stared for several minutes in shock before hailing someone, "What has happened?"

"A wave from the Sea destroyed the Temple!" came the reply.

Frantic, but still dizzy from his bout with Trogzar thugs, Sindle ran as fast as his legs would carry him. Soon he was breathless, and his heart hammered against his rib cage. Buildings swirled above him at the same time the whirlpool of unconsciousness tried to suck him under. When he reached Stargazer Street, a shouting, fist-waving mob blocked the way to his house, so he had to detour through a back alley and climb over walls to get there. After gaining entry, he rushed through the library to a window and carefully pulled back the curtains. What he saw next horrified him. The angry mob had his grandfather and Lord Dargad surrounded, and a dark, hooded figure was interrogating them. Sindle forced the scene into view. When the dark figure removed his hood, Sindle could not believe his eyes. The face revealed was that of the handsomest and best loved of Zil's magistrates—the Grand Inquisitor of the Holy Task!

"What is the meaning of this?" Wizdor demanded. His visage was noble and courageous.

"You know too much, Lord Protector," the Inquisitor replied. "The liberation would have gone smoothly if the woman hadn't informed you of our plans. Now Finsterna is offended. You must become one with her."

Sindle at first watched in terror. Then his terror turned to fury. He wished he still had the Zarafat of Zil Magnus. He would rush out and drive it through the Grand Inquisitor's heart. The traitor!

"Are you mad?" shot Wizdor.

"Devotion must not be confused with madness," the Inquisitor responded. "The magistrates threaten our success. We have no alternative but to sacrifice each of you to the Queen of Shades."

Sindle's heart sank when he heard these words. He could not believe the Grand Inquisitor would do this to his beloved grandfather.

"What?" muttered Lord Dargad, his jowls quivering with fear. "You cannot be serious."

The Inquisitor's eyes shot fire at Dargad. "You had your chance to join Prince Neblas early this lumen-flow! Instead you scorned him!"

"Is this true?" Wizdor probed Dargad.

"Yes. I mean, no." Then he said to the Grand Inquisitor, "I am the Prince's Guardian and Advisor. Surely you cannot expect me to stand by and let him commit folly."

"Folly, you call it?" the Inquisitor returned, anger flaring in his voice.

"How was I to know the Prince was guided by your wise hand, Grand Inquisitor? Excuse my ignorance. Had I only known, I would have supported you then, as I most certainly do now."

Sindle burned with fury at Dargad's words. For the first time in his life, he felt the urge to kill.

"You are a fool and a coward," shouted the Grand Inquisitor. "It is Neblas's good fortune to be rid of you."

"You will not get away with this," said Wizdor, glaring at the Inquisitor. Compared to the crowd of Trogzars, Wizdor appeared radiant.

"No?" The Inquisitor issued a command to his guards, "Take them. The sooner they are disposed of, the better."

His guards bound Wizdor and Dargad and started driving them toward the Sea of Darkness. Sindle raised the window and leapt through it. "Stop!" he shouted.

Some of the Inquisitor's thugs beat him and left him lying in the street as the mob followed Wizdor and Dargad. Sindle pulled himself up and staggered after them.

"Please, Grand Inquisitor," Lord Dargad blubbered. "May I see Neblas. I will apologize to him—do anything."

"Do you think he is still in Zil-Kenøth? No, I say! He marches with the Star to vanquish forever he who rules the Hell of Light. In his end will be our beginning!"

"Whose misguided mind concocted such a plan?" asked Wizdor. His voice was confident, and he appeared unafraid.

"A mind more ancient and wiser than yours, Lord Protector," the Inquisitor replied. "She who revealed the light-freezing mysteries to Zil Magnus now guides Neblas and our Trogzar brotherhood. Soon, you, too, shall meet her and learn the meaning of fear."

"You *are* mad!" Wizdor accused.

"Enough!" shouted the Inquisitor. His guards pushed them forward. As they marched in the direction of the Sea, Sindle followed, trembling and weeping.

When they arrived, Lord Dargad became hysterical. "I beg you, Grand Inquisitor. Let me live. I now see the truth of what you do. You are champions of the Holy Task. I did not understand what that meant until now."

Sindle could not believe his ears. Hatred against Lord Dargad surged inside him.

"You disappoint me," Wizdor said to Dargad. "You know as well as I that he has perverted the Holy Task. Neblas cannot vanquish the ruler of the Hell of Light with a star made of light.

Why should light fear light?" Wizdor's words pierced the Grand Inquisitor's dark mind, causing a flood of anger to gush forth.

"Blasphemer!" Lord Dargad accused, taking the cue. Sindle remembered how he, too, had questioned the dogma about the Hell of Light. Wizdor had forbidden him to question any of the dogmas of Zil Magnus. Now his grandfather felt free to speak his mind. Sindle marveled at Wizdor's courage. But why did Wizdor have to speak? Sindle knew his grandfather's words would seal his fate, and that he would be left alone.

"You shall surely die, Wizdor," the Grand Inquisitor seethed. "Dark fire will devour your soul just as surely as Neblas struck his father dead with the Star!"

Lord Dargad covered his mouth.

"So it *is* true," said Wizdor. "The Prince assassinated the High Guardian."

"Such a terrible word, Wizdor," replied the Inquisitor. "Do you not realize it was the only way our plan would succeed? Only a High Guardian could escape the curse placed upon the Star by Zil Magnus. One Guardian had to die so that another could be immune from it."

"Madness," shot Wizdor. "Neblas will not escape the curse. He has violated the moral law. His heart shall be pierced by his own sword."

The Grand Inquisitor's eyes threw flames. "How dare you utter those words!" he shouted. "Dispose of this babbler now." Then he said with utter disgust. "As for you, Dargad, your wish is granted. I will let you live but only so that you will suffer the memory of your cowardice and treachery."

"A thousand thanks, Inquisitor," Dargad groveled. "I am your obedient servant."

"Quiet! You sicken me!" He turned. "Guards! The time has come. He who was Lord Protector must now lose all protection. The wrath of our Queen of Shades awaits him. Make him one with Finsterna."

As the guards carried Wizdor to the end of a light-freezing dock, Sindle screamed, "Stop! Murderers!" A Trogzar knocked him to the ground and pushed his face into the sand. "No," he cried, trying to drive the grit from his mouth.

Then Wizdor shouted his final words at the Grand Inquisitor: "By your sword, too, shall your heart be pierced!" Infuriated, the Inquisitor signaled, and the guards led Wizdor to the Sea. Wizdor's long silver hair seemed to shine like a halo around his head, and his face was luminous. The Trogzars proceeded to hurl him into the Sea of Darkness, and he disappeared as the lips of its frothing mouth closed over him. As Wizdor sank into the Sea, the dagger of sorrow stuck deep in Sindle's heart. He hid his face and wept.

Immediately the winds picked up, followed first by a rumbling sound and then a deafening blast. Sindle lifted his eyes and saw a hideous black hand towering to the sky. Its whirling fingers stretched out, paused for a moment, and then plunged into the midst of the mob. Trogzars scattered like ants. As Sindle covered his head, something hard struck his knuckle causing burning pain to shoot through his finger. He rolled over, grabbing his hand. Lying beside him in the sand, he saw a strange, glowing stone. When he tried to pick it up, he immediately dropped it, for it was too cold to handle. So he ripped a piece of cloth from inside his tunic, wrapped it around the stone, and tucked it in his money pouch. Then he shot to his feet and screamed at the top of his lungs, "Murderers!"

"Finsterna is still angry," the Grand Inquisitor uttered. "All those who do not support the Holy Task must be sacrificed to her." He pointed in the direction of Sindle. "The grandson of Wizdor shall be next."

As Trogzars started in his direction, Sindle sped away. He ran down streets, ducked around corners, and crept through alleyways until in time he was confident he had thrown them off. Over walls and through back streets of the city of Zil, he wandered toward home. Trogzars were everywhere, but he managed to stay out of sight. At last he came to Stargazer Street, but what he saw there drove him to despair. The Grand Inquisitor's thugs now guarded the entry to Wizdor's lodgings. Soon other Trogzars arrived and erected a platform in the street.

In time, the Grand Inquisitor mounted it. Now not only his beloved grandfather, but all memories of him, were off limits to Sindle. He stood out of sight and wept silently.

"Bring forth the banner of liberation," the Grand Inquisitor commanded.

The Trogzars obeyed and unfurled a flag that had on it a white circle pierced by a black sword. That dark sword was now also piercing Sindle's heart.

"No more shall freezers forge their putrid light in Finsterna's sacred depths," said the Grand Inquisitor with hatred grinding in his voice. "Now we shall only sacrifice to her those who would thwart our plan. Go! Round up our enemies! Every last one of them shall pay!"

Sindle knew now he had no choice but to flee Zil-Kenøth. With no food or money, he escaped down a path to the top of the cliffs of Dismar that overlooked the city of Zil, passing the place where earlier that lumen he had watched the Shades gathering for the Star Ritual. He had met Wizdor there such a short time ago. Now the horror of what had happened to his beloved grandfather pierced his mind with unbearable pain. As he escaped into the countryside, he tried to process the unthinkable horrors he had just witnessed. Was Wizdor truly lost forever to the depths of the Sea of Darkness? Trusted friends had turned into traitors, the High Guardian was dead, Prince Neblas was a murderer and a thief, and now all Zil-Kenøth lay in the grip of a power-crazed tyrant.

CHAPTER 7
VIOLINDA

As Sindle shuffled down a path, the horrible events of the lumen tumbled through his head. The Grand Inquisitor's face branded itself into Sindle's mind, searing its dark sore of doom into whatever bright flesh of hope remained. Time and again, his memory played back the image of Trogzars casting his beloved Wizdor into the Sea of Darkness. Grief would build up pressure inside him until it would explode into uncontrollable sobbing. This cycle repeated itself countless times until he fell to his knees, buried his face in his hands, and cried, "Grandfather!"

Suspended in pain, he began to think about the mysterious stone he had discovered beside the Sea of Darkness. Reaching into his money pouch and pulling it out, he found that it was no longer cold. As he gazed into it, he noticed its striking beauty for the first time. Unlike ordinary frozen light, it glittered with the brilliance of a diamond.

"Grandfather," he sighed, shutting his eyes and sitting there numbed by shock and grief. He returned the stone to the pouch, arose, and continued on his way.

As he travelled, he tried to drive the horrible image of the Grand Inquisitor from his thoughts, but the harder he tried, the more it persisted in haunting him. A violent battle began to rage inside him. For a time, his desire to even the score with the Grand Inquisitor and the Trogzars would strengthen rage until rage would drive out sorrow. Then sorrow would counterattack, using the memory of Wizdor's fate as its weapon, and would defeat rage. This cycle would play itself out until Sindle's emotions would become locked in stalemate, causing him to break down and weep, unsure of whether he was shedding tears of grief or fury or both. In time, his voice became too hoarse to cry, and his eyes were reduced to burnt holes.

Weak and miserable, Sindle trudged down the path with no thought of direction or destination. His mind was locked on what had happened in Zil-Kenøth. Then a sudden breeze chilled the tears on his hot cheeks. For a moment, his mind escaped its prison of torment. Wind sweeping through trees and chirping crickets together composed what sounded like a nocturnal string symphony of cellos, violas, and violins. Wiping away tears, Sindle focused on meadows dotted by lilac groves stretching out into the distance from both sides of the road. The groves cast violet shadows across carpets of fallen leaves. Beyond the meadows, purple hills kissed a peaceful, violet sky. Sindle stood amazed, for although he had heard in legends that there was such a thing as color, he had never before seen anything but the blacks, whites, and grays of Zil-Kenøth. Still, he knew he was in Violinda, one of the seven lands of Spectara, for when Sindle was a child, Wizdor had told him stories about the place.

As Sindle remembered his childhood with Wizdor, gentle thoughts of peace drifted through his troubled mind. He shut his eyes, and again felt the cool breeze caress his face. He gazed once more across the meadows at the hills, and wings of memory carried him back to Wizdor's words. "Violinda is the land of autumn, the land of dusk, the land of peace. When I was but a lad," he could remember hearing his grandfather say, "I once travelled with your great grandfather–that would be *my father*– as far as Marus Lazul, the Sea of a Thousand Blues. Violinda and Marus Lazul were the only regions of Spectara I ever saw."

Of all Wizdor's stories about Spectara, Sindle's favorite was that of Veronica, a wicked Queen who once ruled the waters of Marus Lazul. He remembered his grandfather's vivid description of her: "She had awful hair that looked like seaweed, and an ugly, fish face. She lived on a volcanic island. Her dreadful kingdom was always covered with thick, foul-smelling fog, and her people were little more than slaves. She loved to strike terror in their hearts!"

Wizdor's scary tale had always made Sindle want to hide beneath his bed covers. Feeling the urge again, he burrowed into a pile of purple leaves and remembered more of the story.

"The wicked, fish-faced Veronica used a wand to conjure up fierce hurricanes and deadly tidal waves on Marus Lazul. Entire fleets of ships were swallowed, never to be seen or heard from again. Once 'Old Fish-Face' raised a tidal wave so large, it covered all Spectara. Thousands died. But when the wave lashed back, she was not expecting it. Her own kingdom was destroyed too, and she drowned in the sea never to be heard from again."

As Sindle lay beneath his leaf-blanket, thoughts of Zil-Kenøth, the Trogzars, and Wizdor began to torment his mind again. He sat up, removed the stone from his money pouch, and held it to the sky. For a moment, its brilliance penetrated his soul and eased his sorrow a bit. But then its strange beauty reminded him of the light of Asdin, and that hammered back into his thoughts the events that had transpired in Zil-Kenøth. The sorrow returned.

Sindle arose and resumed his journey. However, after walking several hours, his feet ached, and hunger's sharp teeth gnawed at his stomach. He hoped a wood in the near distance would offer the prospect of food, so he went on a search that drove him ever deeper into the forest maze. Eventually, he discovered trees dotted with purple berries, but when he bit into one, his mouth reacted with a bout of violent spitting that lasted for some time. No matter how much he tried to drive out the bitter taste, it lingered.

As his hunger worsened, he suddenly realized he was also lost. When he tried to retrace his steps, trees with thorny branches, like soldiers with spears, dared him to pass. They seemed poised, waiting for his next move before launching their attack. When he tried to breach their perimeter, he imagined that one sprang to life and stabbed him in the belly. He yanked up his shirt expecting to find a wound, but then he realized his mind was playing tricks and that the sword he felt was the sword of hunger.

Fighting his way through the forest, he lost track of time and was on the verge of collapse when through the trees he glimpsed another color he had never seen. Sheer curiosity propelled him forward. He fought through the barrage of trees and ran onto a beach glittering with sand the hue of amethyst. Beyond the beach was a sapphire sea that swirled with every color of blue imaginable. Currents and waves of blue upon blue danced and sparkled, filling his vision with delight. He had reached the shores of Marus Lazul, the Sea of a Thousand Blues. Sprinting into the surf, he let its warm waves massage his aching feet. Like magic, all his pain seemed to melt away. He trotted back through luminous indigo-colored sand to the crest of a dune, looked out over Marus Lazul, and ran down again. Then falling on the beach, he burrowed into the sand and let the sea breeze and the wave song lull him into a much-needed sleep.

CHAPTER 8
THE CAPTAIN

The next thing Sindle knew, Marus Lazul had become as black as the Sea of Darkness, and a foul wind howled across its waters. Dark clouds hung low in the sky, and in the distance a volcanic island smoldered beneath a blanket of dense, gray fog. Fear gripped him as he walked along the shore staring out at the terrifying sight.

In the distance, Shades were lined up on what seemed to be a light-freezing dock. Taking care to stay hidden, Sindle crawled on his belly through gray sand until he was underneath the dock. "Onto the barge, slaves!" a harsh voice commanded, followed by the crack of a whip. Sindle then peeked and saw the Grand Inquisitor, his eyes as sharp as daggers. How had he gotten to Marus Lazul? Sindle was confused. The whip cracked again, and he saw faces of friends and acquaintances from Zil-Kenøth. He made his way to the end of the line, still trying to stay out of sight. To his amazement, Lord Dargad was there. "Where are they taking you?" Sindle whispered.

"To Queen Veronica," he replied. His words trailed off in the gale. "She needs more slaves to fuel her furnaces of dark fire. These death barges take us to her. Her barges are the dogmas of Zil Magnus."

The next thing Sindle knew, he was on Veronica's volcanic island in the throne room of her palace. When he caught a glimpse of her face, it was so hideous, he had to avert his gaze. Someone then approached her. "The people are crying for food again, Your Majesty," came a voice. It was that of Prince Neblas!

"Then let them eat the berries of the Zarafat trees of Violinda!" she replied. "They shall be in their mouths as bitter bile and shall pierce their hearts with swords of sorrow!" Her cackling sent chills up Sindle's spine.

"As you wish," Neblas complied. "And what shall we do with the cursed Star they have worshiped for a thousand lumnus-years?"

"Bring the horrid thing forth, and I shall dissolve it," she replied.

Neblas brought Asdin, still stained with the grey blood of the High Guardian, and laid it before the Queen. Its light revealed glistening slime on her scaly face. With her wand, she touched the Star, and it disintegrated. Darkness fell like a curtain, and her insane laughter pierced the air. "Load more of my death barges with slaves," she commanded. "Let none of them escape."

Sindle awoke suddenly with a scream and shot to his feet. In a daze, he stood ready to defend himself. With blurred vision, he saw a bearded man dressed in a dark blue, hooded robe. The man backed away and drew back his hood. "Good lumen-flow, lad," he said. "Sorry to startle you, but I thought you might be needing passage across Marus Lazul. My ferry is over there," he said, pointing, "and I'm setting sail now. You're welcome to come along if you wish." Sindle hesitated, and the man extended his right hand. My name is Pisces," he said, "Regius Pisces. But most people call me Captain."

Sindle reluctantly shook his hand. "I'm Sindle, from Zil-Kenøth," he replied, staring at the ground. When finally he did look the Captain in the eye, however, he did feel a bit more at ease. His long hair and beard were silver with a slight tinge of blue. His hair reminded him a bit of Wizdor's. The Captain's face also radiated good will. But then Sindle remembered that the Grand Inquisitor had also shown good will to Sindle on the day he messed up the ritual of the Dark Circle. He became suspicious. "I suppose you are taking slaves to her volcanic island," he stated, thinking that the Captain was one of Veronica's slave traders.

"I don't quite understand," remarked the Captain.

"Taking slaves to the island of Queen Veronica," Sindle clarified.

"You must be thinking of Viridia," he said. "Is that where you're headed?"

"No," Sindle stated flatly. "I'll never be one of her slaves."

"Slaves?" the Captain queried. "In Viridia? Its people work hard, true, but none are slaves. Viridia is a beautiful place. Perhaps the most beautiful land in all Spectara."

Sindle paused and scratched his head. "Thank you all the same," he said.

"Suit yourself," said the Captain. "But there will not be another ferry coming this way until mid-lumen-ebb."

Sindle started feeling hunger pangs again. "Do you have any food? I can't remember when I last ate."

"Most of the time I catch what I eat from Old Sapphire— that's my name for Marus Lazul. If you want to eat, you'll have to come along for sure."

Sindle looked out over Marus Lazul and saw no sign of a volcanic island, storms, or death barges. Maybe the Captain was not a slave-trader after all. "I have no money for passage," said Sindle.

"That is not a problem," the Captain said. "I would welcome a companion."

At this point Sindle's hunger outweighed his mistrust. "All right," he relented. "I guess I'll come along."

"Good," said the Captain. He turned and made his way toward the ferry, and Sindle followed. "Make yourself comfortable," the Captain said after they had climbed aboard. He whistled a tune as he untied the moorings, pushed off, and hoisted up the sail. Sindle looked out toward Violinda as wind carried them out to sea. Soon gulls were flocking around the ferry. Their calls pierced the air as they dived for fish.

"I wish I was one of them," Sindle remarked to the Captain. "They look well fed enough."

"Right," he replied. "I'll teach you how to fish this very minute. You'll give those gulls a bad name in no time." The Captain stood up, cupped his hands around his mouth, and called out, "oowissss....oowissss...."

That instant, a fish jumped into the boat. The Captain called out again, this time with the call "oouummmm." Fish started flipping onto the deck by droves. "I've got to be careful, or we'll have a job on our hands throwing them all back." Sindle stood speechless and amazed at the whole spectacle. "What's wrong?" asked the Captain, observing him. "You look as though you've seen a ghost."

"How did you do that?"

"You've never seen fish called?" asked the Captain. Sindle shook his head. "You said you're from Zil-Kenøth," the Captain continued. "Have you never left home before now?"

"No."

"I should have guessed. Then you likely have never seen color before. No wonder you look so confused."

"I'm not confused, I'm just..."

"A fish out of water," the Captain interrupted with a chuckle as he looked at fish flopping on the deck. "That explains a lot. All right, Sindle. How can you expect to learn how to fish if you're still one of them? Now, call out and let them know who the master is."

Sindle stood up, cupped his hands around his mouth, and cried out, "Oowissss," but nothing happened. "It's no use," he said, "I don't have the knack."

"I know the problem. You're not in tune," said the Captain. He cupped his hands and shouted, "oooowammmmm...."

Just then, about twenty fish, one after the other, jumped from the water smacking Sindle right in the face with their tails.

"I told them you were hungry," said the Captain, chuckling, "so they all tried to jump into your mouth. Why didn't you just catch them with your teeth and swallow them whole?"

"What? Eat them raw and alive?" Sindle looked disgusted.

"Is there any other way? Of course, raw and alive! Now eat one. I know you're starved." Sindle hesitated. "Go ahead, it won't bite."

Sindle bit into one of the fish, and it squealed. "Whole, Sindle, whole! You don't want the poor thing to suffer."

Sindle obeyed the Captain and swallowed it with one gulp. To his amazement, it tasted delicious. "You see," the Captain went on, "they're better that way."

Sindle swallowed another. "They're very good," he remarked. Then he swallowed several more.

"Don't eat too many now," the Captain warned. "If they get to wiggling around in your tummy, you'll get sick."

Sindle ignored his warning and kept eating. "When I was young," he told the Captain, "my grandfather used to tell me about the delicacies his father would bring him from Marus Lazul. These fish must be what he was talking about." He kept swallowing one fish after another. In time, however, he became queasy, just as the Captain had warned.

"You don't look at all well," remarked the Captain.

"Maybe you were right about the fish," Sindle admitted.

"You'll have to take the cure, I'm afraid."

"Cure?"

"Yes. Into the water with you."

"What?"

"Just do as I say, and you'll be fine."

Sindle jumped overboard into the sea.

"Now put your head under and take deep breaths."

"What? I'll drown!"

"Calm yourself," said the Captain. "The waters of Marus Lazul are enchanted. Now do as I say."

A reluctant Sindle submerged, breathed the water, and soon surfaced. "You're right!" He dove back under.

"You'll need to take a breath for every fish you ate above the limit," the Captain yelled. "Then you'll be cured."

In no time, the deep breaths had made Sindle feel better, and he popped up out of the water. "I feel all right now. I'm ready to come aboard."

The Captain threw out a rope, and told him to grab hold.

Sindle pulled himself to the side of the ferry, and the Captain hoisted him up. "That was amazing," Sindle remarked.

"My, oh, my," said the Captain staring at him, "you've got an interesting tan my boy."

Sindle looked at his hands and feet. "They're blue! Have I been poisoned?"

"No," laughed the Captain. "You've just been 'colorized'. Maybe the time will come when you will learn how to control how you look. Let me show you what I mean." The Captain suddenly turned from purple to blue to green to orange to red. "Oh, I almost forgot," and he turned yellow. "Sometimes it helps when you're traveling through Spectara to be a chameleon," he continued. "And sometimes," he said, changing back to a bluish color, "when it comes to what is really true and important, the chameleon way backfires."

Sindle stared at him with his mouth hanging open.

"Yes, my boy," the Captain continued. "What is really true can only be found in pure light, not in the shadows and divided colors of this world we call Spectara."

Sindle hung his head and said, "I know what you mean. I thought I knew what the truth was when I lived in Zil-Kenøth, but I only found out how terrible lies can be. A group of liars called Trogzars killed our High Guardian, stole Asdin, our Sacred Star of Frozen Light, and sacrificed my grandfather, Wizdor, to the Sea of Darkness."

A painful look crept across the Captain's face. "That is an even deeper lie than the one that has gripped the Shades of Zil-Kenøth for over a thousand lumnus-years, the lie that the Star is shield and protector against the Hell of Light."

Sindle's eyes brightened. "My grandfather had similar doubts about the Star, but he did not voice them for fear of what might happen. But then, one of the last things he said before they took him to die was 'Why should light fear light?'"

"How often do the wise keep silent until it is too late," remarked the Captain, shaking his head. "He was right, of course—about the Star, I mean. Light will never fear itself. Never."

"Then Prince Neblas and the Trogzars may not succeed in their plot after all?" inquired Sindle, staring out over Marus Lazul.

"Prince? Plot?" queried the Captain.

"Prince Neblas was son of the High Guardian of Asdin," Sindle explained. "He was involved in a Trogzar plot to steal the Star, journey to the Hell of Light, and use the Star as a weapon to destroy its ruler forever. He killed his own father in order to get control of the Star."

"That is terrible news," said the Captain, frowning. "I think I know the one you speak of. I can't believe I didn't see it before. He was very quiet, that one. The bag he held, too, seemed to have contents he wished to keep secret."

"That does sound like Neblas," said Sindle. "How did you meet him?"

"I regret to tell you that he was among my passengers last lumen-ebb," answered the Captain, hanging his head. "I can't believe I helped him with his sordid quest. It makes me sad that I did not know of his conspiracy."

"But surely his quest will not succeed if what you have told me is true," said Sindle, trying to reassure him.

"Still, we can't be sure that he won't do great harm before he is finished with his misguided mission," the Captain remarked. "It is not his damage to the Light I fear most, but his damage to Spectara. Spectara is vulnerable. The ruler of that place you people of Zil-Kenøth call the Hell of Light may have to take extreme measures to save Spectara from ruin and possible annihilation."

Sindle shuddered. "I had no idea."

"The balance of power has now been upset in Spectara," explained the Captain. "You should know, my boy, that truth always exists in compassion, while hate spawns those lies that attack truth. Sometimes hate erodes truth to the point that love must sacrifice itself in order to reverse the lie and restore the truth. Surely you can see that your own grandfather's death was such a sacrifice of truth to undo hate and the lie."

"I don't understand that at all," said Sindle. "If anything, Wizdor's death has made me hate more, not less."

"That must be because your heart is still chained to the shadows of your netherworld," said the Captain. "Forgive me for saying it, but such chains are quite difficult to break. People sometimes prefer chains to freedom, you know. Of course you have taken the first step by leaving Zil-Kenøth behind. In time you will understand more. After all, you did not know what other colors there were beside black, white, and gray until you saw them, right? And you did not know what it was like to be made well by the waters of Marus Lazul until you breathed them. Is that not correct?"

"I suppose," replied Sindle.

"In the same way, you cannot know truth until you are immersed in it as you were in these waters. Maybe you should take a journey, like your misguided friend Neblas. Not the same kind of journey, mind you, but a journey of a different sort. A quest for truth, perhaps? If your heart remains open, then I'm sure that quest will lead you to the right destination."

"Then again," replied Sindle. "My quest might turn out to be just as misguided as Neblas's. How can I know what is true or false anymore. How can I believe anything?"

"You can believe this," replied the Captain. "Neblas has already succeeded in bringing death and tyranny to the Shades of Zil-Kenøth, and the farther he ventures away from there with the Star, the more death and tyranny will spread to other regions of Spectara. We can only hope that the forces of good will unite instead of fighting each other, for if the colors of Spectara become more divided than they are now, they all may finally sink into the abyss you call the Sea of Darkness where they will cease to exist."

Sindle sat looking out over Marus Lazul with its blue waters of a thousand shades dancing together in its waves. How could such beauty ever be swallowed up by the abyss of darkness? Sindle could not fathom how it was possible. Still, the Captain's words frightened him. What if he did speak truth? Sindle couldn't bear the thought that the evils unleashed in Zil-Kenøth might follow him and that in the end he and the rest of Spectara might not escape them.

"My words have upset you," the Captain said, observing his sadness. "Cheer up. I happen to know from experience that where there is light there is hope. You must not give up."

"I know," said Sindle. "But I have no idea how to fight the darkness. I feel like a soldier being sent to battle without shield or weapons or knowledge of how to fight. What am I to do?"

"The light will be your shield and your weapon, and the light will teach you how to fight," said the Captain. Suddenly the Captain caught a glimpse of a shoreline in the distance. "Look," he shouted. "Viridia is coming into view. It's a wonderful place where you will find solace and healing for your wounds of grief. Viridia is known for its healing arts, you know."

"But I have no place to go or stay," replied Sindle.

"Viridians are not like the hordes of Kenøth," said the Captain. "They are hospitable and generous to a fault. I'm sure you will be welcomed with open arms."

The Captain stood and adjusted the sail. Soon an emerald coastline covered by patches of gray-green fog that hovered close to the water came into view. Fog billowed up and swirled behind the stern as the ferry cut through it. The bay was dotted with fishing boats. When they reached a dock, the Captain tied the ropes to the moorings, climbed out on the pier, and extended his hand to Sindle with the words, "Welcome to Viridia!"

Sindle climbed onto the pier. "I do have something I could pay you with after all," said Sindle, removing from his money pouch his beautiful stone of frozen light and handing it to the Captain.

The Captain held the stone to the sky and squinted. "It's very valuable, I'm sure," he said, "but it is no ordinary piece of frozen light. You may need it on your journey, so here."

"Thanks," said Sindle, taking it back and returning it to the pouch.

"It's good-bye, then, I suppose," said the Captain, shaking Sindle's hand, "until our paths cross again."

"I hope that time will come soon. Well," said Sindle looking at the shore, "I guess I had better get going. Thanks, Captain, for helping me."

"Don't mention it, my boy."

Sindle walked along the dock to the shore, and the Captain cried out one more time, "Don't forget the quest we talked about!"

"I won't," he said, waving back.

CHAPTER 9
KELDON

Sea gulls piped, waves roared, and the harbor bustled with Viridians loading and unloading barges. Sindle wandered down a path strewn with broken shells toward a string of thatched-roof huts that were joined together like a patchwork quilt. Like peas from a pod, green-skinned Viridians were spilling out of the huts, carrying chartreuse bags filled with vegetables. Sindle watched one man who was sitting in front of one hut, carving small objects from what appeared to be jade. After watching him for several minutes, Sindle finally mustered the nerve to go and ask him for information.

"The carvings are beautiful," said Sindle.

The man stood, clasped his hands and bowed.

"Forgive me for interrupting your work. I've just arrived in Viridia. Do you know where I might find an inn?"

The man smiled. Then he rattled off a confusing train of words, and bowed again. Too embarrassed to ask him to repeat his words, Sindle uttered a polite, "Thank you," and walked inside the market. Without warning, his senses were assaulted by pungent and earthy aromas together with chattering. The market had the sound and odor of a bird sanctuary. Just then, from the center of the chirping throng rose the clear voice of a woman. "May I help you?"

She must have noticed his oscillating head and guessed that he was a stranger. "Thank you," replied Sindle. "I've just arrived in your land and need a place to stay. I asked the man sitting in front of the shop, but I'm afraid I didn't understand his accent. Do you know where I might find an inn?"

"You had best go to the city of Chartra," she answered, smiling. Her beady, close-set eyes were the color of fireflies. "Only vegetable and fish markets can be found in these parts. Chartra is a beautiful place. You will love it there. I'm sure you will find many inns to choose from." After she spoke, she clasped her hands together, brought them up to her chin, and bowed. Then she grabbed Sindle's arm. "Come, I will show you the road."

By now everyone in the market was smiling and bowing in Sindle's direction. Leaving the market, the woman led him down a narrow path to a road paved with gravel the hue of turquoise. "If you follow this road," she instructed, "you will arrive in Chartra in a few hours. I am sure you will find an inn there." Her tiny eyes glowed as she smiled, brought her hands up to her chin, and bowed.

"My sincerest thanks," he said, bowing in return, and he bade her farewell.

As Sindle walked down the road, he glanced back several times to see if the woman had returned to the market, but every time he would see her still standing there waving at him. So he would wave at her and bow; then she would do the same in return. Finally, he rounded a bend and noticed that the turquoise path was beginning to be spangled with emeralds. He stooped down and ran his fingers through it. He could not believe such beautiful gems were but common gravel in this land! He straightened, and his eyes roved the countryside. Rich meadows of grass and clover stretched into the distance beneath a pale, green sky.

As he continued to travel, he started seeing odd trees with small leaves and smooth, olive-colored trunks. Curious, he walked over to one and touched it. It had a velvet, spongy feel. He caressed, squeezed, and punched it from its branches all the way down to its soft roots. Beside its roots grew cool clover. Though it was not yet low lumen-ebb, this was enough to invite him for a nap, so he crawled into the clover, laid his head on a large root that protruded from the ground, and let the gentle, warm breeze waft over him. He was nearly asleep when he heard distant harp music that faded in and out in concert with the gusting of the wind. Sitting up, he tried to locate its source, but seeing no one, he lay back down and soon drifted to sleep.

When Sindle awoke, he heard instead of harp music a sound of buzzing in the air like that made by swarming bees. He sat up and gazed across the meadow. Several dense clouds of vibrating green light were drifting toward him. Alarmed, he hid behind a tree until they passed. Scarcely a moment had passed when he heard a distant cry for help. He darted off in its direction, hearing the plea several more times as he ran. Then, in the nick of time, he caught himself just before plummeting headlong over the edge of a bluff. When he stared into the gully below, he saw a man, sprawled upon the ground, holding his arm and grimacing in pain. "Please, help me," the man cried.

Sindle crawled down the side of the bluff, and then came and knelt beside the wounded Viridian.

"My arm is broken, and my flock is scattering. Please, hand me my harp. It's there," he said, pointing, and Sindle retrieved it quickly.

"There's no time to lose. Can you hold it as I play?" As Sindle held the instrument, the man began strumming its strings with his good arm. "Please, hold it tight while I tune it," he said, and Sindle complied. "There," said the man, "let's hope it's not too late."

The Viridian's fingers ran quickly across the strings, but they made no sound.

"It must be broken," Sindle remarked.

"No," he replied. "My zoas are returning now. Listen."

Sindle again began to hear the harp music he had heard earlier.

"All will be well now," said the man. "By the way, I'm Keldon." He extend his good arm only for a second to shake hands.

"I am Sindle," he replied.

Keldon quickly returned to his playing. "Here they come! See!"

When Sindle looked, his eyes widened. The green clouds of light he had seen earlier were heading toward them. Now their light formed intricate patterns and shapes, and harp music rang from inside them. "Amazing!" exclaimed Sindle. "How is it that the harp makes no sound but the creatures do? What are the creatures called again?"

"Zoas." Keldon was so preoccupied that he must have noticed Sindle's appearance for the first time. "Forgive me," he said. "I see now that you are a stranger in Viridia. No doubt I have much explaining to do. Follow me to my cottage, and I shall tell you about the zoas. I shall need you to hold the harp as we travel if you don't mind."

"Not at all," replied Sindle.

As they walked, Sindle noticed that Keldon had light green skin, a large nose as sharp as an eagle's beak, small close-set eyes that glowed green under high-arching eyebrows, and a thin slit for a mouth. Keldon's thinning hair lay plastered firmly against his head, giving him the appearance of an onion.

"Where were you headed before you came to my rescue?" Keldon asked Sindle.

"To Chartra," he replied. "I was hoping to find an inn there where I could stay."

"You will stay with us, by all means," said Keldon. "You may not yet realize the great service you have rendered to the kingdom of Viridia. Those were not just any zoas you helped save. They are the zoas of Queen Veronica. I am certain she will reward you handsomely for your heroic act!"

When Sindle heard the name 'Veronica', Wizdor's story of 'Old Fish Face' raced through his memory, and he became fearful. "That's kind of you, really," he responded, "but it won't be necessary. A nice place to stay will be reward enough."

"You will at least enjoy a wonderful dinner with us, then," said Keldon. "My wife, Biona, is the best cook in all Viridia, despite my looking like skin and bones."

Sindle and Keldon talked and laughed as they wandered down the path to the Viridian's cottage. Keldon never ceased playing his harp as they chatted. He seemed to play it automatically. With a nod of his head here and there, he pointed out sites of historic interest. Like a cross between a schoolmaster and a tour guide, he explained the traditions and lore of Viridia to Sindle.

In the fields, on either side of the road, Sindle observed zoaherders tending their flocks. "Why do you herd zoas?" he asked. "What good are they?"

Keldon smiled, and a light switched on in eyes that made him appear quite intellectual. "Zoas are the most important things we raise in Viridia," he replied. "It takes many lumnus-years of practice to know how to control them because they are wild by nature." He nodded in the direction of a group of zoaherders, "The lads you see there are as young as four lumnus-years. I myself started when I was that age. I am now close to two-hundred." Sindle was intrigued as Keldon, using his head as a pointer, continued his lecture without pause. "If you will look over there, you will see zoas in their vegetable form—and over there," he nodded again, "crystalline zoas are ready to flower. See the reapers with their harps?"

"Yes. But why are some vegetable and other crystalline?"

"Most zoas pass through three stages," Keldon explained. "These I herd now are animal zoas, but soon they will lay their egg-seeds in the ground and die. Then the tiny egg-seeds will grow into vegetable zoas. In this form they must be tended like any other plant. Some will be uprooted before they flower. When they are dried, they become crystalline zoas. Some become jade, some tourmaline, some emerald, and some beryl, depending upon what combination of notes was played while their parents were in the animal stage."

"Remarkable," said Sindle. "What do you do with the crystalline ones?"

"We build with them for the most part," Keldon replied. "You should see the buildings of Chartra. We shall go there tomorrow."

"That would be wonderful." Sindle looked at a field where zoaherders stood ready to reap, and asked Keldon, "How are the new animal zoas born?"

Keldon laughed. "They're not born, exactly. They blossom, you see. When the buds of the zoas open in that field over there," he said, nodding, "new animal zoas will emerge. The zoaherders even now stand ready to harvest them."

"Do any ever escape before they are harvested?"

"Oh, yes," replied Keldon. "It's terrible when that happens. These would have gotten away, you know, if you hadn't come to my rescue. We have to play these harps constantly, or they will wander off to Zanthis where they become wild and quite dangerous. Also, the right combination of notes must always be played, or they will become deformed. That, too, is a sad end for a zoa."

"Where is this Zanthis you speak of?" asked Sindle.

"It borders Viridia. It is a horrible desert land. I've never been there, mind you, but I hear it's a dreadful place. Truthfully, I have no wish ever to go there."

Zanthis sounded to Sindle like the Hell of Light, and the thought struck him that maybe the Hell of Light was real after all.

"See there?" said Keldon, nodding toward zoaherders who were playing flutes. "They tend silk zoas. We use their cocoons for thread to make our clothes."

"Are they different from other zoas?" asked Sindle.

"Only in the sense that a flute is used to herd them instead of a harp. We do not allow silk zoas to lay eggs. Instead, they are unwound the moment they finish spinning their cocoons."

Sindle thought for a moment, and then asked, "Are some offspring of the zoas you herd converted into silk zoas when they flower?"

Keldon's eyes lit up. "Theoretically, yes."

They walked along in silence for awhile. Then Sindle remarked, "If you ask me, zoaherding is much more interesting than light-freezing."

"Light-freezing?" queried Keldon.

"Yes," Sindle replied. "That is how we make the raw material for our buildings and clothes in Zil-Kenøth where I am from."

"Fascinating!" exclaimed Keldon. "You must explain it all to me."

As they journeyed, Sindle expounded the science of light-freezing to Keldon, who in turn asked him many questions. In time, their conversation drifted to the subject of the dire events that had transpired in Zil-Kenøth and to the tragedy of Wizdor's demise in the Sea of Darkness. "How terrible," Keldon at last commented.

"Yes," said Sindle. "The Sea of Darkness is a dangerous place, and light-freezing is a dangerous science. My father died there there, too, many years ago in a light-freezing accident."

"How did that happen?" asked Keldon.

"The platforms beneath the light-freezing houses rest on piers that extend far out into the Sea. Different sizes of wells in these platforms are open directly to the Sea. A special kind of liquid light is then placed inside molds and sealed. After this is done, light-freezers stand on the platforms and submerge these molds which are attached to cables. They must be submerged slowly, or a sea-surge might result. The substance from the Sea of Darkness freezes on contact. It always maims and usually kills whomever it touches. The form being submerged by my father's light-freezing circle was very large and heavy, and had to be suspended by eight cables. As the light-freezers were lowering it, one of the cables snapped. The weight of the form proved too much for the rest to handle. The form plummeted into the well. The sea-surge lashed back. All eight light-freezers, including my father, were killed. I was only three when it happened, so I don't remember him at all. I only know the story of how he died. Since my mother died giving birth to me, I was left an orphan. My grandfather, Wizdor, took me in. So when he was sacrificed to the Sea of Darkness, the story of what had happened to my father returned, and I felt my childhood terror of the Sea of Darkness return. I loved my grandfather more than my own life. He reared me, taught me everything I know. Now the dearest person in the world has been taken from me forever."

"How terrible," remarked Keldon. "I've heard that people could in fact die, but I've never known it really to happen—at least not until now."

Sindle appeared startled. "Do you mean that no one ever has died in Viridia?"

"Not in recorded memory," Keldon answered. "Our Queen would never allow it. She wields power over every sickness, disease, and malady. In rare cases where death does occur, she easily reverses it."

As they walked along, Sindle began to doubt what he had learned from Wizdor about Queen Veronica. So happy a man as Keldon could hardly be a slave, and so beautiful a land as Viridia could hardly be ruled by so evil a Queen.

At last they came over the crest of a hill, and Keldon exclaimed, "We're home!"

Sindle's eyes settled upon a peaceful valley, and in its midst a little thatched-roof cottage seemed to grow from the landscape as though it were a living thing. The enchanting scene beckoned them to come and rest.

CHAPTER 10
THE VERDIS TREE

As Keldon and Sindle meandered down the path to the cottage, the door sprang open and out ran a stout little woman. She trotted toward them, shouting with motherly urgency, "Keldon! Oh, my dear! What has happened to you?" When she reached him, she doted. "You're hurt. Hurry inside, and I'll call Garn to take the flock, Garn! Garn!" she shouted. "Oh, Keldon!" she exclaimed, seeing his wounded arm, "you need Verdis ointment on that this minute! Garn!" she shouted again.

A tall man came running from a barn. "Keldon has had an accident," she said, handing Garn the harp.

"Is the arm broken?" he asked.

"I'm afraid so," Keldon answered. "Biona and Garn, this is Sindle. If he hadn't shown up, the herd would have been lost."

"How can we ever thank you, Sindle?" the stout woman remarked. Turning, she said, "thank you," to Garn and then looked at Sindle. "Please do come with us into the cottage so I can doctor Keldon's arm."

Once inside the cottage, Biona ordered Keldon to sit as she hurried to get medicine for his injury. The interior of the cottage resembled a greenhouse. Plants with thick, fleshy stems and leaves looked like gentlemen dressed in green tuxedos. Other plants having lacy leaves and plumed flowers seemed like ladies waiting for the gentlemen to invite them to waltz.

Soon Biona returned with a jar, unscrewed the cap, dipped her fingers in some clear, green salve, and started smearing it on Keldon's arm.

"Sindle is a stranger in Viridia and needs a place to stay," Keldon informed Biona.

"You are most welcome to stay here with us, Sindle," she said. Her eyebrows had now become two half circles, and the pudgy cheeks of her moon face protruded when she smiled. "Thank you again for saving Keldon and his zoas."

"It was no trouble, really," said Sindle.

"There," said Biona as she finished smearing the ointment.

Before Sindle's very eyes, the bruises faded, and Keldon began to move his arm and fingers about freely. "That's better," he said. "Now it's as good as new."

"Amazing!" exclaimed Sindle. "What was that you put on him?"

"Verdis ointment," replied Biona. "It is named for the tree it's taken from that grows in the center of the city of Chartra."

"The people of Viridia call it the Tree of Life," Keldon added. "Our ancient sages believed that it was the ladder between our world and the realms of eternal light we call *Vernesda*. That is the place all Viridians aspire to go when the regions of Spectara cease to be."

"Where is Vernesda?" Sindle asked.

"No one knows, really," answered Keldon. "I hear tell that the Queen knows the way and that she may go there if she wishes," Keldon answered. "But her love for the Viridian people keeps her here where she can use the power of the Verdis Tree to cure every disease and restore life to the dying and the dead."

"I wish the Queen could have helped my grandfather, Wizdor," said Sindle, "but I'm afraid Verdis salve would do no good now."

"True," remarked Keldon, "but the Queen has more than just the Verdis Tree, you know. She possesses an ancient wand that gives her power over death."

Sindle's dream of the Fish-Faced Queen flitted again through his memory. "Would she ever use her wand to cause evil?" he asked Keldon.

"Knowing Queen Veronica, that would be very unlikely, if not impossible," Keldon replied. "She is known for her kindness and wisdom."

"Could she use it to bring my grandfather back to life, do you think?" Sindle asked.

Keldon's eyes lit up. "I see no reason why she couldn't!" he exclaimed. "Why didn't I think of that before? You deserve to be rewarded by the Queen for saving her zoas. What better thing could she do than restore your grandfather to life? It would be such a simple thing for her too!"

"But Wizdor's body has been lost to the Sea of Darkness. How can she restore his life if his body is no more?"

"There have been cases such as this in the past," returned Keldon. "I don't believe it will present a problem to our Queen. Her knowledge of such matters is unsurpassed."

Sindle sat on the edge of his chair. "Could we see her before the lumen is over?"

Keldon hesitated. "I'm afraid not. We shall have to wait until tomorrow at Wittistide, for she can be approached only then. I feel certain, though, that she will grant you audience."

Keldon, noticing Sindle's disappointment, added, "I know how anxious you will be until the morrow's lumen-flow comes. As for now, we have just the thing to keep you from fretting. Biona!" he called out.

She trotted into the room. "Yes, dear?" she inquired.

"May we have a spot of coolum?" he requested.

"How terribly rude of me," she remarked. "I should have offered you coolum, Sindle. Forgive me." She left and a few minutes later returned with a teapot, cups, and saucers. After pouring two cups of dark green liquid, she handed one to Sindle and another to Keldon.

"You must sip the coolum slowly until you get use to it," Biona instructed Sindle. "It has been known to make people see stars if they are not use to it."

Sindle received the cup with a "thank you," and Keldon piped in. "Biona is only kidding. Some people find the taste offensive at first, but it has a way of growing on you."

When Sindle took a sip, he immediately wrinkled his nose, and a look of disgust came over his face.

"The first cup tastes bitter," Biona commented. "But one does adjust to the second. It is always much better."

While Keldon and Sindle finished their coolum, Biona left for the kitchen, set the table for dinner, and a little while later announced, "Dinner is served." The table they gathered around looked as though it had been sliced from a large tree trunk, and the stools had the appearance of overgrown toadstools. Biona placed a generous helping of food on a large banana leaf and handed it to Sindle. The food looked vaguely like the plants he had seen growing in another part of the cottage, but since it was attractively prepared, he decided to be adventurous and try it. At first, he took only small bites, but finding Biona's cooking quite delicious, he began eating heartily. Biona kept offering him additional helpings as soon as he would finish, and he complied by eating several more. However, remembering his bout with the fish on Marus Lazul, he stopped short of becoming too full.

"Care for more coolum?" Biona offered.

"No, thank you," he replied, grimacing.

"My dear Sindle, you must try another cup," Keldon insisted. "I promise the second will not be bitter."

In order not to offend his hosts, he complied, and when he did take a sip, his eyes lit up. "It's delicious," he said with amazement. He gulped it down, and went on to ask for several more refills. Each time Biona would freshen his cup, she and Keldon would chuckle. At length, Sindle lost count of the number he had drunk.

"Careful," Keldon cautioned. "People have been known to overdo it on the coolum. Too much may make you drowsy."

"Indeed?" yawned Sindle. "Then I will stop with one more." He poured himself another cup from the teapot, but as soon as he finished drinking it, he drifted to sleep. "Come," Keldon said to Biona. "Help me get him into bed." They guided Sindle to the bedroom, and Biona pulled back the green silk bedcovers. Then Biona tucked him in. "Good lumen-ebb, and sleep well," she whispered, smiling, and they tiptoed out of the room.

CHAPTER 11
VERLIN

When Sindle awoke, music from harps and flutes wafted through the window on the crisp breeze of early lumen-flow. Sitting up, he stretched and looked around. In keeping with the rest of Keldon's cottage, the bedroom resembled a jungle. Sindle swept back the green silk covers and dangled his feet over the edge of the oddly shaped bed. At least he supposed it was a bed; he had never seen anything quite like it before. Using his toes to probe its base, he discovered that it grew out of the floor. It had the texture and feel of the velvet sponge-wood he had used for a pillow when he napped in the meadow upon first arriving in Viridia.

Sindle rose up, stretched again, and yawned. He then heard Keldon and Biona clattering about in another part of the cottage and realized he had overslept. He ambled over to the mirror to freshen up before breakfast, but when he saw his face, he was shocked. His skin—indeed his whole body—had turned green! Now only his eyes kept him from looking Viridian. They were not close-set enough.

Sindle emerged from the bedroom to find Biona and Keldon sitting at their table chatting. "Oh, good lumen-flow, Sindle," Biona tweeted.

"Good lumen-flow," he replied.

"We were getting worried about you." Biona's tiny eyes showed a mixture of triumph and pleasure as they roved back and forth across Sindle's new skin tone.

"Sindle must be hungry," Keldon hinted to Biona.

"Of course, I'll get him breakfast." She rose from the table and went to prepare his food. Keldon followed and whispered to her, "I'm afraid he had too much coolum last lumen-ebb."

"It's just as well," Biona whispered back. "Now people won't stare at him when we go to Chartra."

Sindle, overhearing, was relieved that they hadn't made a fuss over his appearance. "When shall we go?" he asked.

"Oh," started Keldon, blushing dark green and straightening his pea-pod coat, "Immediately after breakfast if that is all right."

"Yours is ready now," said Biona, handing him a banana leaf full of vegetables similar to the ones he had eaten the previous lumen-ebb. She and Keldon hovered over him, waiting for him to eat.

"Aren't you going to join me?" Sindle asked.

"We've already had our breakfast," Biona replied.

Sindle blushed. "Sorry I overslept. I'll hurry." Sindle stuffed his mouth, swallowing half-chewed bites. Biona rummaged through her pantry, emerged with a basket, and placed it on the table. Sindle gulped down the last morsel of food, wiped his mouth, and sprang up. "That was delicious, Biona. Thank you."

"You're welcome," Biona replied. "Would you like anything else? Some coolum, perhaps?"

"I had better not," he replied. "Thanks all the same."

"Then I suppose we had best be off to Chartra," she said.

"I'll make sure Garn will tend the zoas while we're away," said Keldon, and he left the cottage. Meanwhile, Biona put on a hat that resembled the banana leaves she used for plates. The ends of the leaves had green vines attached to them, and she tied these in a bow under her chin.

"Let's be off, Sindle," she said, picking up her basket, and with that she walked out the door with her green skirt rustling. "Keldon!" she shouted, "we must leave now if we are to arrive in Chartra by high lumen-flow!"

Keldon came running from the barn. "Garn has agreed to tend the zoas," he informed her.

In a few moments, they waved good-bye to Garn and were on their way to Chartra. For several miles, they followed an emerald-peppered, turquoise path that wound from Keldon's cottage through the meadows and hills of Viridia. As they climbed the crest of a hill, Keldon informed Sindle, "In a moment you will see Chartra."

As they journeyed over the hilltop, the grass carpet gradually sank before their eyes, revealing in the valley beyond a beautiful city that seemed like an immense wheel. The city resembled an ancient forest; yet, despite its antiquity, it basked in a thin, bright, youthful haze of vibrant light.

"I've never seen so lovely a city!" exclaimed Sindle.

"Just wait until you see the Verdis tree at Wittistide!" Keldon remarked.

As they strolled into the valley, exquisite gardens came into view. In the near distance, the city's pillars, domes, turrets, and spires seemed to move back and forth like priests performing silent rituals. Low hedges swirled in intricate designs from either side of the path. Soon they were entering Chartra's delicate emerald gates. Beyond them, buildings rose with elegance and grace above sculptured gardens.

"It's early yet, and I want Sindle to meet Verlin," Keldon informed Biona.

"Then I shall go along to market and see you two later," said Biona. "Where shall we meet?"

"In front of the palace after Wittistide would be best, I suppose," Keldon replied. Then he and Biona exchanged a brief kiss, and she trotted off down the street.

"We'll have to hurry, Sindle, if we are to meet Verlin," said Keldon, and they started down the street in the opposite direction from Biona.

"Who is Verlin?" Sindle asked.

"Verlin is a Grand Maestro of the zoaherding art," Keldon replied. "He's quite old and lonely, so whenever I come to Chartra, I look in on him to see how he is getting along. I was Verlin's apprentice for many a lumnus-year. He taught me almost everything I know about zoaherding."

As they traversed Chartra's ancient streets of jade cobblestone past elegant buildings of turquoise, tourmaline, jade, and emerald, Keldon told Sindle stories about his experiences with Verlin that made Sindle look forward to meeting him. In time they came to a vast, domed building. "This is the academy where zoaherding is taught," Keldon told Sindle as they climbed a mountain of steps to the building's colonnaded porch. When they passed between the vast columns, Sindle gazed up in awe.

"It is here, my dear Sindle," Keldon began with his school-master's voice, "that I began to learn the principles of zoaherding almost two-hundred lumnus-years ago." The porch opened up into a quadrangle with gardens, shrubbery, and ivy-covered walls. "There," Keldon pointed to a window, "is where musical horticulture is taught. To the right, just above you, the proportions of perfect, harmonic, and inharmonic tones and melodic sequence to lapidary zoa forms and symmetry are studied, not to mention the theories of musical embodiment. There, also, experiments are performed that show the effects of bass and treble energy transference on zoa mass and size, and the effects of emotive dynamics and logical form and rhythm on substance quality."

Keldon's explanation brought Sindle's face to a quizzical point. "I see," he replied, not actually seeing at all.

"And just ahead are practice rooms," Keldon continued. "When the theories are learned after thirty lumnus-years of schooling, then the practice of the zoaherding art must be perfected. All this begins, of course, at age four, but one cannot herd zoas unsupervised until one can perform perfectly."

As Keldon and Sindle passed beneath an arch at the opposite end of the quadrangle from the porch, a melange of harp and flute notes assaulted their ears. "How ghastly," remarked Keldon, grimacing. "Please don't pay any attention to that. Verlin's quarters are this way," he said, directing Sindle through an archway. They walked down a long corridor, and midway came to another corridor that led to still another. Sindle lost count of the number and direction of turns they had taken, and since all the corridors were identical, he began to wonder and soon asked Keldon, "Are we lost?"

"Not at all," he replied. "You're probably thinking there must a shorter way, but there isn't. Since Verlin is a Grand

Maestro of the art, he is protected by a labyrinth. No one would be able to find him who does not know the labyrinth's secret."

Eventually, when they came to an ancient wooden door, Keldon rapped three times. Moments later, three raps sounded from the other side, and Keldon rapped again in some kind of code. Then the door popped open with the shout of "Keldon, my son!" and there stood an ancient green-skinned, gray-bearded, wrinkled-faced man clothed in forest green robes and wearing a pointed, light green hat on which a tree, the same color as his robes, was embroidered. When his close-set eyes focused on Keldon, they sparkled, and he said, "Please, do come in!"

"Maestro Grandioso," Keldon addressed him. "Allow me to introduce you to Sindle."

"Sindle, is it?" Somehow, Verlin's look was sharp and soft at the same time. "Let's see." He stroked his long beard. "Yes, that's a Kenøthic name if I ever heard one."

"How did you guess that?" asked Sindle.

"My dear child, I'm eight hundred and thirty lumnus-years old," he said with a chuckle. "You do learn a few things during such a span. Besides, your looks give you away. Your eyes are not those of a Viridian."

Sindle laughed. He instantly liked Verlin.

"Welcome to Viridia," Verlin said to Sindle. "You are welcome here despite what your people have done to so many of our zoas. Right, Keldon?"

"Right," he replied, smiling. It was just like Verlin not to lose time getting to the point.

Sindle was confused. "I'm afraid I don't understand," he remarked. "What do we do to the zoas? I never knew they existed before coming here."

"Then you must not come from the upper echelons of the light-freezing guilds," Verlin commented. "I should have known. Only a select few know the real origins of the liquid light you people of Zil-Kenøth freeze in your dreadful Sea of Darkness."

Sindle's mouth hung open, and at the same time he felt insulted that a foreigner would know more about light-freezing science than himself.

"Surely you must have been suspicious at some time or another about the relationship between those horrid Ophis horns and liquid light," Verlin continued. "Yes, indeed. Those infernal tooters use their dark music to sap the zoas of their energy, transforming them from green living things into dead, gray, inert liquid."

"I had no idea," said Sindle with a look of shock and sadness.

"After they have committed such criminal acts," Verlin went on, "they transport the liquid on secret barges across Marus Lazul and through Violinda back to Zil-Kenøth where they freeze it mercilessly in the Sea of Darkness."

"They should be killed for their crimes!" Sindle blurted. "Why don't you fight them?"

Keldon and Verlin shook their heads in disdain, and Sindle immediately realized he had said the wrong thing.

"That may be the way of the Kenøthic hordes," said Verlin, "but it is not the Viridian way. Ours is a way of peace. We believe that life will ultimately triumph over the evils of vengeance, war, and death. Our people are forbidden even to touch a weapon. War is completely out of the question."

"I should have known Ophis horns were evil," said Sindle. "No wonder the Trogzars love to play them."

"The Trogzars killed Wizdor, Sindle's grandfather," Keldon informed Verlin. "He barely escaped Zil-Kenøth before meeting the same fate."

"Then you are their victim too, poor man," Verlin remarked. "I cannot fault you for what your people have done. You are not to blame."

"We are going to request an audience with the Queen this lumen in the hope that she will restore Sindle's grandfather to life," Keldon explained to Verlin. "He deserves to be rewarded because he saved my zoas from ruin after I had an unfortunate accident and broke my arm."

"Saved the Queen's zoas, did he?" inquired Verlin, stroking his beard. "Then you should know, Keldon, that you have made the right decision to present him to the Queen. If he were like the others, he would have found the perfect opportunity to steal your entire flock, but he is not like them. Sindle is a good man."

"Thank you, Maestro," said Keldon. "Your wisdom has given me light as usual."

"You're most welcome, Keldon."

"Well," said Keldon. "The time grows short. It will be Wittistide soon, and Sindle and I must be sure to arrive early."

"Then you had best be off," said Verlin. "Do come again soon."

They exchanged farewells, and Keldon and Sindle made their way back through the labyrinth of corridors, through the quadrangle, and down the steps of the academy to the street.

"I really like Verlin," Sindle remarked. "He reminds me of my grandfather."

"His wisdom is great, second only to the Queen's," Keldon commented. "I never cease to be amazed at what he knows. Take those Ophis horns, for instance. I had no idea they had anything to do with light-freezing. I wonder how he knew about them."

As they walked down the jade cobblestone street, Sindle began to worry. In time, he asked Keldon, "Is it possible the Queen will view me as her enemy when she finds out I am from Zil-Kenøth?"

"I should think not," answered Keldon. "To my knowledge, the Queen has no enemies, not even the players of the Ophis horns."

As they continued down the street, Sindle's dream of the wicked Fish-Faced Queen kept running through his mind, and he wondered if the story was just another lie of his homeland. Still, despite Keldon's reassuring words, he would not rest until his visit with the Queen of Viridia was over. Sindle was confused and still not sure whom or what to believe.

CHAPTER 12
ZOELLA

Within earshot, a crystal-clear stream danced across a bed of mossy stones. Along embankments ran emerald-gravel walkways crisscrossed by jade-cobblestone streets. Plants with feathery leaves and lacy, pale green blossoms pirouetted in the gentle breeze as thick-stemmed plants clad in dark green foliage and variegated plumes stood at attention like soldiers. The stream and the paths on its embankments soon disappeared into an entrance within a massive wall surrounding the city center.

"Just ahead, Chartra's streets meet at the hub of the city like spokes of a great wheel," Keldon explained. "The wall you now see separates the sacred garden where the Verdis Tree grows from the rest of Chartra. Follow me, Sindle."

The stream echoed like an opera singer as they entered a tunnel that ran through the wall. Moments later, they emerged into a forest of velvet sponge-wood trees. "We Viridians believe four living walls separate the Verdis Tree from the rest of Chartra," Keldon lectured above the noise of the rippling stream. "Each wall has a meaning for our people. As we pass through them, we imagine we are on a journey from Viridia to Vernesda. We call the first wall–the wall of 'living stone' we just walked through–the *wall of Vera*. It reminds us of the solid things of our world—such as rock, and the soil that everything in Viridia grows from." Keldon pointed to the wall of sponge-wood trees they were standing in. "And we call this the *wall of Verda*. When we pass through this wall, we remember the gifts that grow from our land—our food, our clothes, our zoas, and other things that make our lives comfortable." Soon they exited the forest of sponge-wood trees and entered a forest of palms. "This wall," Keldon explained, "is called the *wall of Vernda*. See how the palms form a canopy above our heads? The palms remind us of our green

Viridian sky." Keldon stopped and looked at Sindle. "Can you see how each wall builds on the preceding one? Each is like the rung of a ladder. The first gets us to the second, the second, to the third, and so forth. We think of all of them together as forming a ladder that stretches between Viridia and Vernesda. Now we are coming to the last rung. As we pass through the next wall, we imagine we are leaving Viridia behind and are entering Vernesda."

"I don't see how you keep all the names straight," Sindle remarked.

"It's not as hard as it seems," said Keldon. "Each name builds on the one before it. Vera, Verda, Vernda. We are about to come to the final wall—the *wall of Verneda*—but I must warn you. We are not allowed to speak from this point on. The most sacred silence must be observed."

"I understand," said Sindle.

"I shall tell you the meaning of the Vernedan wall before we enter so you will know. It stands for the last rung of the ladder of life that joins Viridia to the eternal world. We shall soon enter a circular clearing that reminds us of that world. That is why we call this clearing *the Vernesdan Circle*. In its center grows the most sacred tree, Verdis, also called the Tree of Life. We believe that the Verdis Tree contains the spirit that lives in the four walls and the Vernesdan Circle combined. When we reach the Verdis Tree, you will see performed an ancient ritual we call *Wittistide*. At high lumen-flow, Queen Veronica will arrive to water Verdis with her wand. You will see her enter by the Eastern Gate, for that is the direction most sacred to our people."

When they approached a forest of fir trees, Keldon halted. "We have now come to the wall of Verneda. From this point on, we must keep the most sacred silence." Sindle and Keldon walked down the path that led through the forest of firs and entered the large round clearing Keldon had called the Vernesdan Circle. It was carpeted with fine grass the texture of velvet. The forest of firs bordered it all the way around, and in its center stood an immense crystal pyramid in which grew a tree, hundreds of shade-lengths in height, having thick fleshy leaves, and resembling a jade plant.

The stream they were following had its source from beneath one side of the pyramid, and three other streams flowed from its remaining sides, dividing the Vernesdan Circle into quarters. On either side of each stream ran paths like the one they had followed through the four walls. A circular path, midway between the circumference of the clearing and the Verdis Tree, intersected these other paths, and four footbridges, crisscrossing each of the streams, connected the circular path's four quarters. When Keldon and Sindle reached this path, they crossed a footbridge and headed east.

Keldon halted, however, when he saw an entourage of women entering the Vernesdan Circle from the Eastern Gate. The women were clothed in green silk and bore standards and pale green banners embroidered with images of the Verdis Tree. In the midst of the entourage, four men with clean-shaven heads carried Queen Veronica on her throne.

After the attendants lowered the throne, Veronica arose. Her chartreuse regalia had been woven from the finest of silk, and she wore on her head a crown carved from jade and encrusted with emeralds. Her face was veiled and hidden from the people. As though floating on a cloud, she proceeded toward the Verdis Tree. Two female attendants, bearing standards, preceded her, while two, following, carried her train. The remainder of her entourage knelt on the emerald-gravel paths with their hands raised and palms turned outwards toward heaven.

When the Queen reached the pyramid, she extended her wand and slipped through one of its walls without need of a door. Her four attendants knelt, facing the pyramid, with their hands extended in the same position as the others. As Veronica pointed the wand toward the roots of the tree, sparkling white light flowed from it. The Verdis Tree at first glowed. Then it grew several inches before their very eyes. The attendants and all present, including Keldon, fell prostrate.

After the Queen exited the pyramid and joined her entourage, Keldon and Sindle started from the Vernesdan Circle back through the four walls. Keldon told Sindle to wait as he ran ahead to speak with an attendant. Moments later, he returned with the news, "I've spoken to Biona's sister, Zoella. She will relay your request for an audience to the Queen."

When they emerged from the four walls, they heard glorious music. Hundreds of harpists and flautists from the Academy of Zoaherding played a festive Baroque composition as the Queen returned with the procession to her palace. Then a tall slender woman approached Keldon and Sindle. She wore a forest-green chiffon gown, and a tiara that shone with the cool brightness of the moon. Beneath the tiara, her hair cascaded in soft curls like moonbeams onto her delicate shoulders. Sindle was at once enchanted by her beauty. He was dumbfounded at first, but then, finding his voice, he awkwardly blurted out the words, "Your Majesty," and bowed.

The woman laughed softly and replied. "I am not the Queen, my dear Sindle. I am Biona's sister, Zoella." Her laughter was to Sindle's ears more pleasant than the bubbling of any Viridian brook.

"Do you have news from Her Majesty?" Keldon asked.

"You are most fortunate," she replied. "She has agreed to grant Sindle audience this lumen-ebb."

"I am grateful," said Sindle, bowing. "Thank you for bearing her my request."

"I could not have done otherwise," replied Zoella. "You did, after all, become a hero when you saved the Queen's zoas. Now follow me, and I shall guide you to her palace." Turning, she led them down a street. As she walked, she seemed to float like a cloud, and her gown flowed in the gentle Viridian breeze. Sindle, who could not take his eyes off her, tried to make polite conversation. "Is your husband a zoaherder like Keldon?" he asked.

"I am not married," she replied. Her statement came as a relief to Sindle.

"Zoella is a follower of the Vernesdan Way," remarked Keldon.

"What is it like living in the Queen's palace?" Sindle asked.

"It is a delight," Zoella answered. "The Queen is very gracious."

"I've heard the wand she uses to water the Verdis Tree has many miraculous powers," Sindle stated. "What other things does she use it for?" He had in mind the story of the Fish-Faced Queen.

"On occasions she has used it to raise persons from the dead," replied Zoella. "Other than that, she only uses it to water the Verdis Tree."

As Sindle turned his head, he caught a glimpse of the Queen's palace through the trees. Its massive emerald pavilion was surrounded by towers with spires that rose until they pierced the gentle green Viridian sky. In front of the palace stretched an immaculate lawn with hedges, gardens, and jade statues that sparkled like jewels.

"I've never before seen anything so beautiful," Sindle remarked.

"Most would agree with your opinion," said Zoella. "The palace took two centuries to build. No other building in Chartra can compare." Soon they climbed its steps to a massive porch supported by hundreds of jade pillars. Inside, the courtyard was surrounded by an enclave carved with friezes that told the story of Viridia. Suddenly, Sindle saw an image that triggered shock. His heart raced, and his eyes became locked in terror on an image about which he could not be mistaken. It was an image of the Fish-Faced Queen! The woman, the wand, the tidal wave–all were there!

But if the image on the mural were not enough to frighten him out of his wits, he smelled a fragrance that caused his mind to regurgitate the memory of the bitter berries from the trees of Violinda. His dream of the Fish-Faced Queen raced again through his mind. Could it now be coming true? He glanced at Zoella. No, it was not possible–there was too much beauty in this place. Then the herald blasted a trumpet, and the page cried out, "Keldon of Viridia, and Sindle of Zil-Kenøth!"

When the page cried, "Sindle of Zil-Kenøth," a dagger of fear stuck and twisted in Sindle's stomach. As they proceeded toward the Queen's chamber, terrible thoughts kept flashing through his mind–thoughts of his grandfather's death, of Trogzars, of the Fish-Faced Queen and her slaves. Could he be headed toward the same fate as Wizdor? He looked around. Zoella had not followed. Where was she? Panic struck him. Why had he agreed to meet the Queen? What was he thinking? He felt helpless, and was scared out of his mind.

CHAPTER 13
VERONICA

As the page led Sindle and Keldon down a corridor lined with magnificent murals that told more of Viridia's history, Sindle tried to suppress his mounting fear. Soon they reached the throne room, and porters opened massive, ornately carved doors of jade. The page entered and announced their presence to the Queen. As Sindle and Keldon entered, a vista of grandeur opened before them. Sindle's fear gave way to wonder as the room's beauty and immensity overwhelmed him. Delicately sculpted jade pillars supported fan-vaulted ceilings highlighted with a kind of precious phosphorescent gilding.

Then Sindle caught sight of the Queen, and his fears returned. He thought he could see glistening fish-scales on her face. She motioned for them to approach. Weak-kneed and trembling, he started toward her, but as he drew closer, fear gave way to relief. He saw that her face was covered not with scales, but with beautiful glittering skin. When they reached her throne, they bowed.

"Arise," the Queen commanded.

"Your Majesty," Keldon began. "Your zoaherder is in the debt of this man, Sindle of Zil-Kenøth."

"Welcome, Sindle, to the Kingdom of Viridia."

"I am honored to be here, Your Highness."

"I know of your service to my realm. You shall indeed be rewarded." The Queen's face radiated kindness and goodwill, putting Sindle at ease, but he could also feel her eyes penetrate his soul like light passing through glass. "I know you wish to have the life of your grandfather, Wizdor, restored." Sindle's eyes widened. "You needn't be surprised," she continued. "I wield the power of knowledge as well as that of life. I see and hear all that is done and spoken in Spectara."

"Then Your Majesty knows how much Sindle has suffered from the hands of the Trogzars, and how he lost everything dear, especially his grandfather," said Keldon. "Your Highness can restore Wizdor's life if it be her pleasure. Your servant, Keldon, begs that you grant Sindle his wish."

The Queen rose. "Nothing would please me more. If I were able to restore Wizdor, I would not hesitate, but to do so lies beyond my power." Her words cut Sindle to the quick.

"Do you not have the power to restore life to the dead, Your Majesty?" asked Keldon.

"In most cases, yes," she responded, "but the manner of Wizdor's death prevents me in his case. I cannot grant Sindle's request because his grandfather died in Finsterna's dark depths. I have no further power over my evil sister."

"Your sister?" remarked Sindle. "I don't understand, Your Majesty."

"She who now is melded with the element you call the Sea of Darkness is my sister, Finsterna, who once ruled Pyrath, Land of Fire. She now dwells in the Sea of Darkness and controls it with her thoughts. What power I once had over her was exhausted long ago. I cannot interfere again."

"Is she to blame for what is happening in Zil-Kenøth?" asked Sindle.

"Yes," replied the Queen, "Like a long-extinct volcano, she is again erupting. Her flow of evil has only just begun. If it continues, what it may do to all the lands of Spectara may defy description."

"Can you do *nothing* to stop her, Your Highness?" Sindle asked.

"Nothing," replied the Queen. Her eyes darkened, and she seemed to grow older before their very eyes. "You must understand that in the aeons before time as you know it existed, there were three of us who ruled Spectara's primary regions. I, the youngest sister, ruled Marus Lazul, the Sea of a Thousand Blues. To me was given the power of life. My eldest sister, Lucia, ruled the yellow lands of Zanthis, Land of Truth. She possessed great wisdom, superior to mine in every way.

Finsterna, my elder sister, ruled Pyrath, the red lands. Unto her was given power over fire so she could test and purify souls. Her task was to prepare Spectara's inhabitants to enter Lux Aeternum, the regions of eternal light. At first she used her power only for good. In those times she was not wicked as she is now. The inhabitants of her kingdom were great forgers of metal, and they guarded the way past the Crystal Mountains of Arete Vitrea with their swords of purity. They allowed only worthy souls to pass through Arete Vitrea, whereafter they would dwell in the presence of the Telarch of Light who rules over Lux Aeternum. It was he who fashioned Spectara and its inhabitants. It was his light that gave the queens of Spectara their powers. Indeed, his light illumines and sustains Spectara even now."

"I know nothing of this Telarch," remarked Sindle.

"That comes as no surprise," said the Queen. "Your people have long lived in darkness."

Sindle hung his head. Then he looked up and asked, "Why did Finsterna become evil?"

"I have yet to understand." Fighting to restrain her emotions, she continued. "Finsterna was impatient and restless. She was not satisfied to possess power over fire alone, she desired wisdom too. Envy of our sister, Lucia, burned in her until at length she determined that she would take what she was not meant to own. Impatience turned to ruthlessness. Finsterna commanded her thralls to forge weapons in the cracks of fire that lay deep within the volcanoes of Pyrath. Then she sent her armies to make war against the inhabitants of Zanthis, Lucia's kingdom. Countless Zanthans were slaughtered without mercy until Lucia was captured and brought to Finsterna. Finsterna at once demanded that Lucia relinquish her power over wisdom. Lucia refused, so they tortured her. When that failed, Finsterna had Lucia's all-seeing eyes seared out with a sword that had been heated in the cracks of fire. Still, Lucia refused to relinquish her powers. Enraged, Finsterna shot a flaming arrow through her heart and burned her body to ashes. Still Finsterna was not satisfied. If it were not enough to destroy wisdom, she determined that she would destroy life as well. She waged war against me and my kingdom, raising her hateful armies of fire against us in great numbers. However, I possessed a weapon my sister Lucia did not. Because Finsterna had lost all reason, Lucia's weapon of truth was useless against her. But I held a more formidable weapon—absolute power over the waters of Marus Lazul. But in using this weapon, I committed a horrible deed that I shall forever regret. I raised the sea against my evil sister and quenched her fiery power, but my action came at a great cost. Much of Spectara was destroyed, and the backlash from the wave destroyed my kingdom as well. Many of my subjects perished. Those who survived migrated here to Viridia. This was the first and only time I used my power to destroy, and I have mourned ever since because of it. That is why I enchanted Marus Lazul so that it could never destroy again."

"Is that why it is possible to breathe beneath its waters?" Sindle asked.

"Yes," replied the Queen.

Sindle remembered again Wizdor's story about the Fish-Faced Queen. A tidal wave was sent by Veronica, true, but not as a result of any evil intention on her part. The Queen with wicked intentions was not Veronica, but her sister, Finsterna. Somehow the stories about the two Queens had become muddled in his grandfather's tale.

"With her powers quelled," the Queen continued, "Finsterna fled into the Sea of Darkness. Her people thought her dead, so they tried to return to Pyrath. But Pyrath was in ruins, and the peoples of Spectara would not allow them entrance. Instead they became refugees who had no choice but to settle by the Sea of Darkness. Little did they know that their Queen had lived and made her abode in the Sea's dark depths. Eventually, Finsterna would learn to control darkness as she had once controlled fire."

"Wizdor said the name *Finsterna* meant *dark fire*," Sindle remarked. "Now I understand why. Instead of forging metal in the cracks of fire as the Pyrathans once had done, our people in Zil-Kenøth now use Finsterna's dark fire to forge light and freeze it. Everything is now starting to make sense."

"Then, my dear Sindle, you can also understand why I cannot grant your request," said the Queen. "My power does not extend over the realm of darkness as it did over the fire she formerly controlled. Only the Telarch of Light who reigns over the regions of Lux Aeternum possesses such power now."

Sindle's eyes revealed both sadness and understanding.

"There is, however, one thing I can do," added the Queen with some hesitation. "I could allow you to speak with your grandfather; though I warn you–to do so may bring you great pain."

"I would gladly risk it if I could speak to Wizdor even for one minute!" exclaimed Sindle.

"Very well," said the Queen. "Follow me. But Keldon," she said, turning to him, "you must remain here, for what Sindle shall see is not for your eyes."

"As you wish, Your Majesty," he said, bowing.

The Queen proceeded to a wall of polished jade and held up an emerald pendant. A door mysteriously appeared. As it opened, it squeaked and roared through the tunnel behind it. "This way," she pointed, and they entered a narrow cavern of smooth, glowing green stone. The Queen led Sindle through a damp and musty chamber, and down a spiraling stone stairway. As he descended, the sound of bubbling water grew ever louder until he laid his eyes on a spring of liquid, silver light that cascaded into a pool. The Queen led him over to it. As they looked into its center, its reflection rippled across their faces in strange patterns.

"This," said the Queen, "is the spring of Zoa Aeonum called forth from the eternal depths by the Telarch who reigns in Lux Aeternum. This spring is the source of my power. In it resides the power of life that sustains all Viridia. From this source the Verdis Tree is nurtured. What I now must ask you will seem strange. You must give me the stone you found lying beside the Sea of Darkness."

With a curious look, Sindle reached in his pouch and pulled out the stone.

"Do not let my request surprise you. Remember that I see and hear all that is done and spoken in Spectara."

When the Queen received the stone from Sindle, lines of anguish became etched on her face.

"This stone is Wizdor's *scintilla*, the indestructible spark of his soul that animated his shadow-shell while he yet lived. Now, frozen by Finsterna's power, Wizdor is imprisoned in it."

The Queen cast the stone into the midst of the fountain, raised her wand, and chanted. "By the power granted me e'er Spectara began to be, e'er there was Verdis or Wittistide, when first the elements of chaos did vie and life emerged victorious as Zoa Aeonum from its depths, created by Telarch, Source and Goal of Life, arise Thou Spring of everlasting Lumen-Flow to thy summit at Vernesda's gates and reverse the eternal Lumen-Ebb of death! Arise, O Spring of Zoa! And pierce the darkness with thy light!"

The moment Veronica finished speaking, the fountain bubbled and churned. Then white light gushed up and cascaded until it subsided, revealing in the midst of the fountain a figure, tall, erect, and bright as an angel. "Grandfather!" Sindle shouted for joy. He started to climb into the fountain.

"You must not!" warned the Queen, grabbing him and holding him back.

"Your Majesty! You said you couldn't restore my grandfather Wizdor to life, but you have done it!"

The Queen shook her head. "It will not last! What you see is only an apparition!"

Sindle refused to listen. "Grandfather! Is it really you?"

"It is I," spoke the figure. His voice, which had the sound of a distant echo, seemed sad and full of pain.

Sindle stepped onto the rim of the fountain and held out his hand. "Here! I will free you!" The Queen held Sindle back. "You must listen!" she admonished. "If you dare touch the apparition, Finsterna's darkness will infect your soul and destroy it! From such darkness no soul can recover! See if what I tell you isn't true. Wizdor's image withers before our very eyes."

Sindle watched as the image shriveled and turned black like burning paper. "Grandfather!" Sindle cried. "No!"

Wizdor spoke in sad and mournful tones. "Find Prince Neblas and recover Asdin. Asdin was Zil-Kenøth's shield not against the Hell of Light, but against this Hell of Darkness that is now my prison." Wizdor cried out in pain as his flesh withered.

"Wizdor! Please let me save you!" cried Sindle.

"Return Asdin to Zil-Kenøth," spoke the image. "Or all Spectara will become as I am now. Find the Star. Find Asdin."

"Your Majesty," Sindle pleaded. "You cannot let this happen to him! Is there nothing you can do?"

The form in the fountain disintegrated. "Grandfather!" Sindle cried. "I promise, I'll find the Star! Just speak to me!"

A dark and horrible shadow filled the chamber and crept across the faces of Sindle and the Queen. The Queen at once removed the stone from the fountain. "It was as I feared," she said. "This spectacle has caused you much grief." She took him by the arm and began leading him up the spiral stairs. "I am sorry, my dear Sindle," she said. "Now only the Telarch who reigns in Lux Aeternum can free Wizdor from Finsterna's evil grasp. He alone has the power to free Spectara from her awful curse."

"Then I must go and plead with him!" said Sindle. "Just tell me what I must do?"

"It is not that easy," replied the Queen. "First, you will have to pass through the Crystal Mountains of Arete Vitrea."

"I will do it," he stated. "Just tell me how."

"The way is barred," she replied. "No one has passed through Arete Vitrea since the flight of Finsterna to the Sea of Darkness."

Desperation filled Sindle's face. "There has to be some way, surely," he said with a determined voice. "If there is a way, I'll find it."

The Queen looked upon him with pity. "Should you not first find the Star as your grandfather has asked?" she advised. "You must know that what your people have unwittingly called the Hell of Light is none other than Lux Aeternum where the Telarch dwells. Prince Neblas will be headed toward the source of light. Of that you can be sure. He will come to the foothills of

Arete Vitrea and attempt to pass so that his plan may succeed. But he will fail."

The Queen stopped at the foot of the stairs and unhooked the chain on which her pendant hung. "What I do now is against better judgment. This," she said, grasping his hand, and placing the pendant in it, "is the only way to pass through Arete Vitrea." Closing Sindle's hand around the pendant, she held his hands in hers as she spoke. "Because I fear what damage Finsterna may do in Spectara, I will let you use this most precious object. However, you must swear that you will keep it safe at all times and guard it with your very life. No one but Keldon must know you carry it. No one but Keldon. Do you understand?"

"Yes," he replied, kneeling and kissing her hand. "Thank you, Your Majesty."

"There is one other thing," she said. "Without the password, the pendant will not work and you will not be allowed to pass through Arete Vitrea. The password must be kept secret even in the face of torture or death. Do you vow to keep it sacred and inviolable?"

"I do," he pledged.

"Then kneel."

Sindle fell to his knees, and Veronica touched him with her scepter on both shoulders. "I now create a new order and ordain you to it. I dub you a Companion in the *Order of the Quest for Asdin*," she said, touching him on both shoulders with her wand. As she spoke, the password mysteriously formed in Sindle's mind. "I will also ordain Keldon to this order and commission him to travel with you. Remember the promise you have made," she repeated. "Trust no one with the pendant, and do not divulge the password to another, not even to Keldon. Is that clear?"

"Yes, Your Majesty."

"Now, a final warning," the Queen continued. "If my pendant should fall into the wrong hands, or if the password should become known, then grave peril may come to your soul and to mine as well. Remember that my sister Finsterna has powers that even now are awakening and growing stronger. She may know already what I now do and say. That is why you must take the greatest care."

"I promise, I will, Your Majesty," said Sindle.

"Then arise," commanded the Queen. "My power goes with you."

Sindle and the Queen emerged from the passageway, but Sindle's thoughts still clung to the fountain in the cavern below. The image of Wizdor kept withering in his mind. Each time it did, Finsterna's evil sword of darkness would rend his heart. If he could but succeed in passing through Arete Vitrea, he could go to the Telarch in Lux Aeternum and plead with him to make Finsterna release Wizdor from her grasp.

As they entered the throne room, Keldon bowed, and the Queen again mounted her throne. "Sindle must journey to Arete Vitrea," she told Keldon. "He is to find Asdin, the Sacred Star of Frozen Light, and return it to Zil-Kenøth. His mission is urgent and of the gravest importance, so I am sending you, Keldon, to accompany him." Keldon's face grew pale. The thought of leaving Biona and his zoas dismayed him. Why was the Queen asking *him* to go with Sindle. Why could she not send someone like Garn?

"Kneel," she ordered Keldon, and he sadly obeyed. "I dub you a Companion in the Order of the Quest for Asdin," she said, touching him on his shoulders with her wand. "Henceforth you and Sindle will be called *Companions of the Quest.* Sindle also carries my pendant. You both must guard it with your lives. Only you and Sindle must know that Sindle carries it. The pendant will allow Sindle to pass through Arete Vitrea. But until he enters, you must promise me, Keldon, that you will accompany him always. Encourage him and help him remain strong in his mission. Promise me."

"I will always obey Your Majesty's wishes," replied Keldon. "But what am I to do about my wife, Biona, and my zoas? Who will care for them? Would it not be better to send someone more suitable than I?" He was hoping the Queen would change her mind and not ask him to go.

"You are the one most suitable for the task, Keldon," she informed him. "Your wife will be brought to my palace to live with her sister in the Vernesdan quarters until you return. As for your zoas, they will be tended by your apprentice, Garn." The Queen's decision disappointed Keldon. He now realized there was no way out. The Queen then turned to Sindle. "Remember what I have told you. The Telarch possesses fully what powers the Queens of Spectara have possessed only in part. This means the powers of truth and destruction are as much his as are the powers of life. Should you choose to pass through Arete Vitrea, you must do so with great humility and care."

"I understand," Sindle replied.

"Then be on your way with my blessing," said the Queen.

After they bowed, they exited the throne room, and the page escorted them back through the corridor, across the courtyard, and down the steps to the front of the palace. Zoella was there waiting, and when Sindle saw her, his sadness temporarily melted away. Keldon, still reeling from the Queen's decision, remained silent.

"Did the Queen grant your request?" Zoella asked Sindle.

"She was unable to do so," he replied.

"I am sorry." Her words, like Verdis salve, seemed to ease his wounds of disappointment, but only for a moment. She turned to Keldon. "What happened?"

"It's a long story," he answered in a sullen voice. "Let's find Biona, and I shall explain."

Biona had been waiting at the palace gates, and when she saw Zoella coming with Keldon and Sindle, she hurried toward them. When they met, Biona embraced Zoella and kissed her on the cheek and greeted her.

"Hello, sister," Biona responded. She anxiously turned to Keldon. "What news do you bring?"

"It is bad, I'm afraid," he said. "The Queen was unable to grant Sindle's request." He did not want to tell her the rest of the story.

"Why couldn't she?" Biona asked with disbelief.

"Come along, and I shall explain."

As they walked through the streets of Chartra, Keldon told her why the Queen could not honor Sindle's wish. Biona listened with sad and sympathetic eyes as they relayed to her the substance of their visit with the Queen. Zoella also kept telling Sindle how sorry she was that the Queen wasn't able to help.

In time, they arrived at the cottage. "So this is why Sindle must go and search for the Star of Frozen Light," said Keldon. He opened the door and they entered. "But now comes the hard part. My dear, Biona, the Queen has asked me to accompany Sindle on his journey. The Queen has created a new order, the *Order of the Quest for Asdin*, and she has ordained me to it as a Companion."

Her disbelieving eyes started to fill with tears. "I don't understand? Why must you go?"

"It is the Queen's command that I be a *Companion of the Quest*, my dear. I have no choice. What she been spoken cannot be undone."

Sindle suddenly felt awkward. He had not anticipated that Keldon and Biona would show such reluctance. Then Keldon quickly noticed Sindle's downcast face and said, "Oh, Sindle, my friend, I have upset you. Please forgive me. Biona and I have been apart for sometime now because of the harvest. That is all."

"I understand," said Sindle. "I know how hard this must be for you."

Biona, who was at the point of tears, took heart and brightened. "Oh, my dear, Keldon, it won't be such a bad time for me, living with Zoella in the Queen's court and all. I'm sure I will be fine."

"Yes," said Zoella, embracing Biona. "It *will* be good for us to be together again."

"Indeed," said Keldon. "But what shall I do without my Biona?" Tears formed in his eyes, and Biona came to his aid.

"It won't be so terribly long, my dear," she encouraged. "You'll see. Being in the Queen's court with Zoella will make the time pass quickly for me. And you will be busy helping Sindle on his quest."

"You're probably right," said Keldon.

"I'll go and pack some provisions for their journey, Biona," Zoella volunteered.

Biona nodded. She was struggling to hold back tears. "Keldon, please promise to be careful and not to have any more accidents."

"I'll try not." Just then, Biona could no longer restrain herself and burst into tears.

Keldon took her in his arms. "You mustn't cry so, my love. Everything will be fine. You'll see." They stood there for some time in silent embrace.

Soon, Zoella returned. "I've packed some fresh vegetables and a jar of Verdis salve," she informed them, "just in case you run into trouble. And two canteens of water," she added. "You will need them in Zanthis."

"I worry about you going there of all places," said Biona, dabbing her eyes with a handkerchief.

"Try not to fret," Keldon encouraged her. "We'll take the greatest care."

Biona and Keldon kissed. "I suppose we should be off, then," said Keldon, and he kissed her again. "Farewell," he then said to Zoella, pecking her on the cheek. "Please take care of Biona for me."

"I will, Keldon," Zoella said. "Don't worry. Everything will be fine."

"Before we go," interrupted Sindle, "I wonder if I might have a word with Zoella."

Keldon and Biona glanced at each other and then at Zoella. "Of course," said Zoella.

When Keldon and Biona had left them, Sindle stood for a moment, peering silently into Zoella's eyes.

"Well, Sindle," she said, breaking eye-contact. "It may be a long time before you're in Viridia again."

"It's with great sadness that I leave your beautiful land," he said. "Everyone here has been so kind, and you most of all. You made it possible for me to see the Queen. I've grown so fond of Viridia, I really don't want to go on this quest now at all, but I know I must."

"Your quest is of the utmost importance, Sindle," said Zoella. "I know Keldon well. No better friend could accompany you."

"I'm sure that's true." Sindle wanted to tell Zoella what was really in his heart—that he believed she would be a better companion for him than Keldon. He wanted to tell her that he would miss *her* most of all after leaving Viridia. But he was afraid to speak his mind. This was not so much out of fear of offending her as fear that she might rebuff him. He decided for the time being to keep his feelings for her secret.

"Farewell, then, Sindle," said Zoella, extending her hand.

Sindle took her hand and kissed it. The touch of her soft skin upon his lips was almost too much to bear. He felt the impulse to take her in his arms and kiss her, but Keldon interrupted before he could act so foolishly. "Everything is ready, Sindle. We should be on our way."

Sindle's eyes became filled with sadness. "Good-bye, Zoella," he said.

Just then, Biona joined them. "Sindle," she said, teary-eyed. "Please take good care of Keldon. Don't let anything bad happen to him or to yourself."

"I promise, I won't," he said.

Keldon and Biona gave each other one final hug and kiss good-bye. Then he and Sindle started down the path. Biona and Zoella waved at them until they reached the crest of the hill. They all exchanged final farewells, and Keldon and Sindle were on their way.

CHAPTER 14
ZANTHIS

Keldon and Sindle climbed a ridge overlooking the valley of Chartra and said their good-byes to the fair city. The gentle harmony of zoaherders' harps wafted across rolling hills patch-worked with ten-thousand shades of green. Zoas danced and flickered like fireflies on a summer's eve, and formed patterns like snowflakes on a winter's morn. Now and then, a zoaherder would remove his hand from his harp long enough to wave at Keldon and Sindle, and they would return the gesture. Further along, herders of silk zoas played flutes beneath groves of trees. Humming zoas, hanging from branches, spun cocoons from tiny fibers of green light. In fields, too, vegetable zoas were ready to flower, and zoaherders stood poised with harps in hand to harvest new animal zoas as they emerged.

Along the way, Keldon, who now was in better spirits, delivered to Sindle an in-depth lecture about Viridian philosophy. "See how hard the zoaherders work? It would be impossible if it weren't for our *Code of Cooperation*. We, Viridians, view competition as the greatest of evils in Spectara. Our *Code of Cooperation* is based on our belief that every Viridian is but a ray of the One Light that shines in and through everything. The light is all and in all, and the many things we see in Spectara are but illusions. When we begin to realize this, then we can say we're well on our way to Vernesda. When a person finally can look past the darkness that divides our world to see only the One Light—we believe that is when he *reaches* Vernesda."

Sindle lifted an eyebrow. "It seems Vernesda would be a very difficult place to get to."

"It *is*, I assure you," replied Keldon. "I believe some have made it. My master, Verlin, is very close. Zoella has dedicated her whole life to the pursuit of it. That's why she joined the celibate order that attends the Queen."

Celibate? Shock and disappointment struck Sindle when he heard this word. "Does that mean she can never marry? I didn't know." For awhile he was silent and angry. Then he asserted, "Why would anyone join such an order?" His question startled Keldon.

"My dear, Sindle. Surely you realize she's chosen the better path. Marriage is a thing of darkness. It divides the unity of thought. Her happiness will be greater because of the direction she's chosen."

"But *you* chose to marry," Sindle stated. "Does this mean *you* will not reach Vernesda?"

Keldon answered defensively, "I can only hope I will reach it. I'm trying very hard."

Sindle looked out into the fields, trying to get his mind off Zoella. He did not want to face his deep disappointment.

No more zoaherders could be seen now, and fingers of parched grass retreated before sand dunes. Emerald-spangled turquoise-gravel roads also began to give way to tans and yellows, and a hot dry wind drove the cool Viridian breezes into retreat. Keldon wiped his forehead with his sleeve and remarked. "We must be in Zanthis now. Didn't I tell you it was horrible? And we're just now on the borders. I dread to think what lies ahead." They left the road, climbed on a boulder, and sat down.

"Maybe this is the Hell of Light," Sindle commented.

"Let's hope you're wrong," Keldon returned. "It is almost low lumen-ebb," he said. "This would be a good place to camp."

Early the next lumen-flow, they started out again. By high lumen-ebb, the last blades of grass were now far behind, and wretched dunes of burning, yellow sand stretched ahead into the far distance.

"I can't breathe," remarked Sindle. "How can we survive this heat?"

"Just think of it as a mirage. That should help." replied Keldon.

They climbed to the top of a dune and gazed across the vast desert expanse. There was no sign of civilization.

"Maybe we should turn back," suggested Sindle.

"I made a promise to the Queen, remember," Keldon returned. "She is depending on me to help you find Asdin and return it to Zil-Kenøth." Keldon's optimism perturbed Sindle.

"It's too low in the lumen-ebb to press on," said Sindle.

"I suppose you're right," Keldon agreed, and they set camp again.

The next lumen-flow, they started out again, journeying past shifting sand dunes that lurked beside the road like silent predators. Their canteens were now almost empty. By mid-lumen ebb, they were deep in the land of Zanthis. Burning sand had scorched the soles of their feet. Pain ripped through their calves and stabbed into their knees. Their hair smoldered on their heads, and acid sweat ran from their foreheads into their sand-scoured eyes. Sindle's tongue had started shriveling into a hard, dry piece of leather that kept uselessly probing his mouth for moisture. "I can't go on," he told Keldon. Earlier that lumen, Sindle had drained the last reluctant drops of water from his canteen. Even then, there had been only enough water to fuel the fire of thirst. In desperation, he tried to find one drop to bathe his parched tongue. Then in anger, he threw the canteen to the ground.

"I've run out too," remarked Keldon.

Sindle's face revealed disgust. They traveled several more hours when the road, which had been gradually dissolving into segments beneath the sand, finally disappeared.

"What are we to do now?" Sindle asked. "It is again time to set camp."

"Perhaps we should press on," replied Keldon. "It will not be as hot if we travel through low lumen-ebb."

With fatigued eyes, Sindle squinted as he looked out over the desert. In the near distance, a wall of yellow sand, driven by a fierce wind, was headed their way. "What is that?" he asked.

"We had best take cover," answered Keldon. They found shelter at the foot of a rock formation. When the sandstorm hit, they drew their garments around their faces and huddled together, coughing as they tried to breathe. The storm raged throughout low lumen-ebb, and kept them from sleeping. By early lumen-flow, it had passed, but when they started out again, they could not find the road. They wandered until the heat of early lumen-ebb began to bear down on them. The desert's hot jaws had devoured their remaining strength. There was still no sign of life or civilization. The lash of the desert's whip stung their raw flesh until they were driven to their knees. Sindle's tongue was now as hard as a stick. He pointed to his mouth and groaned.

Keldon, who was not much better off, realized Sindle was on his last leg. "The Ver'is oi'men," he smacked like a toothless old man. Keldon removed the jar from his pack and opened it, releasing an awful stench that drove the air from his lungs and made him gag. Without warning, Sindle grabbed it from Keldon and gulped it down.

"No!" Keldon cried.

It was too late. Sindle fell to the ground unconscious. Keldon knelt and shook his limp body. "Sin-le. Sin-le."

Then a screeching sound ripped through the air. Keldon peered into the sky. Terrible, dark creatures circled overhead. He tried pulling Sindle's limp body through the sand, but the creatures drew closer. "S-ew! S-ew!" he cried, but his voice was too weak to frighten them away. Keldon's head started spinning. Then a curtain of darkness fell.

CHAPTER 15
HELANTHIN

Through dust-matted eyes, Sindle glimpsed a black form sweeping up into the dingy sky. The voices of men, swelling then fading, mixed with the ringing in his ears. The light dimmed, and the curtain of darkness fell again.

Sindle was jolted back to consciousness when he felt cold water splash against his face. His eyes struggled to open. Someone lifted his head and poured water into his mouth. It seemed to sputter at the back of his throat as water does on the surface of a hot skillet.

"This one's alive," came a voice. "What about the other?"

"Barely."

Water again bathed Sindle's parched tongue.

"Slowly!" came a voice.

"More," he begged. His throat fried with pain when he tried to speak, and his head pounded. The precious liquid arrived again.

Sindle tried to focus. When he shut his eyes, he was left with the imprint of a long tan beard and piercing golden eyes.

"Quick! Get them to the wagon!" said the voice.

Hoisting Sindle up, they stretched and twisted his body. Pain darted through it, but he was too weak to dodge it—his flesh merely hung like limp rags from his bones. Men carried him and laid him inside the wagon. The cool, musty smell of leather filled his nostrils, and he soon fell asleep. Later, someone woke him and cradled his head so that he could be made to sip from a bowl of broth. When Sindle had finished, the person placed the bowl on the stand next to his bed and was gone.

On the other side of the tent, Keldon, with a hoarse voice, scratched out the story of their ordeal in the desert. Sindle turned his head and managed to focus. Keldon was talking to the man with the tan beard and golden eyes. Sindle tried to speak but couldn't.

"You're lucky to be alive," the man told Keldon. "You and your friend were almost food for thandoos."

Sindle remembered the dark forms sweeping up into the sky, and a shudder ran through his limp body. He imagined the thandoos were somehow fragments of Finsterna's hideous claw that struck the city of Zil on the fateful lumen-ebb of Wizdor's execution.

"What are thandoos?" asked Keldon.

"Unholy creatures whose food is death. They dwell in the deserts where death is plentiful. You had nothing to fear from them as long as you were alive. They rarely attack living things."

Sindle, forcing himself to sit up, took the bowl in his shaking hands and sipped more broth. His aching head was as heavy as a sack of rocks. A faint feeling came over him, and he collapsed again. Then the rhythm of the wagon rocked him back to sleep.

When he awoke the next time, the wagon had come to a standstill, and he realized that it was near low lumen-ebb. His head felt a couple of pounds lighter, though pain still pulsed through it. He looked around the wagon and saw for the first time that it was a crude wooden rig covered with a worn leather canopy. He would have drifted to sleep again, but his curiosity was aroused when he heard men's voices outside. Their words seemed to hit with dull thuds against the thick canvas, making their speech difficult to understand. He sat up, pulled back the flap, and peered outside. Sitting around a campfire and eating were yellow-skinned men whose crude laughter mixed with the sound of their smacking. They were draped with ragged tunics and capped with turbans, and beards drooped from their leathery faces. The beards, all of varying lengths, were tan or yellowish-white in appearance. One peculiar-looking man, however, had no beard, and his head looked something like a yellow onion. After staring at the man for several moments, Sindle realized it was Keldon. The poor Viridian's green skin had turned the color of parchment. Sindle glanced at his own hands and shook his head. He had suffered the same fate. He climbed out of the wagon and started toward the campfire.

"Ah! ha! Your friend has finally awaken after half a lumnus-week!" one of them blurted. Keldon arose and trotted over. "Come, Sindle. Meet the man who saved our lives. This is Helanthin."

Sindle remembered the image that five lumens earlier had been imprinted on the inside of his eyelids. But now he also saw lines running across the man's face, making it look like a detailed road-map. Helanthin stood up and shook Sindle's hand coldly. In his eyes was a look that could have shattered stone. Then he sat back down.

Sindle's mouth was still as dry as cotton. "Could I have some water?" he asked. Helanthin tossed him a skin, and Sindle started drinking.

"You're lucky we found you before the thandoos ended their death vigil!" said the Zanthan.

Sindle wiped the dripping liquid from his mouth with his tattered sleeve. "Thank you," he uttered in a quivering voice.

"Here," he said, removing a leg of some unknown animal from the spit and throwing it at Sindle. "Eat. I hope you're not like the vegetable man here!" Helanthin looked at Keldon. "Can you believe he asked for celery?"

Laughter sloshed from the bellies of the men sitting around the fire, making Keldon feel uncomfortable.

As Sindle nibbled at the leg, the eyes of Helanthin and his troop puckered with amusement and teased him. A few moments later, Helanthin shouted, "You eat like a girl! Here!" He whipped out his paw toward a man who poked at the fire. "Give me one of those." He jerked one of the legs from the man's hand. "This way!" he said, tearing into it with wild jaws. As he smacked, the corners of his mouth drooled.

Sindle tried his best to imitate Helanthin's actions, but the men's burning stares teased him, and their mouths spewed out crude, coarse laughter.

Sindle kept eating as Helanthin watched. The Zanthan's pointed eyes refused to blink. "Your friend doesn't look Viridian," he said to Keldon.

"I'm not," said Sindle, chewing.

Anger flashed from Helanthin's eyes and silence struck the camp. Helanthin jerked his head around and glared at Keldon. "You told me three lumens ago that you were from Viridia?"

Keldon shot a quick glance over at Sindle. Sindle's chewing slowed, and he looked back and forth at Helanthin and Keldon.

"We are from Viridia," replied Keldon with a nervous gulp. "We're on a special mission from Queen Veronica. I wasn't trying to deceive you."

"Queen Veronica, eh?" The Zanthan sprang to his feet and hardened his face. "Liar! I'll wager you are spies!"

"You're wrong," said Sindle, laying down the half-eaten leg and wiping his mouth.

"You'll have to prove you're not, or you will be burned alive!"

Sindle remembered Queen Veronica's pendant. That would be proof enough. But he had promised the Queen to tell no one that he carried it. Still, if it came to a choice between death by fire and showing Helanthin proof, he knew he would have no choice but to reveal the pendant. Sindle reached into his shirt to be sure it was safe, but when he did, panic bolted through his eyes. He stood up and felt through every inch of his clothing. "No!" he shouted.

Keldon rushed to his aid. "What's the matter?"

"I can't find the pendant!"

"What?" exclaimed Keldon.

"Maybe it fell off in the wagon." Sindle got up and started toward it.

"Halt!" ordered Helanthin.

"Please let me search the wagon," Sindle begged. "I was carrying the pendant of Queen Veronica, I promise you. That will prove we are not spies."

"Very well," said Helanthin, "but don't try anything sneaky. He and two of his men accompanied Sindle and Keldon to the wagon. Sindle and Keldon made a thorough search, but the pendant was nowhere to be found.

"I don't know what could have happened to it," said Sindle. "I had it with me in the desert before I blacked out."

"Enough of your deceit," said Helanthin. "The pendant is a lie, and so is your identity. You are spies, both of you!"

"I'm telling the truth!" shouted Sindle. "I did have the pendant! I swear!"

"We're not lying," Keldon stated. "I *am* from Viridia."

"Is your friend also a Viridian?" Helanthin asked.

"No," replied Sindle. "I'm from the city of Zil in the land of Kenøth, by the Sea of Darkness."

Helanthin's eyes flashed fire. "ZIL-KENØTH?" He choked on the word. "That settles it!" Helanthin drew his sword and held it to Sindle's throat. "You shall die, Zilish swine." He called his men. "Bind them. They shall be burned at once."

"But we have done nothing!" Sindle shouted.

As the men grabbed and bound Sindle and Keldon, fear boiled in their stomachs.

"Why will you not believe us?" Sindle cried out.

"Does the name *Pyrath* mean anything to you, Kenøthian scum?" Then he ordered his man, "Tie them to the stake!"

"Do you want innocent blood on your hands?" Keldon shouted.

Helanthin and others heaped the wood around them.

"No *Pyrathan* is innocent," Helanthin bellowed.

Keldon whispered to Sindle, "They must harbor resentment against your people from the time when Finsterna murdered their Queen."

"Silence!" Helanthin ordered. "Plotting your escape will do no good. Your death will be swift, murderers of truth!"

Keldon tried diplomacy. "Sir, what evidence do you have against us to warrant our execution? We have committed no crime but have come on a mission of peace."

"Quiet, fool. You've both committed crimes punishable by death!"

"Does your law say nothing about false accusations? Suppose you execute us and later learn that we were innocent of the crimes of which you accuse us. Would not your law demand that you suffer the penalty of death, as well?"

"Bargaining will buy you no time, Onion Head!" Helanthin signaled to one of his men. "Bring the fuel!"

"No! Please!" Panic flashed from Sindle's eyes as he struggled against the ropes, but Keldon, remaining calm, kept his Viridian composure and started muttering a monotone Viridian death chant.

Helanthin lost no time. He reached into a pouch, drew out sulfur-colored powder, and threw it on the wood, causing it to burst into flames.

"Please! Do not do this!" screamed Sindle. A wall of fire closed in about them, and they cringed as they waited to be devoured. But amazingly they felt no pain, and the fire did not harm them.

Helanthin broke out into hysterical laughter. Then he turned serious. "You wonder why the flame does not destroy you. It is kindled with wood from the sacred groves of Ameth. But I warn you just this once, so hear me well! Speak only the truth, and the fire will not harm you, but lie, and it will devour you skin, flesh, bone, and hair! Now, answer my questions carefully if you value your life! You, Onion Head! Are you really on mission from the Queen of Viridia?"

"My name is not Onion Head, it's Keldon," he answered calmly, "and the answer to your question is *yes*."

Helanthin, bracing himself, expected the flame to consume Keldon, but the Viridian remained in tact. "So," remarked Helanthin with surprise. "What you say is true."

"I tried to tell you that," said Keldon.

Helanthin turned to Sindle. "And you! Are you a spy, swine?" Again Helanthin braced himself for the spectacle of burning flesh.

"No," Sindle declared.

Amazed that nothing happened to him, Helanthin asked, "Then why have you come to Zanthis?"

"We are on a quest to find the Sacred Star of Frozen Light that we call Asdin."

"Asdin, eh? Tell me of this Asdin."

"Asdin shielded Zil-Kenøth from the Sea of Darkness—that is, until it was stolen. If it's not found, all Zil-Kenøth will perish."

A cruel smile crept over Helanthin's face, and he squinted. "Then at last Zanthis would be avenged! Our ancient foe would be annihilated! So, you are not a spy, but you are loyal to Zil-Kenøth! That is just as heinous a crime in our eyes! The Viridian shall live, but you, pig of Kenøth, shall perish nonetheless."

"But you're wrong," said Sindle. "I am not loyal to Zil-Kenøth. Not after all the lies I was told there, and not after they killed my grandfather, Wizdor, by casting him into the Sea of Darkness."

Helanthin, bracing himself, waited for the fire to consume Sindle, but nothing happened. "Hmph!" he grunted. "First you tell me you're on a mission to find a Star and save your people. Then you tell me you don't care what happens to them? This wood must be bad! Tell me. Why would you want to save people you care nothing about?"

"When we were in Viridia, the Queen used her magic to allow me to speak to my dead grandfather," explained Sindle. "It was his wish that I find Asdin. He pleaded with me to return the Star to the city of Zil. I only wanted to do his bidding. Through the power of the Queen's pendant, I hoped that we would be able to pass through Arete Vitrea and plead with the Telarch who reigns over Lux Aeternum to restore life to my grandfather. Now that the pendant is lost, I have little hope of ever seeing my grandfather again. He may be imprisoned forever in darkness."

Sindle's story moved Helanthin, because in Zanthis the devotion of sons to their fathers, grandfathers, and great grandfathers was the highest of virtues. The fact that Sindle hated the Shades of Zil-Kenøth was also clear. "I see now that you are neither spy nor Kenøthian loyalist," remarked Helanthin. "From now on you shall be called friend. But you must abandon your absurd quest for this Star you speak of. The people of Zil-Kenøth deserve their fate." Helanthin turned to his men. "Untie them! We must return to search for Queen Veronica's pendant so Sindle may hope to save his grandfather from Finsterna's grip." Then he spoke to his men sitting around the fire. "Prepare three parjars for travel! And you," he commanded another. "Array my friends in appropriate apparel for their journey."

Sindle and Keldon returned to the wagon. A few minutes later, someone threw in old, ragged robes, tunics, and turbans, and Sindle and Keldon started changing. "I can't believe you said what you did," whispered Keldon as he removed his tattered pea-pod coat.

A frown came over Sindle's face. "What?"

"About not wanting to help your people," he specified. "Is that truly how you feel?"

Sindle didn't answer.

"Of course, it must be," Keldon reckoned. "Otherwise, you would have been burned alive. I find your attitude most perplexing."

Sindle, pretending to ignore Keldon, kept dressing.

"Sindle, you must not give up on finding Asdin. We're Companions of the Quest, remember. We've come too far for you to quit trying."

"I would rather not discuss it," Sindle stated flatly.

"Very well. Perhaps later." Keldon removed his shirt and examined his bare, yellow body. "I can hardly believe what's happened to my skin."

"Believe me, you'll get used to it in time," said Sindle, trying to wind his turban. "We should be glad we still have skin."

When they had finished changing, they stepped outside the wagon and immediately focused on bright clouds of golden light that hovered near the ground like zoas. The clouds vibrated and whistled, and at their center was an eye that shot out flashes of bright, yellow lightning. The lightning wove elaborate patterns inside the clouds that reflected on the sand. Helanthin and his two servants made the parjars obey.

Keldon had already seen the parjars attached to the wagons, but Sindle, who had not, watched with wonder. "What are they?"

"Parjars," Helanthin responded. "We use them to travel." Helanthin's face hardened like stone. He reached into the cloud and the lightning patterns converged into a single bright golden arc that ran from his hand to the creature's eye. Then he climbed into the parjar's center, and its appearance changed. Helanthin took the place of its eye, and the lightning ceased flashing. Helanthin's body became one with the parjar's eye, and he glowed golden and bright as if he were on fire. "My will is now its command. It will go wherever I choose."

"It is amazing how you do that," remarked Keldon, and then he said to Sindle. "The parjar is a kind of zoa, you know."

"But I thought the zoas that migrated to Zanthis were *wild*," Sindle stated.

"If this one *had* been wild, I would now be dead," replied Helanthin. "It might have been so once, but now it's perfectly tame. Go ahead, Keldon, and mount yours."

"All right, if you're sure it's not dangerous," he said. "Of course, it shouldn't be too difficult for me since I was a zoaherder back in Viridia." Keldon reached into the center of the cloud, but when he did, lightning crashed and thunder roared from inside it. He jerked back his hand, screamed, and fell to the ground in pain.

Helanthin belched out coarse laughter. "You Viridians may tame zoas with harps and flutes. But only a Zanthan can break a wild one with his bare hands! I know your problem. He doesn't respect you. He must be made to know who the master is. Now try again, and this time, let it know you mean business. Your will must be strong, or it will bite again!"

"I'd rather not, thank you," replied Keldon, massaging his hand.

"Don't be a coward," Helanthin chided. "The parjar won't bite you a second time if you have confidence. Now do as I say, and try not to let it think you fear it."

Keldon mustered the courage and reached into the cloud again. This time the lightning formed an arc from his hand to the parjar's eye. As Helanthin had done, he managed to step into the eye at its center.

"Well done," Helanthin congratulated him. "Now it's Sindle's turn. Remember. Let it know from the first who has the upper hand!"

Sindle's eyes became fixed with determination, and his face hardened. He reached his hand into the cloud toward the eye. The arc formed, and he stepped in.

"Well done!" Helanthin applauded. "You'll be Zanthans yet! Now comes the easy part. To make them go, you simply *will* them forward. Now try it. Just *will* them to follow me!"

Helanthin started out. Willing their parjars to proceed, Sindle and Keldon sped out like whirlwinds over the dunes and across the blowing, stinging sands.

As they rode, Keldon shouted to Helanthin, "How did you manage to tame wild zoas? We could never do that back in Viridia."

"It's not easy," replied Helanthin. "They're dangerous when they're without form—vibrating clouds of energy that kill anyone who dares touch them. Fortunately, they're afraid of people for the most part and try to escape whenever you chase them. But rounding them up is a hard and dangerous job. Sometimes they turn on you when you corner them. That's why brands are used to tame them, and not brands heated in just any fire. They've got to be heated in the sacred flame at the city of Ecrusand. When we brand them, the eye appears in their center. When that happens, they become parjars, and there's little reason to fear them after that."

Early the next lumen-flow, they had reached the place in the desert where Helanthin had earlier found Sindle and Keldon unconscious. They stepped out of their parjars and started searching for the Queen's pendant. "It's no use," said Keldon. "By now it lies buried in the sand."

"Nonsense," said Helanthin. "We lose things in the desert all the time. If it's here, I promise I shall find it."

The Zanthan trudged through the sand with his eyes closed and his palms turned downward. Sindle and Keldon watched as Helanthin's hands began to shake and his body trembled.

"There's something here, all right!" he cried. He stooped down, ran his fingers through the sand, and pulled up something.

"That's the chain the pendant hung on!" exclaimed Sindle. "The pendant can't be far away."

Helanthin scoured the sand. "There's nothing here."

"Could you search a bit longer?" suggested Keldon.

Helanthin shut his eyes, put his palms downward, and roved back and forth over the dunes. Finally, he gave up. "If it were here, I know I would have found it. It must really be lost."

"Then we have no hope of passing through Arete Vitrea," said Sindle. "What will the Queen say when she finds out I've lost her pendant? She made me promise to protect it with my life!"

"I'm sure she will understand," Keldon reassured him. "After all, you could not have protected it when you were unconscious and dying in the desert."

"Do not admit defeat yet," said Helanthin. "There resides in the ancient city of Ecrusand a very wise man whom we call the Patriarch of Zanthis. If anyone can help you, he can. I encourage you to go to him. You are welcome to take my parjars. Will them to go to Ecrusand. They know the way and will get you there by mid-lumen-ebb. I only ask one thing. Parjars are valuable. When you get to the city, say to them, 'return to your master!' and they will obey."

"How can we ever repay you for your generosity?" asked Sindle.

"It's our custom," stated Helanthin. His eyes sharpened and he spoke to each of the parjars. "You will take my friends to Ecrusand." Lightning flashed from their eyes as if they understood.

Keldon and Sindle climbed into the parjars and bade farewell to Helanthin. Soon they were sailing over the wild jaws of the desert that before had threatened to devour them, but in their parjars they felt safe and protected. Still they would be glad when the desert was behind them, and glad to be in Ecrusand.

CHAPTER 16
ECRUSAND

By mid-lumen-ebb, the silhouette of an ancient city on a distant rise sifted into view through dust-filled air. Broken lines gradually became colored in with tans and dull yellows revealing buildings that mourned lost glories of a bygone age. Across waves of sand and up ravaged roads, Sindle and Keldon sped toward Ecrusand. In time they entered its gates and rode between several shriveled old men engaged in furious debate. One of them jumped up and shouted at Sindle and Keldon, "Have you no respect for the ancient philosophies?"

They halted and glanced back. The old man's leathery face puckered with anger. "Sorry!" Keldon apologized. He glanced over at Sindle. "Should we ask him where to find the Patriarch?"

"That might not be a good idea," he replied. "He seems pretty angry." They decided to continue on.

As they rode, Sindle observed Ecrusand's inhabitants. "They seem a none-too-happy lot," he remarked. Zanthans shuffled through the streets like puppets controlled by some invisible hand. With clothes soiled by sulfur-colored dust, and scowls hardened upon their faces, they were the very definition of misery.

Keldon and Sindle eventually arrived at a dilapidated inn afflicted with a leprous facade of peeling paint, broken windows, and a crooked, weather-beaten sign. They thought it abandoned until a large woman paraded out the front door and started shaking dust the color of sulfur from a threadbare rug. The woman's face was no less hard than those of the other Zanthans they had seen.

"Shall we ask her?" inquired Keldon.

"What could it hurt?" Sindle returned.

They leapt from their parjars, and walked over to her. Acting at first as though she did not notice them, she kept shaking out her rug. Keldon, dodging the yellow clouds, made his best diplomatic effort. "Excuse me, please, Madam. Do you know where we might find the Patriarch of Zanthis?"

She suspended her shaking, placed one hand upon her hip, and asked in a suspicious tone, "Who wants to know?"

"Never mind," said Keldon, and he changed the subject. "We noticed this is an inn. Do you have a vacancy? We've traveled far, and are quite tired."

"Are you desert people?" she probed.

"No," Keldon replied.

She scoured them with suspicious eyes. "Then where did you get that garb?"

Sindle grew angry. "Is that any business of yours?" Then he said to Keldon. "Come, we'll find lodging elsewhere," and he returned to his parjar.

"He's a rude one," the woman snorted at Keldon loud enough for Sindle to hear. She stormed inside and returned several minutes later. "We have a room, but it's not much to speak of."

"Let's find another inn!" Sindle shouted to Keldon.

"We *are* the only inn in Ecrusand," the woman growled.

Keldon smiled. "Thank you. We would be grateful to have the room."

"Follow me," she said in a snooty tone.

"Excuse me, but I must take care of something first," Keldon told the woman. He trotted over to the parjars. "Return to your master," he ordered, and immediately they sailed off.

Keldon and a reluctant Sindle followed the woman into the inn, up rickety stairs, through a beaten-up door, and into a dingy room. As she thumped across the floor, she left what looked like hoof prints in the yellow dust. Then, passing a table, she cut a trail across it with her finger and flicked it. Proceeding to the bed, she tried to force stuffing back into a mattress. Then she puffed up the stained pillows, creating a yellow nimbus cloud. She coughed and shooed it away with a flap of her hand. Gaping holes and cracks covered every inch of the walls, and in places plaster from the ceiling had snowed upon the floor.

The woman walked up to Keldon, slapped the key into his hand, and said with a tinge of sarcasm, "Enjoy."

"Thank you," he replied with a forced smile.

As the woman marched out, she gave Sindle one last disapproving stare. After she was gone, he yanked the turban from his head and collapsed into a chair. Dust rose from the cushion and hovered in the atmosphere. Meanwhile, Keldon, drew a circle on the table next to where the woman had left her mark.

"I've never been to such a terrible place or met such horrible people!" Sindle griped.

"It must be the dust," said Keldon, trying not to cough. "How do they live with it? I feel sorry for them."

Sindle frowned. "You would, of course. The sooner we leave this place, the better."

Keldon brushed off a chair and sat in front of Sindle. "I'll agree, Zanthis is not the most hospitable place in Spectara. Still, I suppose we should be grateful that everything has worked out for the best."

Sindle stared with disbelief at Keldon. "Worked out for the best?" he shot back. "We *lost* the pendant of Queen Veronica. How can you say everything has worked out for the best?"

"There's still a Patriarch in Zanthis, remember."

"If he's like the other Zanthans we've met, we might as well abandon all hope."

"Maybe he will be different," said Keldon.

Sindle stared into space. "I'm worried. I have a feeling the pendant has fallen into evil hands. The Queen feared such a thing might happen."

"I don't see how," Keldon returned. "Surely it lies lost in the desert. No one could have found it under all that sand, not even Helanthin."

"Still something the Queen said makes me worry. She told me Finsterna might gain greater and greater power. What if the pendant was stolen?"

"Are you suggesting Helanthin or one of his men might have taken it?" Keldon asked.

"I doubt that Helanthin would have done it," replied Sindle. "He refused at first to believe there even was a pendant. Still, one of his men could have stolen it without his knowledge, I suppose."

"But why would the thief take the pendant and leave the chain behind?" asked Keldon. "Somehow that doesn't make sense."

"Very little does make sense anymore."

"Surely the pendant is lost," said Keldon. "That would be the most reasonable explanation."

Sindle was silent for a moment. Then he asked. "What if the Telarch doesn't *want* us to pass through Arete Vitrea? Could he have willed the pendant to be lost?"

"The Telarch is good. I don't think he would will such a thing."

"How can you be so sure?" Sindle questioned. "What if the beliefs of Zil-Kenøth and the Trogzars turn out to be true, after all we've been through? What if the Telarch *is* the Hell of Light's evil ruler? I'll admit, the idea of the Hell of Light could have been made up just to keep the Shades of Zil-Kenøth chained in their traditions. But could not the opposite also be true? The idea of a good Telarch may have been dreamed up by your Queen to keep the Viridians satisfied with *their* way of life. How can anyone know what is true or false anymore?"

Keldon was offended. "The Queen would never lie."

"Maybe not. But she could withhold part of the truth, just as she did with you, Keldon."

"What do you mean?"

"She tried to shield you, remember? She didn't want you to see the image of Wizdor shrivel in that fountain, so she protected you from having to look upon death." Sindle's memory of the event choked him up and made it difficult to speak.

"I believe you're wrong about the Telarch and wrong about our Queen."

"The Telarch's fire may destroy us quicker than the fires of Ameth would destroy a liar. Think of that."

"There must be a logical reason why things have turned out the way they have," Keldon asserted. His eyes showed that he was distressed. "Who are we, anyway, to fathom the mind of light? We are mere Shades in this mirage we call Spectara."

"Mirages evaporate, you know, and so do Shades when they are struck by light that is too bright."

Sindle's words made Keldon so angry he was speechless, and a tense silence filled the room. Finally, Sindle spoke. "I'm sorry, Keldon," he apologized, rising from his chair. "I'm tired, discouraged, and confused." He walked over to the bed and collapsed. As he lay staring at the ceiling, questions about the Telarch tormented his mind. Could the Telarch do nothing about the evil that now was infecting Spectara? Zil-Kenøth had fallen to Trogzars, Asdin had been stolen, the pendant of Veronica had been lost, but the Telarch had done nothing to prevent these evils. A terrible thought occurred to Sindle. If the Telarch couldn't stop these events from happening, then how could he bring Wizdor back to life? Would the Telarch turn out to be as powerless to avert Finsterna's evil as Veronica had been? As Sindle mulled over these thoughts, he wondered again about the Kenøthic belief that the Telarch ruled over the Hell of Light. If this were true, then the Telarch, not Finsterna, would be the one who threatened Spectara. Neblas would then be correct in his decision to go vanquish the Telarch with Asdin. Sindle's mind churned with confusion and doubt. Finally, he became so weary of thinking, he resigned himself to fate and fell asleep.

Meanwhile, as Keldon sat in his chair, his sand-sore eyes became fixed upon a hole in the wall. At first his thoughts traveled back to Viridia. Then he started worrying that he might never see Biona or his Viridian paradise again. Worry was gradually driving out hope, and Sindle's doubts were poisoning his mind. He had tried to be strong for Sindle's sake. He also knew that to abandon the quest for Asdin would betray the Queen's wishes, and *this* he could never do. But inwardly, he longed for home, for the simple life of herding zoas, for their carefree dancing through the fields, and for the comforting sound of harps and flutes. Now the Verdis Tree and the glories of Wittistide seemed but a distant dream. Keldon felt his soul sinking beneath a flood of sadness.

CHAPTER 17
THE PATRIARCH

Sindle and Keldon had slept through the next lumen-flow, and it was already mid-lumen-ebb when there was knocking at the door. Keldon rose and opened it. Outside stood an imposing man wearing golden robes and a skull cap. His skin was the color of honey, his platinum hair and beard were long and wavy, and his deep-set, piercing eyes stared from beneath thick, dark brows. "I seek the strangers from Viridia and Zil-Kenøth," he said. His voice was deep and abrupt.

Sindle awoke and joined Keldon at the door.

Dwarfed and intimidated by the man's muscular appearance, Keldon issued a nervous response. "*I* am from Viridia. My name is Keldon, and this is my friend, Sindle, from Zil-Kenøth."

"I am Amaril, son of the Patriarch of Zanthis. There is little time. It is urgent that you come with me." He turned, expecting them to follow. Frightened, Keldon and Sindle glanced at each other. Not too keen to join the imposing Zanthan, Sindle asked, "*What* is urgent?"

Amaril turned and said sharply, "Your questions will be answered by the Patriarch. Come."

Afraid of angering the Zanthan, Sindle and Keldon followed him down the stairs, out of the inn, and into the street. However, before they had ventured far, they heard footfalls through the gravel followed by shouting. "You cannot leave! Your bill is unpaid!" They turned. It was the woman who had given them the room.

Amaril flipped a gold coin into the dirt. "There!" he said without breaking his stride, and continued on. The woman stooped down and retrieved the coin.

"Thank you. You are most generous," Keldon said, but Amaril paid him no heed.

"How does the Patriarch know we are here?" Sindle asked.

"He will explain all when we arrive," replied Amaril. As he swept down a narrow passageway between two very high walls, Sindle and Keldon followed. "This way," he said, pivoting around a corner. He paced across a street and over a large sandstone plaza toward a round building made of rough, yellow brick. Its high tower was capped by a splendid, golden dome held aloft by five pillars.

They entered the building through heavy oaken doors carved with immense eyes. "Through here," Amaril commanded. He led them down a yellow brick corridor, under dark, beamed archways, and past a second pair of doors. These were smaller than the first but were also carved with eyes. After following an alcove along the outermost wall of a round chamber, their eyes focused on a strange fire burning in the chamber's center. Extending out from the location of the flame was a floor made of concentric cobblestone circles that sparkled gold in the firelight. As Amaril rushed through the alcove that ran around the circumference of the chamber, the flame kept drawing Sindle's and Keldon's eyes toward it.

Emerging from the alcove, they saw an old man sitting on a gold and bronze throne. His long beard reflected the color of the flame, and his golden garments and skullcap glittered in its light. The throne, the flame, and the man all seemed as one until the moment he saw Amaril and the others. He then leapt like a spark from the fire, sailing in their direction. "Wonderful! You've found them!" He ran and embraced first Sindle and then Keldon. "I am the Patriarch of Zanthis. Welcome to Ecrusand! You have come just in time! Behold, the flame burns crimson, blue, and gold!"

Sindle and Keldon were at first speechless as they stared at the flame burning in its three colors. Its beauty was hypnotic.

"Tell me," the Patriarch said, looking at Sindle, "are you the Kenøthite or the Viridian?"

Sindle hesitated and glanced at Keldon.

"Don't be frightened," said the Patriarch. "I promise your treatment here will be better than what you received in the desert. I heard this mid-lumen-flow of your dreadful trial by fire there.

The desert clans mean well, but they are often extreme in their zeal for truth."

Sindle took care not to incriminate himself. "I am Sindle from Zil-Kenøth, but I no longer consider myself a Kenøthite. I'm a refugee, not a loyalist."

"And you must be the Viridian," said the Patriarch.

"Yes. I am Keldon, Chief Zoaherder to Queen Veronica," he replied.

"Wonderful," said the Patriarch. "Now I suppose I should tell you that we already know why you've journeyed here. A messenger from the desert tribe informed us of your misadventure. I understand that you intended to pass through Arete Vitrea using the power of the pendant of Queen Veronica but that it became lost. I regret that I have no way of helping you find it. Such a feat lies beyond my powers. But there may still be a way. Come now. Look closer at the flame."

They peered into its center. The flame had a red, blue, and yellow metallic luster. Strange and effervescent, it wove itself into magnificent patterns. A look of awe came over their faces as they gazed into it. Its magnetic power was hard to resist. Then in its center, a mysterious object was unveiled—an eye with a blue iris, a golden retina, and a crimson outline. The eye drew them into itself, urging them to become one with the flame, but as it drew them nearer, they also felt anguish rising up in their souls. The feeling finally became unbearable. They didn't want to stop looking at the flame, but they had no choice but to tear their eyes away from it.

"You have beheld the mystery at the source," remarked the Patriarch. "You feel its power, and this means you surely have been chosen."

"Chosen for what?" asked Keldon.

"The purpose cannot be spoken now. It is a purpose yet to be made known. But you should be aware that few have seen the eye that is the source of the eternal flame of wisdom. Beneath this flame lie the bones of blessed Lucia our Queen. The lumen fast approaches when an ancient prophecy shall be fulfilled— the prophecy once spoken by our Great Patriarch Helis who lit this flame. 'In those times,' saith the Prophet, 'great darkness shall come upon the world, and all Spectara shall languish. Then the descendants of the peoples of the three lands shall journey up to Ecrusand to seek the wisdom of the great flame. In that time it shall burn crimson, blue, and gold until the way through Arete Vitrea shall be revealed. Then it shall come to pass that they shall dwell under canopies of light and find shelter in the tents of truth. The Zarafat of Zil Magnus shall be broken, and the swords of the mighty men of Pyrath cast down. They shall no more wage war, for all Spectara shall be at one with him whose name may not be uttered.'"

"How will this way be opened up?" Sindle inquired.

"It is a secret that will be revealed to you in the groves of Ameth. This too has been prophesied in the sacred Vestar, our holy book: 'In Ameth the things of the end time shall be made known, and the shroud of darkness shall be lifted before the eternal lumen-flow of the One Light dawns.' This is why you must journey to Ameth to sleep in the sacred groves. My son, Amaril, will be your guide into the wisdom of the groves."

"Will you not also go?" Keldon asked him.

"Alas, I've long dreamt of this glorious lumen-tide, but I am too old to make such a journey. The paths are steep. The way is difficult. My time is past."

"If the way is too difficult, we may not be able to make the journey either," remarked Sindle. "We're still recovering from our ordeal in the desert. We've had little rest."

"Of course, how rude of me," said the Patriarch. "To ask you to go now would be too great a request. You need time for relaxation and nourishment. You shall stay here and be my guests. I know the inn where you were staying. You will be much better off here." The Patriarch clapped his hands and a servant appeared. "This is Lucius, my trusted adviser. Lucius, please tell the servants that our new friends, Keldon and Sindle, will be joining us for Karash later this lumen-ebb. Have quiet rooms prepared for them as well. They must rest before beginning their journey to Ameth."

"As you wish," replied Lucius, and he exited the chamber.

"I don't know what I would do without Lucius. He's not only my trusted advisor; he's my right arm too. I love him as a brother. Now, my son, Amaril, will escort you to the baths. You will feel much better once you've ridded your bodies of our Zanthan dust and refreshed yourselves."

Keldon's eyes sparkled. "Thank you, my dear sir."

"You're most welcome, of course. We'll expect you for Karash later, then."

Amaril led Sindle and Keldon back through the corridor and down another long passageway. As they walked, Keldon asked Amaril, "What is this *Karash* the Patriarch spoke about."

"It is a ceremonial meal we eat in honor of Lucia, our Queen. We celebrate it on rare occasions, but now that the sacred flame is burning crimson, blue, and gold, we've been celebrating it daily." They came to a door. "The baths are through here," he said, changing the subject. "I will provide you with special Karash robes to wear. They will be waiting in these dressing rooms. I shall leave you now. May the baths invigorate you."

"Thank you," replied Keldon

When Amaril had gone, Sindle and Keldon went to bathe. Upon finishing, they donned robes of yellow linen embroidered with gold borders and wore skullcaps of the same design. Soon Amaril entered and asked, "Do the robes fit?"

"I don't think so," replied Keldon. "Doesn't mine look rather peculiar?" Something about them exaggerated Keldon's onion head.

Amaril examined it. "No," he flatly replied, and without a second thought about Keldon's concern over his appearance he said, "Follow me. There is something you must see." He led them through a corridor toward the chamber of the flame, but before they reached the chamber, he ducked into a passageway. Then they climbed up spiral, cobblestone stairs until they emerged into a round upper chamber. Low tables were set with golden plates, and on the floor, leather cushions were spread about.

"We will celebrate Karash here, but this isn't what I brought you to see. Come." They exited through a passageway, and started up another flight of stairs.

"Where are you taking us?" asked Keldon.

"To the tower," replied Amaril. "You saw the dome of the building when we walked past it earlier?"

"Yes."

"The dome is supported by five pillars. These represent the five books of our sacred Vestar, the holy writings given to our people by Helis after the death of Lucia our Queen. Helis had five visions in the sacred groves of Ameth. He recorded one in each of the sacred books. They comprise the Vestar whose word upholds all things through its truth. That is why the golden dome of heaven rests upon its pillars."

Keldon arched his brow, for Amaril did not speak of the living tree of Verdis but of a lifeless book.

"In here," said the Zanthan, pointing.

When they entered, they were struck by sudden brightness. They squinted up at a dome encrusted with faceted, yellow jewels. These glittered like stars and scattered intense brightness onto gold-plated walls that in turn splashed light onto the floor, making the whole chamber shine with the brilliance of a sun. When their eyes adjusted, they saw in the center of the compartment a golden ark resting upon an alabaster pedestal. The ark was shaped like a pentagon, and on its lid were engraved many eyes identical to the ones they had seen carved on the doors.

"Proceed no further," Amaril spoke in a low and solemn tone. As he continued, his voice was tinged with an aura of mystery. "In this ark rests the sacred Vestar, the original manuscript transcribed by Helis himself. No one has opened it in nine-hundred and fifty lumnus-years, not since the lumen on which it was sealed. But soon the way will be opened up through Arete Vitrea. Then the Vestar will be unsealed, for its truth will no longer need protecting."

"How do you know the way past Arete Vitrea *will* be opened up?" asked Sindle.

Amaril answered defensively, "What has been revealed by the sacred flame cannot be false. That's why we must go to the groves of Ameth and sleep to receive the oracle. Not since the times of Helis has anyone received a vision there. But now the flame burns in the three colors. The time has come for visions to be imparted again. In Ameth the secret way through Arete Vitrea will be revealed."

"I hope you're right," said Sindle. "I have heard that the Telarch alone holds the power to bring my grandfather, Wizdor, back to life."

"Why are you concerned about that?" asked Amaril. "I'm sure he's better off dead."

Sindle took offense. "He is trapped by the power of the Sea of Darkness!" he replied. "He suffers in its prison! He is hardly better off! That is why I must find a way to free him!"

"Come," said Amaril. "I'll show you to your rooms. You will tell me more as we go."

As they followed Amaril, Sindle told him how the Trogzars had sacrificed his grandfather to the Sea of Darkness, how Prince Neblas had stolen the Sacred Star, Asdin, and how the Sea of Darkness had attacked the city of Zil. He explained to Amaril how the power of the fountain of Queen Veronica had enabled him to speak with his dead grandfather, how the Queen had entrusted them with her pendant, and how they had lost it.

"So I understand from Helanthin's men," Amaril commented, and then, without a glimmer of sympathy, added. "No doubt this is part the judgment that will come in the final lumen." Without any concern whatsoever for Sindle's feelings, he then said, "Here are your rooms. I'll return later to take you to Karash."

After Amaril had left, Sindle said to Keldon, "How cold and calloused can a person be? Do we dare go with him to this Ameth he speaks of?"

"Maybe it's just his Zanthan way," remarked Keldon. "There must be an explanation..."

"Please, spare me," Sindle interrupted. "I don't want to hear it."

Keldon stood speechless. "Very well," he finally said. "I'm sure things will seem better after you have rested." Keldon left him. Then Sindle crawled into bed and drifted to sleep.

CHAPTER 18
DARK FIRE

Sindle awoke when he heard knocking. With his mind in a fog, he staggered over to the door and opened it. Keldon and the Patriarch's advisor, Lucius, stood outside. "It's Karash time," Lucius informed him.

"One moment," said Sindle. He had only had two lumen-hours of sleep, and could hardly pry his eyes open. He walked over to the bed, shook his skullcap out from the covers, and put it on his head. Because he had slept in his robe, it now had the texture of wadded paper, so he kept trying to smooth out the wrinkles as he followed Lucius to the Karash chamber. When they arrived, a Zanthan fire priest stood at the door holding a censer of coals that burned golden in color.

"You will need to be purged," Lucius told Sindle and Keldon. His words ignited the memory of their trial by fire in the desert.

"Do not be afraid," said Lucius, noticing the distraught look on their faces. "The fire is not harmful."

The priest held a coal between his thumb and forefinger and brought it toward Sindle's eyes. Sindle drew back in horror.

"Do not be alarmed," said the priest. "Remain still."

A servant forcibly held Sindle's head so that the priest could touch the burning coal to his eyes. Sindle screamed and struggled to break free as the burning coal approached his right eye. The priest mumbled a strange incantation as he held the coal first to one eye and then the other. Sindle was relieved and amazed when the coals caused him no pain.

"These coals are from the sacred flame," said Lucius. "They contain the fire of truth and wisdom. All other fire destroys sight, but this fire restores sight to the blind soul." Afterward, the priest placed the coal on Sindle's lips and chanted. "This is the fire that purifies speech and transforms words into gold," Lucius explained.

Sindle felt the fire's power penetrate to his bones. He had felt this way earlier when he looked upon the eye in the sacred fire, but the anguish he had felt then had caused him to tear his eyes away. Now, however, he felt united with the flame. The lies of his past seemed to catch fire and burn to ashes, releasing him from all remaining addiction to the ways of Zil-Kenøth. In the empty darkness that remained, a sudden passion for truth and justice ignited in his breast. Sindle fell to his knees and wept.

Now it was the Viridian's turn. Keldon calmly stood as the priest touched the coal first to his eyes and then to his mouth. Keldon immediately erupted with joyous laughter, but in keeping with his reserved nature, he kept apologizing for his reaction.

"You should not be embarrassed," said Lucius. "To some, it is the fire of penitence; to others, the fire of ecstasy. But above all, it is the fire of truth. Now you both may enter into the joys of the Karash."

Inside the chamber, reclining on cushions around low tables, were the Patriarch, Amaril, and seven other Zanthans, their somber faces flickering in the torch light. The Patriarch caught sight of Sindle and Keldon as they entered, and he motioned for them to join him. Soon the Patriarch stood and addressed the assembly.

"My friends, we have gathered to partake of Karash, the sacred festival of our people. We have witnessed the omen foretold in olden times by the Great Patriarch, Helis, and written down in our sacred Vestar. In the chamber below us the sacred flame burns crimson, blue, and gold. Helis prophesied that this omen would herald the final age. Many generations have longed to see what we have witnessed. At long last, the ancient prophecy is reaching fulfillment. It is the wish of him who dwells beyond Arete Vitrea that an aeon of peace should at last return and that the lands of Spectara should become one as they were before the death of Lucia our Queen. It is his wish to bring an end to the present world of division and to establish a new Spectara. For this purpose, he has brought together the descendents of the three lands so that they may journey to Ameth to receive the full vision. Soon, the way past Arete Vitrea shall be revealed to all Spectara. In celebration of this great occasion, we shall partake of the Karash. May the time swiftly come when the Karash shall be eaten on every lumen-ebb."

At these words, the guests lifted their hands and responded, "So mote it be!"

"Lucius, bring forth the sacred fire!" the Patriarch commanded.

Lucius received the fire censer from the priest, covered it with a lid, and brought it to him. As Lucius and a servant extinguished the torches, darkness crept into the room. Soon the windowless chamber was pitch-black, and the Patriarch began speaking in a voice low and mysterious. "It is now as it was before time began, before light emerged from the gulf of darkness, and the eyes of wisdom awoke. Then, behold!" The Patriarch plucked the lid from the censer. "An island of truth spread over the abyss, and the lies of darkness fled before it." The Patriarch lifted the fire and then lowered it. "Still the eyes of truth had not been opened, not until the Nameless One who dwells beyond Arete Vitrea commanded them to awaken, and behold..." The Patriarch removed a black napkin that concealed two round white wafers of the same size. "...they awoke and beheld the light. This was the first Karash, the first awakening to wisdom. Let us now eat of the wafers of the Karash with the hope that we, too, may be awakened. First, we partake of the wafer of the lesser truth. Shall we eat this wafer in hope that we may know and be one with the lesser truth."

The Patriarch passed the wafer through the sacred fire several times before distributing it to his guests. Sindle nibbled his piece. It tasted as bland as paper. When the wafer returned to the Patriarch, he spoke again. "May all who have eaten of the wafer of the lesser truth come to know the wisdom cradled in our traditions, the wisdom of the past and the present."

The guests again lifted their hands and said, "So mote it be."

"And now we must partake of the wafer of the greater truth. Let us partake of it in hope that we shall be enlightened to the greater wisdom and be one with it." He passed the second wafer through the fire and distributed it as he had the other. When Sindle nibbled it, his eyes brightened. It tasted sweeter than honey.

"May all who have eaten of the wafer of the greater truth come to know the wisdom that no dweller of Spectara yet knows— the wisdom that will soon be revealed."

Again, those assembled lifted their hands and responded, "So mote it be."

"And now, may the wisdom of the lesser truth and the wisdom of the greater truth, the wisdom of the two eyes of Lucia, enlighten the eye of the soul and the eye of the spirit. May the wisdom of the sacred fire that burns from the bones of Lucia our Queen burn in our bones. May we become one with the Eternal Flame that burns beyond Arete Vitrea."

The guests responded. "As it was for our fathers, so may it be for us. And as it is for us, so may it be for our children and our children's children."

"And now, as the spark of holy fire is retired to the flame, may we all remember: The wisdom that has been entrusted to us shall return to him who gave it. May we become one with this wisdom that we might also become one with the flame."

The Patriarch's advisor received the censer and then exited to return the coals to the flame in the chamber below. Those assembled raised their hands for several moments, and silence settled in the room. Then the voice of the Patriarch ripped through the silence. "The time has come for rejoicing!" He clapped his hands, and immediately, several servants relit the torches. Others sprang in great numbers through doors carrying trays of food. Musicians entered playing drums, pipes, and stringed instruments. The guests clapped their hands and sang a Zanthan folk song about Karash, while servants spread multitudes of trays upon the tables.

Amaril shouted above the rabble to Sindle and Keldon. "The song is not difficult! Try to join in!"

Sindle and Keldon gave each other a curious glance and started clapping to the beat. However, the words to the Zanthan folk song were tricky, and each time Sindle and Keldon thought they had them in the right order, the rhythm would change.

Trays of food soon began to pass before them, and Amaril made certain that both Sindle and Keldon got generous helpings. Sindle stared at the food on his plate. By now he had learned not to ask about what he was eating, so he tried his best to enjoy it. But then Keldon made the mistake of commenting on the delicious mushrooms.

"Mushrooms!" Amaril exclaimed, and he heaved with laughter.

The Patriarch overheard and butted in. "Have you never tasted eye of karagus? They are good, are they not?"

Sindle had just popped one into his mouth, and this put him in the awkward position of how best to dispose of it without appearing rude. As it rested in his mouth, its feel grew more and more disgusting. Finally he mustered courage and swallowed it whole. It slid down his esophagus with the reluctance of a large marble.

"Indeed," replied Keldon. His pleasant smile disappeared. "Do you mean I've just eaten the eye of some poor creature?"

"Yes," the Patriarch informed him. "The karagus is a lizard that lives in the caves of Ameth."

What could be worse than eating lizard eyes? Sindle thought.

"But I was under the impression I was eating a vegetable," remarked Keldon. The guests stared curiously at the distraught, onion-headed Viridian. "Still it *was* delicious," he admitted. "I suppose another wouldn't hurt."

Everyone except Sindle applauded and roared with laughter as Keldon popped another eye into his mouth. Sindle watched squeamishly as the Viridian devoured one after another of the horrible eyes without a second thought. Sindle's appetite now had vanished, and he dared not touch any other food. Instead, he sat silently, staring at the karagus eyes on his plate, wondering how the Zanthans could tolerate such sinister looking things at so sacred a meal.

The Zanthan folk song curiously began to remind Sindle of the Ophis horns of Zil-Kenøth. Dark images of Trogzars casting his grandfather into the Sea of Darkness crept through his mind. He recalled the stone he had found lying beside the Sea and removed it from his pouch. Sudden anguish struck his heart. It looked like one of the karagus eyes! He now understood what Queen Veronica had felt when she gazed into the stone. She had felt Finsterna's dark fire, and now Sindle felt it too. Whether it was the effect of the coals of fire on his vision or the Karash meal, he now understood more clearly just what it meant that Finsterna's power had frozen Wizdor's soul and imprisoned it in darkness!

Then, without warning, the Patriarch shrieked with terror, "No! It cannot be! It cannot be!"

A hush fell over the celebration. The Patriarch jumped up and rushed from the chamber with Amaril. All the guests ran after them, shouting, and Sindle and Keldon followed. They soon entered the chamber of the flame where they again heard the Patriarch's voice rip through the air like cracking ice. "No! No!"

When they beheld the flame, a look of horror crept across their faces. The crimson-colored part of the fire now burned black.

"What can it mean?" Amaril asked.

The Patriarch's eyes swelled with terror. "Find Sindle and Keldon!"

"We are here," Keldon responded. He and Sindle pushed their way through the crowd. Sindle needed no explanation of what he saw. *Dark fire* was taking over the flame. The thought of it slithered serpent-like through his mind.

The Patriarch's face convulsed with horror. "When did this happen?" he asked Lucius.

"When I returned the coal to the flame after the ceremony," he replied.

"This can only mean one thing," said the Patriarch. "The time is growing short. The descendants of the three lands must journey to Ameth at once."

"I'll arrange for parjars," said Amaril, and he hurried off.

The crowd continued to stare in silence at the flame. Anguish built up pressure in the Patriarch's eyes and throat until it exploded into tears and sobs. He tore his robes, fell to his knees, and wailed.

A short time later, Amaril returned. "Come. Our parjars are ready."

"Hurry, hurry!" the Patriarch urged. "Maybe there is time to reverse this evil omen. I will stay with the flame and pray for its deliverance from this hideous contamination."

The Companions of the Quest, which now included Amaril, proceeded to the plaza, mounted their parjars, and in no time were sailing again across the deserts of Zanthis.

CHAPTER 19
AMETH

Miles of desert stretched before the Companions of the Quest as they rode. Eventually, monotony produced fatigue, and fatigue sapped their wills, slowing them down. The urge to give in to sleep crushed down on them, but they knew they had to remain vigilant if their parjars were to obey. Sindle seemed the most laden by fatigue. He found it ever harder to keep pace.

"How much further?" Keldon asked Amaril.

"It is almost lumen-flow now. We should be there by low lumen-ebb," came the reply.

Sindle's heart sank. "I'm thirsty," he declared, thinking that a sip of water might help him stay alert. Amaril drew a skin from his pack and tossed it to him. "Save some for later." The memory of almost dying of thirst in the desert tumbled through his mind. Sand stretched as far as the eye could see. Sindle guzzled the water. "Enough!" Amaril warned, and Sindle tossed back the skin.

In time, a sense of helplessness tightened its grip on Sindle's mind. He now fathomed that he and his companions had reached a point of no return. It mattered not to him whether the ancient prophecy was true or false. Faced with the prospect that they might be chasing a Zanthan mirage, the thought occurred that he had lost control of his destiny. The only choice that now remained was between continuing on and death. Sindle might have been willing to accept the latter alternative had it not been for the fact that Wizdor was still imprisoned by Finsterna's dark fire. If Wizdor were ever to be set free from her prison, Sindle knew he had to endure, and this somehow gave him strength to carry on. Eventually, a sense of endless hanging between uncertain destiny and oblivion set in.

Sometime early in the lumen-ebb, Amaril pointed. "Look!" he exclaimed, "The crags of Ameth!" The words flew from his mouth like birds long imprisoned in a cage. In the distance, jutting up from the sea of yellow sand, were islands of orange rock.

"Will your parjars to go faster!" Amaril urged.

As they rode, Ameth's crags grew larger, and their outlines became clearer. By mid-lumen-ebb, the Companions reached the first of the formations. Into their orange volcanic ash, shadows seemed to gouge out grotesque features. "Legend has it that a race of giants once ruled Spectara," Amaril told them. "Over the lumnus-years, it is said that they became petrified, and these formations were the result. Look closer. They seem almost alive." The caves in the formations, like hollow eye sockets, reminded Sindle of the karagus lizard eye he had eaten. A chill ran down his spine, and he averted his gaze.

Amaril continued. "The truth is that Pyrath's volcanoes spewed forth this ash thousands of lumnus-years ago. Later, the great flood, followed by wind and sand, carved these forms."

"Was that the flood sent by the Queen of Viridia?" Sindle inquired.

"Yes," Amaril answered. "It was the last in a series of unspeakable tests that Zanthis was made to endure." Anguish lit a fuse in Amaril's eyes and fizzled until the words, "We must hurry!" exploded from his mouth.

Sindle and Keldon tried to keep pace as Amaril sped ahead. On either side of the canyon through which they travelled, honeycombed cliffs, cones, and pillars of volcanic ash cast serpentine shadows across each others' gnarled and pitted surfaces. The formations seemed frozen in pain, as though their mummified flesh still bore throbbing wounds of some terrible, past memory. Through their caverns, winds blustered, piping somber, hollow tones. Rattling noises also echoed from the scurrying feet of unseen karagus lizards.

The path eventually became too steep, narrow, and winding to continue with the parjars, so Amaril willed his to halt. "From this point, we must journey by foot," he informed them. They dismounted, and Amaril commanded the parjars to remain until they should return.

"Are the groves nearby?" asked Keldon.

"They lie deep within these formations," Amaril replied. "Follow me." They climbed a path worn into the soft volcanic ash by centuries of pilgrims' feet. Soon, they entered a small tunnel, and a burst of cool air that carried a hint of the smell of sulfur brushed across their faces. At first the tunnel was dark, but gradually their eyes adjusted to a dim, orange glow that shone from the walls. They crawled through the tunnel into a chamber that was large enough to stand in.

"Where are we now?" Keldon asked.

"The groves of Ameth are protected by many tunnels and chambers," Amaril explained. "When the Pyrathans first marched against Zanthis, our people were unprepared. Zanthis had never before known war and lacked weapons, so she had to protect herself as best she could. Our ancestors tunneled into this ash to protect the sacred groves from the armies of Pyrath. These passageways extend for miles." Amaril ran his fingers along a wall until he came to a carving of an eye that was identical to those they had seen in Ecrusand. "Only someone who knows how to read these emblems can find the way to the groves. Each tunnel leads to another chamber that looks exactly like this one. If a wrong tunnel is taken at any time, it will lead away from the groves. Intruders sometimes become lost in these caverns and die of thirst and starvation." Amaril stooped down and crawled through another tunnel that was almost twenty feet long, and Sindle and Keldon followed.

When they emerged into another chamber, Amaril continued. "If you could look down and see all the chambers together, they would look like a giant honeycomb with many levels. All the chambers look exactly alike, and each one has chambers surrounding it above, below, and around. But there are only three tunnels leading from each chamber to the others. This means you can get to only three of the surrounding chambers at anytime. The others are blocked."

Amaril ran his fingers along the wall, deciphered the eye, and crawled through another tunnel. This time the tunnel slanted downward, and it was longer than the one before.

"In time, we shall come to the throne room of Lucia," Amaril said when they emerged into the next chamber. "The throne room was established here during the war against Pyrath." Amaril found the emblem again, ducked into another tunnel, crawled through, and entered the next chamber. He repeated this until in time Sindle and Keldon became completely disoriented.

"There's one thing I don't quite understand," said Keldon. "How did Finsterna capture Queen Lucia if she was so well protected by this maze? We have heard how Finsterna blinded and then killed her."

"Finsterna didn't discover the secret way, nor did she capture Lucia. Our Queen surrendered of her own accord."

"Why?" Keldon asked.

"The only weapon Lucia had against Finsterna was her miraculous sight. Because of it, she knew when the armies of Pyrath marched and when to warn her people to hide. But despite her warnings, many Zanthans did not escape. The Pyrathans butchered them on battlefields, and captured and tortured others. With her all-seeing eyes, Lucia saw every atrocity, a fact known all too well by her evil sister. To break Lucia's will, Finsterna ordered her smiths to forge instruments of torture so horrible, no tongue in Spectara dared speak of the pain they could inflict. She had her sorcerers brew medicines that would prolong pain by staving off death. The agony of torture the people of Zanthis had to endure became so severe that Lucia could bear it no more. Against her better judgment, she went to Finsterna and tried to reason with her. Everyone discouraged this course of action, but Lucia felt she had no other alternative. Few realized then that Lucia, because of her gift of sight, foresaw what Finsterna would do to her. She knew that reason would have no power to sway her evil sister. But she could hardly stand by in safety while her people were being tortured so horribly. So Lucia surrendered to the Pyrathan army, and they took her in chains to Finsterna."

Amaril read an emblem, led them through a tunnel, and emerged into another chamber. "Finsterna immediately ordered Lucia to relinquish her powers," he continued. "Of course, she refused, so Finsterna threatened her with torture as well. Still she would not do Finsterna's bidding. She could never agree to place wisdom in the hands of one so wicked, so Finsterna ordered that a flaming sword be held up to Lucia's eyes and threatened to have her blinded. Finsterna decided that if she could not have the powers of wisdom, Lucia would not have them either. Finsterna ordered Lucia's left eye to be blinded with a flaming sword."

"The horror is unspeakable," Keldon remarked, shuddering, as they emerged from another tunnel. "How could anyone commit such atrocities?"

"The situation became worse when Queen Veronica failed to give Lucia aid when she needed it."

The words shocked Keldon. "What do you mean?"

"When the news got back to the Zanthans of what had happened to Lucia, they sent an envoy to Queen Veronica, but she would not agree to harm Finsterna. She told the envoy that she had taken a holy oath at the beginning of time never to destroy life. They asked her if she would then allow wisdom to be destroyed for the sake of preserving the life of one so wicked. She could find no answer to this dilemma. Every choice seemed evil to her. She withdrew into her chamber for many lumens and agonized over what course of action to take."

Amaril led them through a tunnel into another chamber. "Meanwhile, news reached the Zanthans that Finsterna had burned out Lucia's right eye, as well. It was then that Lucia told her evil sister that she would bequeath the wisdom of the left eye to her sister, Veronica, and hide the wisdom of the right eye where Finsterna could never find it. This so angered Finsterna that she had Lucia taken to the borders of Ameth where the Zanthan armies were made to witness her excruciating execution. As Lucia's armies watched, Finsterna shot the Queen of Wisdom through with a flaming arrow, burning her to death. Finsterna then rallied her armies to make war against Veronica too. She had already decided that if she could not have the wisdom of both eyes, she would settle for the wisdom of the left eye. Only then did Veronica act. Now that she possessed the wisdom of the left eye of her sister Lucia, she saw what plans lurked in Finsterna's dark mind. She knew Finsterna would try to destroy life in the same way she had tried to destroy wisdom, so Veronica had no choice but to stop her. This she did by sending the great flood that quenched Finsterna's power over fire, but Veronica made a dreadful mistake when she allowed her evil sister to live. Veronica believed that with Finsterna's power over fire lost, her wicked sister would no longer pose a threat. That is where Veronica was wrong. Had she also possessed the wisdom of the right eye she would have known the threat Finsterna would continue to pose, but she did not possess the greater of the two wisdoms. Only the wisdom of the right eye could have given her knowledge of the future. The left eye afforded her only knowledge of the past and the present."

Keldon became defensive. "Had Veronica only known, I'm sure she would have acted differently. You have never met our Queen. She is wonderful and kind."

Amaril ducked into another tunnel without commenting.

"I'm sure she did mean well," Keldon said to him when they emerged into the next chamber. "You must not think badly of her."

"I do not. But I cannot think good of her either. She made the mistake of letting sympathy destroy truth." Amaril ducked into another tunnel without waiting for a response.

"I don't see how that is a mistake," Keldon remarked, emerging into the next chamber.

"If you don't see, then nothing I say will convince you otherwise. It would be better for us not to continue this conversation, at least not here."

"How many more chambers are there?" Sindle interrupted. He was becoming uncomfortable with the growing tension between Amaril and Keldon.

"We're almost to Lucia's throne room now," replied Amaril.

They progressed through several more chambers. "Listen!" said Amaril. The distant sound of rushing water echoed through the passageway. "This way!"

They emerged into a large chamber covered from floor to ceiling with elaborate carvings. "The throne room of Lucia," said Amaril, falling to his knees.

The most prominent carving was of a crown that had seven rays of light descending from it.

"Look at this!" exclaimed Keldon, examining a symbol at the end of one of the rays of light. "The tree is the same as the one on Queen Veronica's pendant! It must be the Verdis Tree!"

Then Sindle focused upon a carving of a sword inside a red circle that was similar to the symbol of the light-freezers.

"The crown," said Amaril, "is the emblem of the Telarch who rules in Lux Aeternum. All the kingdoms of Spectara extend from him, for he is their source."

"I don't understand how he can be the source of something as evil as Finsterna," said Sindle. "Surely that cannot be true."

"Remember that the evil in Spectara is only an illusion," said Keldon. "None of the things of darkness are real."

"We can't waste time with such absurd discussions," said Amaril. It was clear Keldon was offended. Then Amaril stated, "The groves are through here."

They crawled out from the final tunnel into the twilight of low lumen-flow, and their eyes were drawn upward by towering cliffs of reddish-gold rock. Cascading from the cliffs was a sparkling waterfall that emptied into a crystal pool, and from the pool flowed a stream that wound through a deep and narrow gorge. Keldon and Sindle ran into the pool and splashed in the water.

"What are you doing?" started Amaril. "You must stop at once!"

They paid no attention but kept splashing each other. Then they cupped their hands and drank.

"You are on sacred ground!" Amaril growled. "Stop this nonsense and come with me!" Instead, Keldon became deliriously happy when he saw an orange fungus growing from a tree stump.

He trotted over, and, without asking, pulled it from the stump and bit into it.

"Are you mad?" Amaril screamed, running over and slapping it from his hand. "They're poisonous!"

"I don't think they are," Keldon returned. "We Viridians know our mushrooms. It's perfectly safe, I assure you. In fact, I haven't tasted anything so good since I was in Viridia!" Keldon gathered several of the orange growths. "Here, Sindle, try one."

Sindle took a bite. "Keldon's right. It's delicious."

Amaril's brows hung like storm clouds over eyes that threatened at any moment to strike with lightning. Sindle held one of the mushrooms out to him. "Never mind," he growled. "Don't bother anything else here without my say so, is that clear? Come. We must get to the groves."

Amaril stomped through the stream as Keldon and Sindle darted and chased each other back and forth through the water. The stream meandered through the gorge until the gorge widened and an embankment came into sight. On the embankment grew a grove of trees with gnarled umber trunks and orange leaves.

Amaril's face suddenly glowed. "These are the groves," he stated. "Now you must bring your silliness to an end or face the consequences."

Keldon and Sindle did as Amaril requested and tiptoed after him from the stream, onto the embankment, and into the groves. The tree trunks, grotesque and deformed, resembled the formations they had seen earlier. Gnarled branches reached out as though they intended to grab anyone who dared pass. The sight of them gave Sindle gooseflesh, but Keldon's face glowed with awe. "What an enchanting place!" he remarked.

"The groves affect people in different ways," explained Amaril. His eyes narrowed and his brow furrowed. "There have been times that I, too, have feared this place, and other times that I've wanted never to leave. Come with me," he motioned and led them to a place by the stream where orange-colored moss formed a velvet cushion. "This is the oracle that gave the first Patriarch of Zanthis his visions. After the Pyrathans killed Lucia, the Zanthans gathered up her bones and brought them here. On this ground, Helis, the first Patriarch, slept and received the visions that were recorded in our sacred Vestar. He buried the bones of our Queen where we now stand. From this sacred spot the Patriarch uttered the prophecy that locked the wisdom of the right eye of Lucia in the eternal flame that you saw burning in Ecrusand. Since the wisdom of Lucia's right eye was the greater of the two—even greater than what Veronica now possesses—its potential to do harm was also very great. Had Finsterna learned its secret, nothing she purposed to do would have been impossible. With its power, she could have caused untold evil. Now, at long last, the wisdom of the right eye of Lucia will be revealed, and the way past Arete Vitrea will be opened. It will be revealed here to us, the descendents of the people of the three lands."

"Why is the place of vision here and not in Ecrusand where the sacred flame burns?" asked Keldon.

Amaril explained. "After Veronica sent the great flood, the Zanthans returned to Ecrusand. Though war and the flood had destroyed most of the city, it was still their home. So they tried their best to rebuild. They gathered the bones of their Queen along with a spark from the flame and carried them to Ecrusand where the Patriarchs could guard them. But the place of vision has always remained here in Ameth where the bones of Lucia were first buried, and where the sacred fire was first kindled. A trace of the wisdom of the right eye has always remained here since that time. That wisdom imprinted itself that very first lumen upon every tree and stone of Ameth, and its mysterious power has charged them ever since. That power is also recorded in the souls of the first Patriarch and his seed forever. That is why in times of trouble the Patriarchs have always journeyed here and slept in the groves to learn from the oracle. Now that the flame burns crimson, blue, and gold, the time has come to receive the final vision."

Amaril knelt down on the mossy cushion and stretched out. "I have talked enough," he said. "The time has come for sleep." He straightened his platinum beard upon his chest, folded his hands across his stomach, and closed his eyes.

"Sleep well, then," said Keldon, lying down on the moss. "You too, Sindle."

"I'm sure I will," Sindle replied, but in truth he was as confused as he was exhausted. As he drifted to sleep, memories of Wizdor's death flitted through his mind. He kept seeing his beloved grandfather shriveling in the fountain of Queen Veronica—kept hearing his final words, "Find the Star. Find Asdin." But hope of fulfilling this request seemed, like Wizdor's image, merely to shrivel away into dark uncertainty. Tears welled in his eyes as he kept murmuring, "Grandfather...." In time, exhaustion imprisoned him in a chaotic sleep.

CHAPTER 20
THE VISION

"Wake up!" shouted Amaril. A fierce wind whipped through the trees, twisting and tossing their branches. Keldon and Sindle stared upward through half-opened eyes. When Keldon tried to stand, he bent over like a reed in the gale. "Should we get back to the tunnels?"

"No!" Amaril replied. The wind muffled his voice. "It is the oracle! The time of vision has come!"

In a few moments the wind died down, and the leaves of the trees began to glow and glitter like copper. The trees also hummed with deep, mellow tones that the Companions could both hear and feel. The very cells of their shadow-shells seemed to harmonize with the vibrations as the unseen power of Lucia's wisdom uncapped the wellspring of their emotions, causing ecstasy to surge up inside them.

"To the stream!" motioned Amaril. They hurried over and gazed at its surface as it glassed over and became like a mirror. As they watched, strange images flowed by, and their faces glowed bronze in the stream's mysterious reflection. They could not take their eyes off the passing images. Some unseen force compelled them to watch. Then, without warning, a shadow of terror crept across Sindle's face, and he stopped breathing as though someone were choking him.

Keldon's lips quivered. "What's wrong?"

Sindle drew his hand to his neck, grew pale, and let out a scream that sent a dart of terror through Keldon's heart. Amaril, disturbed by the outcry, glared at him. A haze then spread over Sindle's eyes, and his body quaked and rocked back and forth.

Keldon stared into the stream with a look of horror and then shot a frightened glance at Amaril. "What does he see?"

"Shhh! Be quiet and watch."

As Keldon gazed into the stream, his face sparkled in its light. Amaril watched them carefully until the images broke up. The stream soon lost its glassy appearance and started to ripple and foam again. Then Sindle's weary head plummeted into his limp hands.

"What happened, Sindle?" asked Keldon. Sindle didn't answer but sat with his head buried in his hands.

"The oracle gave you different visions," said Amaril. "Sindle must have seen something terrible." Amaril grabbed Sindle by the shoulders and stared into his eyes, "What did you see?" Amaril's words fell on deaf ears. Sindle could say nothing.

"Come," Amaril said to Keldon. "Help me get him into the stream. The cold water will revive him."

They pulled Sindle in and splashed water on his face. Hysterical, he held his hands to his neck again.

"Quick!" shouted Amaril. "Help me get him out!" He placed his hand under Sindle's armpits. "Grab his feet," he ordered Keldon. "Now lift him onto the bank." When they got Sindle situated, Amaril shook and then slapped him.

Keldon gasped. "Are you mad?"

"We must know what he saw," Amaril shot back. "Otherwise the pieces of the puzzle may never fit together."

Sindle began to come to his senses. His mouth moved slowly. "What happened?"

"Something you saw in your vision put you into a trance," said Amaril. "You must tell us what it was."

The muscles in Sindle's face locked in a grimace as he tried to retrieve the memory of his vision. "I can't say."

Amaril's body became as straight as a board. "Then our whole purpose in coming here will be a failure."

Sindle's brow furrowed, and his eyes deepened. "Something dark and evil...I kept seeing the eye of a karagus lizard. The lizard could fly."

"What?" Amaril interjected. "Your vision seems like a jumble of nonsense. Is there anything else?"

"Yes. The creature had wings of fire—like a kind of evil phoenix. Its wings were made of dark fire—the kind we saw in the flame at Ecrusand." Sindle closed his eyes and rubbed his brow. "Everything seemed confused."

"You must tell me more!" Amaril prodded.

Sindle strained to remember. "The creature was hatched from the Sea of Darkness. First it looked like a serpent. Next, it transformed itself into a karagus lizard and finally into a thandoo. It grew feet, then wings. It was horrible!" He shuddered.

"What then?" Amaril inquired.

"The creature attacked me. I carried a seed that it wanted. But the seed was also the pendant of Queen Veronica. The creature took it from me."

"Could the creature have been one of the thandoos that almost attacked us in the desert?" asked Keldon.

"I can't say."

"What happened next?" asked Amaril.

"It took the pendant and carried it into the hands of one so evil, the thought of him made my bones freeze."

"Who was it?" asked Amaril.

"It was not just a Shade. It was a Shade, yes. But not just a Shade. It was also a force of some kind. The evil one planted the seed, and it grew into a large tree. It looked almost like the Verdis Tree of the Viridians, except that the leaves of this tree were every color of the rainbow. Then the evil one climbed to the top of the tree and disappeared. After that the creature perched on the treetop and changed back from a thandoo into a karagus lizard, and then to a serpent that coiled itself around the tree and destroyed it! The next thing I knew, everything had become as black as the Sea of Darkness!"

"Could it be that the creature is going to destroy the Verdis Tree?" asked Keldon in a panic. "If so, then I must return to Viridia and stop it."

"There is nothing you can do back in Viridia," said Amaril. "We must press on toward Arete Vitrea."

"But what if Biona is in danger? I cannot go on. I *must* return!"

"You would never make it across the desert alive," Amaril countered. "No, I tell you. You must follow the destiny revealed to you by the oracle. You must now tell us what you saw."

Keldon's eyes glassed over. "I saw a man with a shining face clothed in a robe of light standing at the foot of the Crystal Mountains of Arete Vitrea. The robe glimmered with every color of the rainbow. For some reason, I couldn't look into the man's eyes because they were cursed with a horrible blindness. In them burned a darkness more terrible than any I have ever seen."

"The dark fire again!" exclaimed Sindle. "Keldon saw it too!"

"Quiet," said Amaril. "Let him finish."

"Something caused me to know the man was kind, in spite of the darkness in his eyes. When he spoke to me, I felt drawn to him. Then I saw a ball of light with a black sword in its center, and that was the end of my vision."

"The ball of light with the black sword is the symbol of the Trogzars," said Sindle. "I don't understand how the man you saw could be kind."

Amaril's eyes widened with horror. "Unless Keldon saw the Telarch who rules Lux Aeternum. That could explain why the flame burned black. The puzzle pieces are fitting together. This Prince Neblas you told me of earlier," he said to Sindle. "Did you not say that he stole the Star from your temple in Zil so that he could vanquish the Hell of Light?"

"Yes," replied Sindle.

"Could this Prince Neblas of yours be the evil ruler? Is he the one you saw?"

"I suppose it's possible," Sindle replied.

"What if he now possesses the pendant of Queen Veronica? That may be all he needs to succeed in his plan. Yes. The pieces of the puzzle fit. The Telarch is he who wears the rainbow robe. This is he whom Keldon saw in his vision. The darkness in his eyes and the Trogzar emblem—these things tell us that the Telarch is in grave danger. The fate of Spectara hangs on a thin thread! The situation is worse than we could ever have imagined. We must act now, or all Spectara will perish. Your Prince Neblas must be stopped before he succeeds in carrying out his evil designs." Amaril started down the stream toward the throne room of Lucia, and Sindle and Keldon followed.

"But Prince Neblas cannot succeed," said Sindle. "He may have the pendant of Queen Veronica, but there is one thing he lacks."

"What is that?" asked Amaril, turning and staring at him.

"The password of Queen Veronica. Without it the pendant will not work. I alone possess that password."

"I knew nothing of this," said Keldon. "Why did you not tell me?"

"The Queen commanded that I keep it secret even from you, Keldon. I shouldn't have said anything about it even now, because I gave her my solemn oath."

"This may buy us the time we need," said Amaril. "Still, we must not underestimate the power of Finsterna's evil. If she manages to tap the source of wisdom in the flame—and it seems she may already be trying—then she may succeed in extracting the password from your very thoughts. This means you must not think about it. You must blot it from your mind."

"I'll try," Sindle agreed.

They entered the throne room of Lucia and soon were returning through the caverns.

"Suppose he does manage to pass through Arete Vitrea with the Star," said Sindle. "If the Star is made of light, why should the Telarch fear it? Can light destroy light?"

"Remember that the light of the Star is not just any light," Amaril countered. "It is *frozen* light–light that has been contaminated because it was plunged into the Sea of Darkness. If the Star passes over Arete Vitrea, the darkness that is in it may forever freeze the vision of the Telarch, thus blinding him. This must be the meaning of the eyes of darkness that Keldon saw. What else could it mean? And the symbol of the dark sword inside the sphere of light must spell victory for the Trogzars. Can there be any other explanation?" Amaril crawled through a tunnel and emerged into one of the chambers. Suddenly his eyes widened with horror. "Now we know why the red part of the sacred flame started burning black. It is written in the sacred Vestar that the Telarch of Light cannot look upon darkness. This must explain why he is calling for us to help him defeat the evil of the Trogzars. We must help him fight the armies of darkness before it's too late. As Sons of Light, we must recover Asdin from your Prince Neblas before he carries it over the summit of the Crystal Mountains."

"What if we are already too late?" asked Keldon.

"Pray we're not," replied Amaril, ducking into another tunnel. Soon he emerged on the other side. "We do have some reason to hope, however. We have no way of knowing whether the visions that you saw are past, present, or future. We can't even know whether we have understood them correctly. One thing may be to our advantage. The flame of Lucia has only recently begun to burn black, and only the red part of the flame has been affected thus far. This may give us the time we need."

"I hope you're right," said Keldon. "I wish I knew what was happening back in Viridia." Sindle remembered Zoella. The thought that he might not see her again filled him with pain and loneliness.

"I don't want to hear another word about Viridia," said Amaril. "We must focus on one thing and one thing only—getting to Arete Vitrea."

They continued through the tunnels and chambers and in time emerged from the caverns. After climbing down the narrow, winding path, they found their parjars and mounted them. By the crack of lumen-flow they were sailing around the citadel of Queen Lucia along the road that led toward Pyrath and Arete Vitrea.

CHAPTER 21
THE CHASM

By early lumen-ebb, when the Companions of the Quest emerged from the formations of Ameth, their parjars came to an abrupt halt. Stretching to the horizon was a vast wasteland webbed with mud-cracks that smelled of blood and glowed like molten lava. The orange formations of Ameth towered over this sea of fire and walled in the ancient evil of Pyrath, preventing it from spilling out into the other lands of Spectara. Hatred hardened in Amaril's face. "Curse this place!" His voice heaved with contempt.

"Is it on fire?" asked Keldon.

"No," Amaril responded with a frown, "though it seems that way. See there?" He pointed at the mud-cracks. "Those must date back to time of the tidal wave sent by your Queen."

"What is that sickening smell?" asked Sindle. "Brimstone, no doubt," Amaril stated. Sindle felt nauseated, as he had after he had eaten the purple berries in Violinda.

"It *is* hard to breathe here," remarked Keldon. "Is there another way through to Arete Vitrea?"

"No," Amaril replied. "And we haven't time to look for another route."

The Companions hovered inside their parjars, glaring at this land of doom. An invisible wall seemed to stand in front of them. Even the parjars sensed it, for when Amaril willed his to move forward, it stuck to its place and quivered. "What's wrong?" Amaril growled. He closed his eyes, and with all the force he could muster willed the parjar to go forward. Then something unexpected happened. Amaril screamed in pain and fell from the parjar's center, shouting, "The blasted thing *bit* me!" He stomped over, reached into its center, and tried to regain control, but lightning flashed from its eye and knocked him to the ground.

Keldon and Sindle leapt from their parjars and ran to his rescue. "Are you hurt?" asked Keldon.

"No!" he barked, standing and brushing off the dust. "What could have possessed it to do that?"

"They may sense danger ahead," guessed Sindle. The parjars became more and more agitated. Patterns of golden lightning flashed from their centers.

"Maybe it's their Zanthan sixth sense," Keldon suggested.

"Ridiculous," said Amaril. "We can't let them get the upper hand. They must be made to mind." He removed a gold rod from his vest and approached the parjar. "This is a branding iron. If it rebels against this, it will die. But it will obey. It knows that the gold rod has been charged by the sacred flame."

Amaril regained control of his parjar and then managed to get Keldon's and Sindle's to submit. Soon they were sailing out across the mud-cracks of Pyrath. By mid-lumen-ebb they caught sight of a trail of what seemed to be ancient footprints, and Amaril willed his parjar to follow them. "These must have been made while the mud was still fresh," Keldon speculated.

"By refugees from Pyrath, no doubt," Amaril added.

"Look ahead," said Sindle, pointing. "Are those the Crystal Mountains?"

"They are volcanoes," replied Amaril. Their cones jutted up on the horizon. "Finsterna's war machine was born in their fiery hearts where she made her people forge her terrible weapons and instruments of torture."

"What kinds of torture?" Keldon asked with a squeamish look.

"Most are too horrible to describe. Only a few Zanthans lived to tell. The Pyrathans strapped their victims to the rack; stretched their limbs until the bones were yanked out of joint and the flesh ripped apart. Sometimes they let stinging scorpions loose in the clothing of their victims."

"How could anyone commit such cruelties?" asked Keldon.

"It's beyond reason," replied Amaril. "I have also heard that the Pyrathans had an antidote for the scorpion sting. Before a Zanthan could die of its poison, the torturers would give the remedy so that the life of the victim would be spared. In this way, they could prolong the torture."

Dark thoughts of the Trogzars raced through Sindle's mind, and he shuddered. "Do you have to talk about such things?"

Amaril paid him no heed but continued his lurid explanation. "They bound their victims with ropes made of stinging nettles, held nests of wasps up to their faces, and threw them into wells filled with deadly ants, centipedes, and serpents. The Pyrathans became experts at bringing their victims to the brink of death, only to pull them back by administering their antidote to the poison. By repeating this cycle many times, they drove most of their victims insane. And when they ran low on Zanthans to torture, they sacrificed countless of their own numbers as traitors to the fires..."

Sindle, horrified, clenched his teeth. "Stop!"

Amaril ceased his flapping, and Keldon tried to ease the tension by changing the subject. "Are the volcanoes extinct?"

"Yes, they were quenched by the great flood," answered Amaril. The volcanic cones grew more immense, and the footprints the Companions had been following trailed off toward them. Two volcanoes stood to the fore, and one stood in the background, forming, as it were, a triangle. The two volcanoes in the foreground guarded its entrance. Like snoring giants, they seemed ready to awaken the moment someone dared disturb their slumber. Their rotten lungs exhaled the suffocating stench of sulfur as the Companions passed.

As they traveled, fear built its tower stone by stone in their minds. Even Amaril appeared apprehensive. Eventually, the mud-cracks and the footprints they had been following vanished. In the valley beyond, strange objects began to appear. But even before they could decipher what they were, the sight of them struck terror in their hearts. Words of scorn then suddenly exploded from Amaril's mouth, "The cursed city of Har Bellak! Feast your eyes, if you dare." Amaril could hardly contain his disgust. Anger flared from his eyes, and his face became hard.

Cemented between the stones of Har Bellak's crumbling walls were the rusted remnants of what were once sharp, iron spikes. These had been its weapons against invaders and had prevented many from escaping its ghastly, totalitarian regime. Implements of iron that had emerged stillborn from Pyrath's ancient forges littered streets, and ruins studded with iron saluted the memory of Finsterna's reign of terror and oppression. These were the gravestones of her kingdom, but their cold hearts lusted nonetheless for some catalyst that would release again the sparks of her ancient evil.

Contempt burned in Amaril's face. "Who could have dreamt up a place so hideous? It defies description."

"I know now what sorrow our Queen must have felt, knowing that she was responsible for such destruction," Keldon remarked.

Amaril's eyes shot fire. "What are you saying? Your Queen should have rejoiced over these ruins, and you should do the same!"

"That is not an easy thing for a Viridian," replied Keldon. "Our people have a hard time grasping the reasons for war and death. Such events and their causes lay beyond our understanding. I know Queen Veronica sent the flood to protect the powers of life entrusted to her by the Telarch of Light. Still, I'm sure she did not wish to cause such horrible devastation."

"Your words are incredible!" Amaril shot back. "Would your Queen let truth and justice be trampled down by pity? How could anyone condone such evil? You should not feel a shred of remorse over what happened here!"

"But the time comes to let bygones be bygones," Keldon stated. "Vengeance, like acid, eats away the soul until nothing is left. I'm sure the Pyrathans did these things out of ignorance and superstition. If they had only known..."

Amaril interrupted with a burst of anger. "It was lust for Lucia's wisdom that drove them to such madness! Had they gotten control of her powers, no barrier could have stood against them! In time, they also would have gained control over Veronica's life-giving power and devised an eternal hell, an inescapable hell where no one could die!"

Sindle, who had been listening uneasily to their argument, suddenly remembered how he had feared meeting the Queen of

Viridia. He had imagined that the Queen might use her powers of life to enslave her victims. Suddenly, a face of evil took shape in his mind that he had not seen before. It was the face of pain and terror forever prolonged by the inability to die.

"This argument is beside the point," Amaril said finally. "We must try to find Prince Neblas before all Spectara becomes like this place."

As they travelled, the path leading to Har Bellak became overgrown with briars, and the Companions had to dismount their parjars. They had no sooner done so than the parjars' behavior turned odd.

"Something has spooked them again," Amaril remarked. "I must bring them under control." He held out his gold rod, and tried to make his parjar obey, but this time, something very strange happened. Its eye began to radiate a strange black substance.

"Look," Keldon cried. "The center of mine is turning black too."

"They are becoming thandoos!" screamed Amaril. "Run for your lives!" Briars walled the path to the city of Har Bellak, and thorns grabbed and gouged the flesh of the three travelers as they tried to pass. Eventually they could see the city's walls. These were varnished with streaks of blood that had gushed from bodies of victims torn apart by spikes. As the Companions traveled, the hot stones of the pavement stung and paralyzed their legs, rendering their joints weaker with each step. They soon entered the city. Its ruined buildings, like skulls, peered out at them with glowing eyes.

"Nothing here can compare with Chartra," said Keldon. "I've seen all I care to see."

"For once we agree," said Amaril.

As they crept through the streets, a feeling of dread slithered into their souls. Then Sindle saw something that made him stop dead in his tracks. "Impossible," he whispered. "My eyes must be deceiving me."

"What do you see?" asked Keldon.

Sindle pointed. "That building is identical to the Temple in Zil where the Sacred Star of Frozen Light was housed. I must go inside and see what is there."

"It is not yet low lumen-ebb," stated Amaril. "We should continue to press on."

"What if Prince Neblas has seen this building? He could not have resisted going in, I tell you. Who knows? He might be inside even now."

"Very well," said Amaril. "We will do a quick search and then be off."

As Sindle led the way up rough stone steps and entered the portal, the dark memory of the awful events in Zil slithered through his mind. A sense of dread weighed heavily upon him as he entered what he expected to be a room resembling the Great Hall of the Temple in Zil. Instead what he saw made his blood run cold. Instruments of torture and death were scattered everywhere.

Amaril's eyes heaved with contempt. "I have heard tell of this place. This is where the cursed Pyrathans tortured our people and slaughtered them on their racks! This is where Finsterna seared out the eyes of Blessed Lucia, our Queen!" Tears of anger formed in Amaril's eyes. He stomped over to one of the torture instruments and pushed it over in a fit of fury. Then he hurled another against the wall. The chamber resounded with the racket. "Listen! Did you hear the echo? The Pyrathans built this temple to magnify the screams of their victims. They did so to give themselves the greatest possible pleasure from their sadistic art!"

Sindle's heart pounded with terror at the scene, but Keldon, who was not at all caught up in Amaril's tirade, had begun searching the chambers that extended from the hall. "Look at this, will you?" he called. The others came and found Keldon kneeling on the floor. "A chasm runs beneath this chamber," he said. "There are steps. See?"

"I sense something down there," said Amaril. The tone of his voice sent chills up their spines. He shut his eyes and extended the palms of his hands in the same way Helanthin had done when trying to find the pendant of Queen Veronica in the desert. "I feel a presence. I'm not sure whether it is man or beast."

Sindle shivered. "If I remember my vision correctly, it could be both."

"Maybe we should leave before something dreadful happens," warned Keldon.

"No," Amaril refused. "If I'm right, we may be close to finding Neblas! We must go down."

"The chasm is too dark," said Keldon. "We could get lost."

"My Zanthan sense will guide us," said Amaril. "If Prince Neblas is down there, I will find him." As Amaril led the way, Keldon and Sindle followed. The steps carried them ever deeper into the chasm, and before long, the light from its opening disappeared as though darkness had closed its mouth upon them.

"I can't see," said Sindle. "Can we go back?"

"No," Amaril answered. "I feel the presence stronger now than ever. We are getting close."

CHAPTER 22
THE GROTTO

As their hands clung to the walls of the dark abyss, the Companions strained to see a faint, red, glowing object in the distant depths. Their cautious feet probed and carried them further down into the chasm.

"What could it be?" whispered Keldon.

"Quiet," Amaril returned. As they descended, the object grew brighter, and its light caused feverish, shrill ringing in Sindle's head. Gradually the ringing made his bones and skull ache. The glowing object also worked on Sindle's imagination. He now thought he could hear the screams of torture victims. After a few moments, Sindle could bear to venture no further, and he collapsed on the steps. Meanwhile, Amaril and Keldon continued their descent, not realizing they had left him behind.

As Sindle sat, he could not drive thoughts about stinging creatures the Pyrathans had used for torture from his mind. His vision froze on the red glow coming from the grotto. As he watched, his fear grew into unspeakable terror. Something could be seen crawling out from the top of the grotto's entrance. Sindle felt paralyzed. He closed his eyes and tried to rid his mind of the image, but when he opened them again, he saw a winged serpent with the tail of a scorpion flying toward him. He turned and with cries of panic fought his way up the steps. About one third of the way along, he stumbled and fell. He wrestled with the steps, but the powerful abyss sucked him down. Sudden fiery pain shot through his side, and he screamed. Something dark and terrible hovered over him. He could hear it breathing.

"Who is there?" he whispered.

"It's a good thing I got to you in time," came a voice. "Let me help get you out."

Meanwhile, Amaril and Keldon stood inside the grotto glaring at an idol that struck unspeakable terror in their hearts. "It is Finsterna's image," Amaril stated with utter disgust. "The people of Pyrath must have worshiped it."

"Could she have really looked that way?" asked Keldon in disbelief. The idol's body and head portrayed a woman with scales on her face. She had six arms, and two horns grew from her head. The lower half was a coiled serpent and had the legs of a dragon.

"It is unlikely," replied Amaril. "This image was meant to strike fear into the hearts of her devotees. I have heard tell that the Queen of Fire always wore a veil so her people could not see her face. They must have been convinced that she really looked this way."

The idol's angry red eyes stared at them, and they could feel its shrill, evil fire invading their bones. Their hearts became heavy, as if they might stop beating and turn to stone at any moment. Amaril eased toward the idol, stooped down, peered at its base, and felt of it. "Why is this hot? The flood should have quenched any power it once had." Just then, Amaril saw something that gave him pause. "Look at this, will you? The Pyrathans sacrificed victims here."

Keldon grew pale.

"And look here," said Amaril. "Do you know what these are?"

As Keldon feasted his eyes, they became filled with horror. "I think I do." Amaril had found blood stains.

"Let's see what else is here," said Amaril. He examined carvings on the wall of the grotto. "Look," he said, squinting. "They must have cut the heads off their victims before burning them before this idol." He turned and glared at it. "The cursed thing must be destroyed." He picked up a large rock from the floor and hurled it at Finsterna's image, but the rock did not harm it in the least. Instead, the image glowed more intensely, and its heat flared in their faces.

Keldon trembled. "We had best leave this place now."

As the earth rumbled, they fled from the grotto's entrance toward the steps.

"Where is Sindle?" cried Keldon in a panic.

"He must have stayed behind," replied Amaril. "He can't have gotten far."

They called out for him, but there was no answer.

"We must go back and search for him," Keldon insisted. "I promised the Queen I would never abandon him. What have I done?"

"I don't sense his presence," Amaril stated coldly as he climbed the steps. "He must have returned to the surface."

At that moment, the earth quaked again, and rocks came rolling past.

"Hurry, or we'll be buried alive!" shouted Amaril. As they scurried up the shifting steps toward the surface, they kept calling out for Sindle, but he did not answer. When they reached the surface, they call out for him again.

"Could Finsterna's idol be interfering with your sixth sense?" asked Keldon. "What if Sindle didn't make it out of the chasm?"

"Do not question my sixth sense, Viridian. I want to find Sindle as much as you do. Remember we need him if the prophecy is to be fulfilled."

"The prophecy?" returned Keldon. "Is that all you care about?"

Amaril's eyes flared. "I warn you, Viridian, or..."

"Or what?" Keldon interrupted. "I'm sure I have nothing to fear from you, for you also need me for your precious prophecy to be fulfilled."

Amaril seethed, and his eyes stared daggers at Keldon. Then he turned and stomped off into the room where they had seen the torture devices with Keldon trailing behind. Just then, they heard the sound of groaning in the corner of the room. They rushed over and found Sindle strung up on a rack. Keldon hurried to untie his arms and feet. "Sindle! How did this happen?"

He did not reply. His eyes were blank, and his body, limp.

"We shouldn't have left him alone," Keldon agonized.

"This has to be the work of Neblas!" exclaimed Amaril. "Now I know it was his presence I felt, not just the idol of Finsterna. He may be headed toward Arete Vitrea. We must go at once."

"We can't leave Sindle behind," Keldon protested.

"I don't intend to do that. Help me get him up."

"He can't be moved in the state he's in."

"Just help me get him off this thing," Amaril ordered.

"What do you intend to do?"

"Stop questioning and help me!"

They lifted Sindle from the rack onto the floor.

"Now help me get this thing apart." Keldon and Amaril disassembled the rack, and Amaril made a stretcher from parts of it and other torture devices. "Grab his arms," said Amaril, and they lifted him on to it.

"He has a fever," said Keldon. He pulled back Sindle's clothing. "What is this?" He found the place in Sindle's side where he had been stung. "Why, it's as hot as fire."

Amaril felt of it.

"He may die if we don't do something," said Keldon. "I wish I had some Verdis ointment. Oh, I shouldn't have left him. How will I explain this to the Queen."

"Quit whining," said Amaril. "Our only hope is to get to Arete Vitrea before he dies. Now grab the other end of the stretcher."

Keldon complied, and they hoisted the stretcher up, carried Sindle down the steps of the Pyrathan Temple, and struck out in the direction of the third volcano. Once outside the city walls, they climbed a rugged and steep path that headed them in the direction of Arete Vitrea. Their fatigue grew greater with every step, but they could not stop to rest. They were now in a race against time.

CHAPTER 23
ARETE VITREA

Amaril and Keldon had now traveled two lumens without sleep. Meanwhile, the fire that raged in Sindle's side had left a numb, empty hole. But the nerveless blackness ate away at more than just his body. Finsterna's dark fire was feeding upon the very essence of his soul. Sindle lifted a weak and trembling hand and placed it in the dark chasm in his side.

"Lower the stretcher!" exclaimed Keldon. "He's coming around!" Keldon knelt down and whispered. "Sindle, can you hear me?" His eyes glimmered faintly through thin slits, and he nodded.

"Tell us what happened to you? Did you see Neblas?"

The slits closed, and he sank back into unconscious. "Enough of this," said Amaril. "We're wasting precious time." They hoisted up the stretcher and started out again. Inside Sindle, a battle against engulfing darkness raged, but the harder he fought, the stronger the darkness grew. As Amaril and Keldon plodded onward, the weight of the stretcher racked their shoulders with pain.

"How I wish I were in Viridia," groaned Keldon. "Will our misery ever end?"

"If Neblas gets to Arete Vitrea before us, it will not," Amaril remarked.

"You could get to Arete Vitrea quicker without us," Keldon suggested. I can stay here and tend to Sindle while you go after Prince Neblas."

"I would not be foolish enough to leave you alone," returned Amaril.

"I'm sure I could manage."

"I'm sure you could manage to go back to Viridia. No, I won't allow the prophecy to die."

Keldon lifted an eyebrow. "It may be the Zanthan custom to abandon friends when they are dying, but no Viridian would ever do that. I don't intend to leave Sindle here, and I certainly don't think I would be able to cart him back to Viridia alone."

As they trudged down a mountain path and argued about what to do, something just over the rise caught their eye. Light, shimmering with every color of the rainbow, interlaced the sky. Amaril's face lit up. "The aurora of Arete Vitrea! We are almost there!"

They picked up their pace, stumbling over loose rocks as they hurried toward the light. As they rounded the path, the pure crystal summit of Arete Vitrea surfaced like an iceberg. Streams of iridescent light flowed from its summit.

"It's more beautiful than the pyramid of Verdis!" exclaimed Keldon.

"And purer than the sacred fire of Ecrusand!" added Amaril.

"I wish Sindle could see it. Sindle! We've come to Arete Vitrea! Try to look!"

Sindle's body lay limp.

"He is dying," said Keldon. "The way down is steep. Surely it would be better for us to remain here. I promise I shall stay until you return."

Amaril squinted and looked out at Arete Vitrea. "You are right. We could never get him down that slope."

"Can you handle Neblas alone?" asked Keldon.

"I'm sure of it," he replied.

Amaril bade them farewell and was soon descending the steep path toward Arete Vitrea. The valley below was infested with a maze of briars that hid the road from view. Soon Amaril was fighting his way through them. The briars towered above his head and cut off his view of Arete Vitrea. The hedge thickened as he journeyed deeper. In time the road disappeared, forcing him to crawl on his belly. Stinging thorns pierced the crown of his head and scratched his shoulders, sending fiery pain through his flesh. Suddenly, he heard a hissing sound. In front of him, a nest of asps glared through thin slits and lashed at him with their tongues. He scurried backward through the thorny tunnel, his eyes fixed upon the brood of vipers. Then a red wasp buzzed past his ear, causing him to jump. Thorns stabbed his scalp, and he let out an angry cry.

The jaws of frustration were now locked on Amaril. When he found the road again, he lay for a moment and rested, but the thought of Prince Neblas getting to Arete Vitrea ahead of him spurred him on. Prince Neblas could not be allowed to blind the Telarch of Light! The thought that the prophecy might die drove Amaril forward! But the harder he pushed, the more the thorns and creatures of Pyrath seemed to feed upon the drive within him, gaining strength with every determined move he took and turning their strength toward his defeat.

Meanwhile, as Keldon lay sleeping on a boulder, Sindle started to stir. Keldon awoke and immediately sprang to his side. "Sindle!" Keldon placed a hand on his forehead. "Your fever has broken."

Sindle pried open his eyelids. "Neblas?"

"No, Sindle, it's Keldon. Did you see Neblas? Is he the one who tied you to the rack?"

Sindle nodded and a tear slipped from the corner of his eye. "He was kind to me at first. He helped me out of the chasm." Sindle's eyes roved, and he rolled his head around. "Where is Amaril?" he whispered. "Amaril must not know."

"Know what?

"I was not in my right mind. I was stung by some horrible creature."

"What creature? Tell me what happened!"

"It looked like the one I saw in my vision. It was hideous. It stung me in my side. Then Neblas came to my rescue. I might have died if he hadn't come. He was the same Neblas I always remembered. He did not seem evil at first. Then I discovered he had the pendant of Queen Veronica! How he got it, I do not know, but it was hanging from his neck by a string. Then the truth of the vision I had received in Ameth struck me hard. I knew without a doubt that Neblas was the evil one I had seen. He not only carried the pendant; he also carried the Sacred Star of Frozen Light. He removed it from a black bag he was carrying,

held it up, and laughed. 'The Star's curse cannot harm me," he
boasted. 'This is proof I was chosen for a great purpose!' I told
him that Spectara was hanging in the balance because of what
he had done. I begged him to return the Star to Zil-Kenøth and
give the pendant to me so that the harm he had caused could be
reversed. His face became as hard as stone, and he asked what
I knew about the pendant. I realized he did not yet know what it
could do. He threatened that if I did not tell him everything, he
would torture me upon the rack with creatures like the one that
had stung me. I could have accepted death willingly, but the
thought of torture turned my soul inside out. Then something
extraordinary happened. The pain in my side grew unbearable,
and I felt all the knowledge I had of the pendant fly from my
mind into the mind of Neblas without my saying a word. I gave
him the password merely by thinking it!"

"Sindle!"

He began to weep. "How could I have done otherwise?
Finsterna's dark fire infected my soul, and that was all she needed
to extract the password from my mind. Please, whatever you do,
you must not let Amaril know."

"I won't," said Keldon. "There is no telling what he would
do to you if he discovered you had jeopardized his precious
mission. That prophecy is the only thing he cares about, you
know. I wish now I had never agreed to come along on this
absurd expedition. I only want to return to Viridia, see Biona,
and herd my zoas in peace."

Sindle started weeping uncontrollably.

"You must not blame yourself," Keldon said, trying to
comfort him. "After all, the Queen did ask me to come with you.
I do not blame her, either. It is just fate, I suppose."

"The light," said Sindle, rolling his eyes around to see it.
"Where is the light coming from?"

Keldon lifted his head so that he could see. "We've made it
to Arete Vitrea, Sindle," he said. Sindle peered out at the Crystal
Mountains, but when he did, excruciating pain flared up in his
side and he screamed.

"What's the matter?" exclaimed Keldon.

Sindle's eyes rolled back in his head, his eyelids shut, and his body became limp again.

"Sindle! Speak to me! Sindle!" Despair cast a pallor over Keldon's face. Gently, he lowered Sindle's head and felt of his brow. The fever had returned and seemed worse than before. Keldon gazed across the valley at the foot of Arete Vitrea and wished for Amaril to return. Tears welled in his eyes. The beauty of Arete Vitrea no longer solaced him.

CHAPTER 24
THE PRISONER

Amaril crawled out of the briars and stood at the foot of Arete Vitrea. Scratches crisscrossed his skin, and his clothes were shredded. He wiped sweat from his eyes and focused on the figure of a man in the distance. Pain stabbed his heart, and poison from the thorns pulsed through his veins as he dashed toward it with all the speed he could muster. As he closed in, hope revived that the prophecy might still be fulfilled. But he stopped dead in his tracks when a pillar of white light sprang from the ground and rose until it was higher than the summit of Arete Vitrea. The light pillar bent in the direction of the Crystal Mountains until it curved over them, separated into strands of color, and formed a rainbow bridge. What Amaril saw next struck terror in his heart. The figure was crossing the bridge. At once, he knew beyond doubt it could be none other than Prince Neblas!

Amaril felt panic bolt through him like electricity. With all his strength, he ran toward the rainbow bridge. When he reached it, Neblas was already a quarter of the way across. Amaril stepped onto the bridge, but when he did, a horrible thing happened. The bottom part of the bridge dissolved into particles of light and quickly evaporated. With desperation, he grasped at its last remnants. He screamed at the top of his lungs at Neblas, "Come back, fool! You are killing the prophecy! Idiot! Scum of Zil-Kenøth! Come back!"

Neblas paid no heed but continued crossing. Amaril fell to the ground and wept bitterly. He envisioned Neblas plunging the points of the cold and evil Star of Frozen Light into the Telarch's eyes. The thought of it froze in his mind and sent stinging, icy pain through his spine. Amaril squeezed his eyes shut and covered them with his hands, as if he felt the pain

himself. Keldon's vision of the Telarch's blinded eyes tortured
his mind. It was now too late to hope that the prophecy might be
fulfilled. Amaril shivered and groaned, glaring at the towering
barrier of Arete Vitrea until fury ignited in him. He could not
allow the prophecy to die so easily! There had to be some other
way to cross. He ran over to the briars he had crawled through
and began stripping thorns from a long, tentacle-like stem. He
tried yanking the stem from the ground, but it held fast like a
cable set in stone. His hands burned as he fought to pull it from
the earth. When finally it snapped, he fell backward, hitting his
head against a boulder and blacking out.

When he revived, his head pounded, and the whelps in his
flesh burned. He stood up, glared at the barrier of Arete Vitrea
again, gritted his teeth, and clenched his fists. With a hoarse,
pitiful scream, he rushed toward it and tried to climb, but his
feet slipped off the glassy slope as though they had been soaked
in oil. Picking up a rock, he pounded it violently against the side
of the mountain, but the rock merely crumbled in his hand,
leaving his fingers bloody and badly bruised. For all his efforts,
the diamond-hard cliffs of Arete Vitrea had not even a scratch.
Amaril collapsed, his head fell into his hands, and he wept
bitterly.

Then Amaril was startled by footfalls. He sprang up,
whirled around, and saw a Shade standing there. He believed
at once that this was Neblas returning from his sordid mission.
Amaril grabbed him, shook him, and screamed in his face. "You
have killed the prophecy, you fool! Now all hope is dead!"

"What are you saying?" came the reply.

"Be quiet! Don't speak again!" Amaril's face was filled
with rage. "Don't trifle with me, or I will kill you!" Amaril drew
his sword and pointed it at the man's heart. "Turn and march!
You will go to Zanthis to stand trial. Every eye there will see
you die!"

"But why?"

"Quiet! Do as I ask or you will die here! And I will make
sure you suffer before you do!"

As they plunged into the maze of thorns, hatred hardened in Amaril's face. The thought that the prophecy would never be fulfilled tormented his mind. As they crawled through the briars, he planned Neblas's execution. First there would be public torture. Next they would tie him to the rack and let stinging scorpions loose in his clothes. Then his eyes would be seared out, just as Finsterna had done to Queen Lucia. As a finale, he would then shoot Neblas through with a flaming arrow, setting his body ablaze.

As Amaril drove his prisoner through the briars, he made sure that the thorns pierced his flesh! Without warning, he would poke him with his sword and cause him to jump, hitting the thorns with his head or back. However, when he did not grow angry or beg for mercy, Amaril boiled with rage all the more. Suddenly, Amaril remembered the nests of asps and drove his prisoner through the briars toward them, but when they reached the nest, the serpents slithered away like streaks of lightning.

"They're afraid of you!" said Amaril. "It is because you wield Finsterna's dark magic, no doubt. Evil sorcerer!"

"What makes you say that?" he asked.

"Silence!" Amaril screamed. "Move on! Your death awaits you!" Amaril forced the prisoner forward, refusing even to let him pause long enough to tend his wounds. When they finally reached the foot of a mountain slope, Amaril, exhausted, stopped to rest. The prisoner took this opportunity to nurse his wounds. He broke off a thorn from one of the briars, picked red berries from a bush, and started mashing the berries on the palm of his hand.

"What do you think you are doing?" shot Amaril.

"Making a poultice for the stings." He stirred the mixture with the thorn and then started over toward Amaril. "Here, let me put some of this on your wounds."

"Stop there!" Amaril barked. "Do you think I would let you work your alchemy upon me? Turn your poisonous arts upon yourself. Then we shall see what brew of evil you have concocted!"

The prisoner drew away from Amaril and started treating his own lacerations.

"Do you think I can be fooled so easily?" Amaril stood and pointed his sword at the prisoner. "Move on!" The prisoner obeyed, nursing his scratches as he walked.

As they climbed up a steep path, loose rocks shifted and slid beneath their feet, but Amaril climbed with the agility of a mountain goat, his sword pointed like a horn at his prisoner's back. As they climbed, however, pain pounded in Amaril's bones like chisels against stone, and his muscles started turning to jelly. Points of fire in his scalp and back now spread through his body and into his skull.

Soon, they arrived at the place where Keldon and Sindle waited, but they were both asleep. "Wake up!" Amaril screamed, "I've caught Neblas!" Awakening, Keldon jumped up, and ran to meet him. "He is our prisoner now." With those words, Amaril fell to his knees. "But it's too late. He has passed through Arete Vitrea! The prophecy is dead! The Telarch has been blinded. You must help me get this criminal back to Ecrusand. He must be burned at the stake!" Then Amaril keeled over and blacked out.

Fear towered in Keldon's soul as he stared at the prisoner in silence. "I tried to help him, but he wouldn't trust me to remedy his stings," the prisoner said to Keldon. "So now, as you can see, he's paid the price."

Now that Amaril posed no threat, the prisoner took charge. He walked over and knelt beside Sindle. "What is the matter with him?"

Keldon sprinted over to explain. "A creature stung him. His fever is high." Keldon gazed pensively at the prisoner. "Sindle was right. You really do seem kind."

The prisoner looked up and asked, "Where did he get stung?"

Keldon pulled back Sindle's clothing and showed him the place.

"The poison has spread. How long has he been this way?"

"A couple of lumens, at least."

The prisoner mashed more berries into a poultice and smeared it on Sindle's side. "It will take some time."

"Will it work?"

"It's hard to say. It depends on how much damage has been done."

Keldon followed the prisoner over to the place where Amaril lay and watched as he dabbed Amaril's wounds with the blunt end of the thorn. "I can't believe this cursed land grows anything with healing powers," he remarked.

"The berries are poisonous by themselves, of course," the prisoner said. "But when you mix the poison of the berries with the other poison of the thorns, the two poisons make a healing poultice. There!" He finished nursing Amaril and tossed the thorn away.

"How long before they recover?" asked Keldon.

"That one," he pointed to Sindle, "will probably come around first. But this other one may take longer because he was so exhausted and angry."

The prisoner sat upon a rock to rest, and Keldon fixed curious eyes on him. "You *are* a kind man," he remarked. "Why then did you destroy the Telarch's sight?"

Just then Sindle began to stir. "Look," said the prisoner. "Your friend is awakening sooner than I expected."

Keldon knelt beside him and shook him gently. Sindle quivered and opened his eyes. "Sindle, how do you feel?"

"The pain is gone for the moment. How long have I been unconscious?"

"Many hours. You've been very ill. If it weren't for Prince Neblas here, you might have died."

When Sindle's eyes focused upon the prisoner, a smile crept across his face and his eyes lit up. "What are you saying, Keldon? This is not Prince Neblas. This is my old friend, the Captain."

"The name is Regius Pisces," said the Captain, introducing himself to Keldon."

"I can't believe my eyes!" Sindle continued. "How are you, Captain?"

"Fine, thank you," he responded.

"We met by Marus Lazul, the Sea of a Thousand Blues," Sindle explained to Keldon. "I can't believe you are here, Captain!"

"I always seem to be doctoring you," the Captain remarked, smiling. "The last time, I caused you to turn blue, remember?"

Sindle smiled. "Of course. How did you get here?"

"Do you remember how I changed from one color to another when we sailed across Marus Lazul?"

"Yes," Sindle replied. "I still don't know how you did that!"

"Well, there's more. Beyond Spectara is a world where all colors unite. This is a world unlike Spectara, because no division between colors exists there as it does here."

"You speak of Vernesda, then, Mr. Pisces," Keldon commented. "We Viridians know of that place."

"Please, call me Captain. Yes, I suppose you are correct, Keldon. Indeed, from that place all Spectara can be viewed together as a whole." The Captain picked up a stone. "All lumens—past, present, and future—can be seen together as one views this rock." He set it down and continued. "By slipping in and out of this other world I am able to travel from one land of Spectara to another. That is how I got here."

Astonished, Keldon stood and bowed toward the Captain. "You are a Vernesdan, then. I am amazed and honored at what you have achieved."

"Not so fast," said the Captain. "You must let me explain. The place I speak of is in the region beyond Arete Vitrea known as Lux Aeternum where the Telarch of Light rules."

Sindle became excited. "He is not only a Vernesdan, Keldon; he is able to pass through Arete Vitrea. This is what we've been trying to do, Captain. To see the Telarch of Light! Can you take us there?"

"You and Keldon are getting ahead of yourselves," replied the Captain. "Going to this world is not that easy, I'm afraid. It is something I cannot simply will to do. It is as though I am one of the fish in this sea we call Spectara, and the Telarch who dwells in Lux Aeternum is the fisherman. When he calls, I answer and *jump into his boat* so to speak! I cannot just decide to go there. It has to be for a reason of the highest importance."

"Is that why you've come here?" Keldon asked.

"Yes. Sindle alerted me to the problem when he told me how the Sacred Star of Frozen Light was stolen by Prince Neblas. I could not stop thinking about it for many days. Then, without warning, I was transported to this other world where the Telarch let me see how the dreadful events in Zil-Kenøth had set off a chain reaction that in time would bring catastrophe to all Spectara. The Telarch conveyed to me that I had been chosen to reverse it, and the next thing I knew, I was at the foot of Arete Vitrea where I met your friend."

"He is called Amaril," said Keldon.

"For some reason, he thinks *I* am Neblas, the one who stole Asdin. There was no use trying to convince him otherwise. He is very hardheaded."

"True," remarked Keldon.

"I can tell you this," said the Captain. "The Telarch is aware that the peoples of Spectara are trying to enter the regions of Lux Aeternum. The pendant of Queen Veronica, the prophecies of Helis—all signs point to an opening of the way past Arete Vitrea. But I regret to say that the events in Zil-Kenøth and the actions of Neblas have complicated matters terribly. By crossing over Arete Vitrea with the Star in an effort to destroy the wisdom of the Telarch of Light, Neblas has sealed Spectara's doom."

"Amaril tried his best to stop him," said Keldon. "The pendant was the only means of getting past Arete Vitrea. We had hoped to cross instead of Neblas and ask the Telarch of Light to restore Sindle's grandfather to life."

"That plan was also misguided," said the Captain. "The Queen of Viridia should have known better than to trust the pendant to Sindle. Sympathy for his grandfather's plight influenced her to remedy the evils caused in Zil-Kenøth by means of a short cut."

Keldon took offense. "Are you saying that the Queen acted unwisely?"

"She did not intend to do so," answered the Captain, "but, yes, unfortunately she did. Sometimes the best of intentions increase evil instead of defeating it. But the zeal of your Zanthan friend was just as misguided. He was under the illusion that he could chisel his way through Arete Vitrea with hatred and rage."

Suddenly, Amaril became conscious and jumped up. "What was *that*? Do I hear the fool Neblas filling your heads full of lies? Amaril started toward the Captain, his eyes spitting fire, and Keldon tried to restrain him. "Stop," shouted Sindle. "He's not who you think he is!"

"Why are you trying to protect him? Are you in league with this devil, as well?"

"You're insane, Amaril!" exclaimed Keldon. "Sindle knows Prince Neblas. Why would he protect someone who tried to kill him only a short time ago?"

"Then who is he, and what is he doing in this cursed land?"

"This is the Captain," said Sindle.

"Regius Pisces," said the Captain, extending his hand to Amaril, but the Zanthan merely stared daggers in return.

"I met him by the blue waters of Marus Lazul not long after I escaped from Zil," Sindle continued.

"The Captain has been explaining to us why he is here," said Keldon.

"Yes," said the Captain. "As I was saying. . ."

"Stop! Do you think I would believe some inane story?"

"You haven't heard it yet," said Sindle.

"Your problem, Amaril, is that you refuse to listen," said Keldon. "If you could but hear him out, maybe you would be convinced. Go ahead, Captain."

The Captain tried to tell Amaril what he had told the others, but to no avail. "Spare me your lies, swine of Zil-Kenøth. I will only hear your story when we are back in Zanthis and you are standing in the fires of Ameth. Then we shall see how your lies hold up."

"Then I'm sure he will have nothing to fear," remarked Keldon.

"We shall see," said Amaril. "Now march!" he ordered. As the Captain proceeded, Amaril followed with his sword pointed toward the Captain's back. Sindle and Keldon kept pleading with Amaril, but they were unable to convince him that the

Captain was not a danger. After traveling one full lumen, they were again in the shadow of one of the volcanoes that guarded the way to Har Bellak. Sindle, meanwhile, had fixed his eyes upon its summit. He seemed again to have fallen into a dark trance.

Keldon recognized something was wrong. "Sindle?"

Sindle's eyes filled with horror. "Amaril, you say you want to take the Captain to Zanthis to test him with the fires of Ameth?" he asked. "There may be no need to do that." He pointed at the summit of the volcano. "Look!" Thick black smoke was billowing from it.

Terror shot from Amaril's eyes. "Her ancient evil is awakening! We must hurry!"

"What you say is true," said the Captain. "We must get to the city at once."

Amaril glared suspiciously at the Captain. "No doubt you have something to do with this?"

Sindle bowled over in pain.

"Can you walk?" asked Keldon.

"Yes." He straightened and staggered down the path.

As they advanced toward Har Bellak, the smoke started flowing down the side of the volcano. Soon they had reached the city gates. Upon entering the cursed city, they heard a deafening explosion. The volcano was belching out more of the foul, black substance.

Horror bolted across Sindle's face. "I have seen this before. That is not smoke. It is Finsterna's *dark fire*."

"Sindle is right," the Captain confirmed. "Her power has now reached through all of Spectara."

Keldon panicked. "What shall we do?"

"Try to escape," said Sindle. "Remember that Finsterna's dark fire froze the scintilla of my grandfather. It might do the same to us."

"We must find the source of her power here if we are to block it off," said the Captain.

"I think I know where it is," said Amaril. "I'll wager it's her idol inside the chasm." Then he glared at the Captain. "But you had better not be fooling us!"

"If I did not mean to help you, I would leave you here to be swallowed by her dark fire," the Captain stated with sternness. "You have no choice now but to trust me."

"Very well," said Amaril. "I will lead the way."

"Look!" cried Sindle, pointing. "The dark fire is moving toward us!"

"Run!" shouted the Captain.

The thick billows reminded Sindle of the tentacle from the Sea of Darkness that had struck the city of Zil after the Trogzars had sacrificed his grandfather. Just then, the ground quaked, causing the travelers to reel and stumble.

"It's closing in fast!" cried the Captain. "Hurry!"

Sindle was having problems keeping up with the others, so the Captain and Keldon helped him. Thick darkness soon covered the pinnacle of the Pyrathan temple itself, and by the time they reached its steps, the substance was a few feet above their heads. They had to crawl up the steps on their bellies to keep from touching or breathing it.

Once inside, they slammed the door and gasped for air. A little of the dark fire entered behind them and formed a thin, black haze that hovered low to the ground and swirled and burned their legs when they walked through it.

"These walls will not keep it out for long," said the Captain. "We must find her image."

Sindle screamed. "My side! It's turning cold again!"

"Hold on to me," said the Captain as they started their descent into the chasm. The deeper they got, the colder the dark hole in Sindle's side became. In time, they could see the red glow in the distance. Its shrill vibrations pierced their skulls. When they entered the grotto, Finsterna's evil force tried to push them back. Sindle clung to the Captain, trembling. He tried not to look at Finsterna's horrible image, but when he finally did take one quick glance, he shuddered and the hollow place in his side froze solid.

CHAPTER 25
THE FORGES

Finsterna's image sapped their strength as its red glow steadily intensified. Upon the walls of the grotto, shadows cast by her idol dripped like blood from the carvings, and her dark fire settled in the grooves making the scenes of human sacrifice come alive.

"Her image is gaining power," said Amaril. "It must be destroyed." He picked up a stone and hurled it at the idol. When it hit, the image flared and singed their hair. The floor beneath them quaked, forcing them to their knees before her. Boulders rolled and thundered through the fissure, crashing against the entrance to the grotto and sealing it.

"We're trapped!" shouted Keldon.

Anger flashed from Amaril's eyes. He picked up another stone.

"Do not," cautioned the Captain. But Amaril did not listen. The stone sailed from his hand. This time, it hit the idol's heart. The image flared again, and the ground quaked. The monstrous thing started coming to life!

"We're going to die!" cried Keldon. "Why don't you listen to the Captain, Amaril?"

Suddenly Sindle screamed, "My side! I can't bear the pain!"

The Captain's eyes grew dark. "There is only one power in Spectara that can stop her now." He extended the palms of his hands toward the idol and touched it. His flesh sizzled.

"Captain!" shouted Sindle. "Let go of it!"

The Captain groaned.

"Has he lost his mind?" Amaril shot.

The image's red light, with acid teeth, ate deep grooves into the Captain's face. Sweat and tears streamed down his cheeks and splattered at its base. Suddenly, intense white light flashed, and the Companions had to shield their eyes. When they looked again at the image, it was crumbling into fine, white, glowing powder. They watched, amazed, until the image of Finsterna disintegrated and all traces of its features were erased. Then, for a split second, a rainbow appeared around the Captain's body. They stood, staring and speechless, until the Captain, without warning, collapsed, causing them to spring to his aid.

"Captain, are you all right?" Sindle shouted.

He sat up, trembling. "Yes," he replied. "Her power was more than I expected. Her will is strong."

"How did you destroy it?" Amaril asked.

"By being in tune," said Sindle. "I've seen him catch droves of fish just by humming a certain way. Now he has dissolved the image of Finsterna."

The Captain's face was serious. "It wasn't an easy thing to do. I felt in her idol a dark power of will that in time could swallow all Spectara whole. Even now, she is learning ways to exert that power and bring her dark designs to fruition."

"The Captain *is* a Vernesdan," Keldon whispered to Sindle. "Only that can explain how he knows such things."

The Captain pulled himself up. "Now we must escape before she regains strength."

"But the idol has been destroyed," Amaril stated.

"Destroying her idol will not stop her. Greater battles must be fought and won if we are to be victorious in the war she is waging against the light. The idol was only one vehicle of her power. There will be others."

As they sought a way of escape from the grotto, Amaril struggled to push away the rocks that had closed the entrance. "There is no use trying this way."

Keldon had been exploring a hole left in the wall behind Finsterna's idol. "Here is some kind of a tunnel."

"Maybe the source of her dark fire," stated Amaril. "We had best not go that way."

"We have no choice," said the Captain. "It is the only possible way out."

As they trudged through the mound of white powder Finsterna's idol had left behind, the luminous residue clung to their bodies, making them glow like lanterns as they ventured into the dark tunnels beneath Pyrath.

They had walked in silence for some time when grotesque shadows started appearing along the walls. The giant apparitions seemed to lie in wait.

Keldon started shivering. "What are they?" he asked.

"Only shadows," replied the Captain. "See?" He moved back and forth to demonstrate. The light from his body shone past carts of ore, causing the huge shadows to move mysteriously across the walls.

"These must have been their mines," Amaril reckoned. As the Companions proceeded, the tunnel became steep and narrow. Through them resounded echoes that sounded like bellows at work. "Their cursed forges must be ahead," said Amaril, who was so angry he was spitting fire.

"Surely they are no longer in use," Keldon said in a frightful whisper. At that moment, their speech, amplified a hundred times, rolled back over them like a wave. Sindle was struck with fear and again began to feel twinges of pain in his side.

"The sounds we are making must collect at the end of this tunnel before rolling back in our direction," observed the Captain. He was right. A few seconds later, his words returned, and he added, "It is a place that resists all reason and logic, a place where Finsterna's madness once reigned supreme and would do so again. That is why our words return to us so forcefully!"

They continued through the tunnel, but when they reached its end, a cart of ore blocked an opening. Amaril tried to push it through. "It's stuck." Then he said to the Captain. "We need for you to dissolve it."

"I must not misuse my gifts, Amaril," returned the Captain. "I dissolved the idol because it was evil, but this cart poses no threat. We will all help push it out of the way."

Amaril's eyes puffed up with resentment, and his face stiffened. The Captain began trying to get the cart loose, and the others joined in. They pushed until the cart broke free, rolled off the track, and crashed into a wall.

"That wasn't so difficult," stated Keldon, but Amaril continued to scowl. As they came through the entrance, he grumbled to Keldon. "I don't understand. The Captain has special powers but refuses to use them when he needs them. That makes no sense."

Eventually they emerged from the tunnel into a large, dome-shaped cavern. The light from their bodies shone upon the floor revealing hundreds of smoke-blackened craters. Anvils and hammers were strewn everywhere.

"The cursed forges of Pyrath," said Amaril with contempt. Hatred boiled in his eyes. "The weapons made here slew many a Zanthan. Now my people will never be avenged."

"Why do you say that?" asked Keldon.

"The prophecy is dead, and we failed to save the Telarch from being blinded by Prince Neblas!"

"Are you sure Neblas succeeded?" asked Keldon.

Amaril frowned. "What do you mean? The vision you had in Ameth revealed that something was wrong with the Telarch's eyes."

"Maybe not."

"Maybe not? Did you lie to me about your vision?"

Keldon was nervous. "No. I just think you may be wrong about its meaning..."

"What?" Amaril interrupted. "Do you dare doubt the power of interpretation given to the Patriarch and his seed forever?"

"Our Queen told us the Telarch possesses in full what powers the Queens of Spectara only have possessed in part," Keldon said defensively. "Surely the Telarch can defend himself against the powers of darkness without our help."

"You would prefer the opinions of your Queen over the wisdom of the Patriarch of Zanthis? If you were in Ameth you could be burned at the stake for such disrespect!"

"That's the way of your people, isn't it?" probed Keldon. "To destroy all who disagree with you."

Anger flared in Amaril's eyes, and he made fists. "I warn you, Viridian."

The Captain spoke. "Keldon is right, Amaril. The Telarch does possess fully the powers that the Queens only possessed in part."

"What makes you the authority?" he shot.

"You saw how I dissolved her image. How could I have done it if my power were based in lies and darkness?"

"You are trying to confuse me!" exclaimed Amaril. "Neblas blinded the Telarch of Light."

"You are wrong. Indeed it was Prince Neblas who was blinded when he saw the Telarch."

"Lies!" shouted Amaril with an incredulous look.

"I speak the truth," said the Captain. "Prince Neblas was not prepared to look upon the Telarch, so he was blinded by the light. But there is a greater irony. The Prince does not know he is blind. He believes he did vanquish the Telarch, and since the Prince can no longer see, for him the Telarch truly has ceased to exist."

"You cannot know such things," stated Amaril. "No one could know unless he himself had passed through Arete Vitrea."

"He did pass through Arete Vitrea," stated Sindle. "He tried to tell you earlier, but you refused to listen. You would not believe anything he said until he could be tested by the fires of Ameth, remember?"

"But surely the only way past Arete Vitrea was through the power of the Queen's pendant."

"You are wrong," said the Captain.

"Then there may be hope for the prophecy! If you know the way through Arete Vitrea, we must return there at once! Maybe we can still help the Telarch fight against the evil Neblas."

"It's too late for that now," said the Captain. "All ways past Arete Vitrea are now closed."

"How do you know?" returned Amaril.

"I was there when Neblas entered," replied the Captain. "Because of what he did, the way past Arete Vitrea is now closed. It can only be reopened after Finsterna's power is quelled."

"Impossible!" said Amaril. If all the powers of Spectara could not stop her, how can she now be stopped?"

"It is of extreme importance that my plan be kept secret for now," the Captain replied. "This place has ears, and I cannot risk telling you anything that Finsterna might hear."

As they started out again, they ventured past the blackened craters of the forges. Sindle shouted into one of them. His voice echoed until it faded in the abyss. Then it came rolling back.

"Those must have once been the cracks of fire," stated Amaril. "I've heard they are bottomless. They may be the source of the dark fire we saw."

Sindle shuddered.

"Over here!" exclaimed Keldon. "Light is shining through a crack in the wall."

Amaril bent down and examined it. "I think it leads out."

"I can wiggle through," Keldon volunteered. When he came to the other side, he was on a ledge. "It's the shaft of one of the volcanoes," he called back, tilting his head upward toward the source of the light. "And there's a path leading out of the cone." As he braced himself against the wall, he gazed first upward and then downward. The path spiraled to the summit and coiled into the abyss. "Be careful!" he warned the others. "The path on this side is narrow."

One at a time, they squeezed through the hole onto the ledge that hung midway between the abyss and freedom. In single file, they then started up the path. Gradually, the small, distant hole of the crater above them grew larger. At one point, Sindle swayed back and forth.

"Don't look down!" warned Keldon.

Sindle closed his eyes, regained his balance, and started again. Upon reaching the surface, they climbed up over the rim of the volcano and gazed out across Pyrath. No sign could now be seen of the dark fire that earlier had threatened to devour them.

"Her power has been stayed for now," said the Captain. "But we must not lose time. She no doubt will muster it again."

"You will tell us your plan now," Amaril demanded.

"It is still too risky," replied the Captain. "We must wait until we are well out of Pyrath."

Behind them, Arete Vitrea shimmered like a cool iceberg rising in front of the fiery sea that was Pyrath. In the valley ahead lay the city of stone and iron, and beyond that the faint outline of the formations of Ameth. They climbed down the slope of the volcano and struck out again over the mud-cracks of Pyrath, this time without parjars to carry them. After they had journeyed for several lumen-hours, they again came to the trail of worn footprints they had followed earlier.

"They are still here after so many lumnus-years," remarked the Captain.

"You know who made these footprints?" stated Amaril. "Who?"

"I cannot tell you now," replied the Captain, "but in time I will explain everything."

"*I cannot tell you now*," Amaril mocked.

As they progressed, they could see the orange cliffs of Ameth rising up in the distance. They hurried in their direction with the hope that it was not too late to escape the tide of darkness that was rising in Spectara.

CHAPTER 26
THE ARCHONS

At low lumen-ebb, the Companions camped in Pyrath, and by early lumen-flow they were off again. By mid-lumen-flow, they were leaving Pyrath behind and were entering Ameth. As they journeyed through a canyon, the rock formations, like mourners around a fresh grave, peered down at them. Winds howled through the caves that were their mouths, carrying their sorrowful wails into the ears of the travelers. By the time early lumen-ebb had come, they had begun climbing through rough terrain, and Amaril remarked, "We will need parjars soon. We will never get through the desert without them." The thought of braving the desert made Sindle shudder. Amaril stared at the Captain and sneered. "Maybe *he* will have a solution," but the Captain said nothing.

At length, Sindle became weak, and the pain in his side returned. Noticing his distress, Keldon asked if he were all right.

"I need to rest," he replied.

"It's time that we set camp anyway," said Keldon.

"Good idea," remarked Amaril, and then added sarcastically, "Maybe thandoos will find us and put us out of our misery."

After they had made a fire and were sitting around it, the Captain said, "We must be on the road by early lumen-flow. I have business in Zil-Kenøth, and time grows short."

"What?" Amaril shot. "What business could you have *there*?"

"The evil that began many lumnus-years ago after the great deluge must now be stopped."

"Isn't it time that you revealed this secret plan you've been keeping?" asked Amaril.

"I suppose it is safe now that we are clear of Pyrath. You remember the footprints we saw? After Veronica sent the flood and quenched Finsterna's power, Finsterna fled to the heart of the Sea of Darkness. The Telarch foresaw then that she would learn to control the darkness as she had once controlled fire, so he convened a council of Archons, emissaries of the seven spectral colors."

"How do you know of this?" asked a suspicious Amaril.

"I have it on good word from the Telarch himself."

A look of disbelief came over Amaril's face, but the Captain continued undeterred. "The Telarch commissioned the seven Archons to devise a plan to stop Finsterna from gaining total power over the element of darkness. The chief and eldest Archon was their leader. He decided the best way to stop her was to take shafts of spectral light, venture into the Sea of Darkness, enter her abode, and drive them all into her heart at the same time."

"An excellent idea," remarked Amaril.

"The Telarch was displeased with the plan."

"Why?" Amaril shot.

"He knew an attempt to destroy her by force would only feed her power. She thrives on the hatred and violence of others."

"Absurd," exclaimed Amaril. "How could that make her stronger?"

"You threw the rock at her idol. Did that not awaken and increase its power?" the Captain asked.

"Maybe, maybe not," Amaril replied.

"Evil in others fuels her power. She inspires evil in others, and they in turn supply her with the fuel she needs to stay alive and produce still greater evil. Like you, the leader of the Archons believed force was the answer, but the Telarch knew better, so he would not agree to it. But when he forbade them to carry out the plan, their leader was indignant. He went against the Telarch's wishes, revolted, and persuaded the others to revolt as well. From the Spring of Lux Aeturnum beyond Arete Vitrea the chief Archon drew a vial of liquid light. Then he convinced his companions to join in his revolt. In secrecy they journeyed through the lands of Spectara until they came to the Sea of Darkness. None knew of their expedition, not even the Queen of Viridia who was deliberately kept in the dark by powerful magic that blocked the vision of the all-seeing eye bequeathed to her by Queen Lucia. The Archons bore the seven shafts of spectral light. One of these is what Sindle's people called the Zarafat of Zil."

"I myself have held it," said Sindle. "But I don't understand what Zil Magnus had to do with the Archons?"

"He, my dear Sindle, was their leader," replied the Captain, "the instigator of the doomed plan."

Sindle sat, shocked and speechless.

"Why did the Archons hide their plan from Queen Veronica?" asked Keldon.

"They feared she would further upset the balance of power in Spectara. After the Archons arrived on the shores of the Sea of Darkness, they intended to carry out their plan. Zil Magnus passed the vial of light to each one and bade them drink lest they become paralyzed by Finsterna's siren song. Although she had not yet gained power to freeze them, her song of deception was even then powerful—so powerful, in fact, that Zil Magnus fell under its spell while the others partook of the flask of light. He would have been the last to drink, but when it passed to him, he deliberately dropped and spilled it. None of the precious liquid could be recovered. He claimed this was an accident, but he lied. Now he had an excuse not to enter Finsterna's dark depths with the others. So he convinced them that their shafts of Spectral light would be sufficient to subdue her. He led them to believe that if they would but drive their shafts into her heart at the same time, her power would be destroyed. The six Archons believed him, so they entered the Sea, hunted her down, and restrained her. But when they drove the six shafts into her heart, she neither died nor lost her power. In her fury, she instead welded the shafts of light together and froze them solid. Their effort to destroy her backfired. Instead of defeating her, in one instant they bestowed on her the power to control darkness as she once had controlled fire. Furious, she then hurled the object of frozen light from her depths, the same object Zil Magnus later found lying upon the shore of the Sea of Darkness."

"Asdin?" Sindle guessed.

"Yes, the Sacred Star of Frozen Light!"

"So Zil Magnus knew its origins all along?"

"He did," replied the Captain.

"So the Zarafat of Zil is the shaft of light that could have defeated her?" asked Amaril.

"Probably not," replied the Captain. "It was only a theory. Yet it does seem that the presence of Asdin and the Zarafat of Zil together were, for whatever reason, enough to protect Spectara from Finsterna's wrath all these many lumnus-years. She wouldn't attack while Asdin remained in the Temple of Zil."

"Wizdor was right then," said Sindle. "The Star was not shield against the Hell of Light, but against Finsterna's hell of darkness."

"Zil Magnus spun his lie about the Hell of Light," the Captain continued, "for he, in the same manner as Finsterna, had become a creature of darkness. Like her, he started to hate the Telarch whom he had once served. Your friend, Prince Neblas, also believed the misguided lie Zil Magnus had spun. This lie caused him to think the Star could be used as a weapon against the Telarch. When Neblas entered the regions beyond Arete Vitrea, he hadn't prepared himself properly, and the light quickly blinded him. In his mind, however, he falsely believed he had destroyed the light. He now truly believes the light no longer exists. The irony is that his mind perceives this to be so. That is why the Telarch released him so that he could return to the city of Zil and proclaim his empty victory."

"The Telarch released him?" exclaimed Amaril with an incredulous look.

"There was no reason to hold him."

Amaril shot to his feet. "But what untold damage will he do now that he is free?"

"The Telarch still has a plan. True, Neblas may do some harm, but he will not win the war against the Companions of the Quest. The Sons of Light have nothing to fear."

"I wish I could have gotten through Arete Vitrea instead of Neblas," said Amaril, pacing. "Things might be different now."

"Had you entered instead of Neblas, you would have been blinded as easily as he was."

He stopped and glared at the Captain. "Impossible. I could never become such a creature of darkness."

"But, my dear Amaril, you already are a creature of darkness," replied the Captain. "All creatures of Spectara have darkness in them. That is their nature. In Spectara, darkness is mingled with light. Like a fire, the light must be kindled so that it can grow ever brighter. Only in this way can the darkness be extracted so that the peoples of Spectara may venture into the presence of pure light without suffering blindness."

"You contradict yourself," Amaril challenged, pointing his finger. "You ventured in, did you not? You even claim you spoke with the Telarch face to face. Why were you not blinded?"

"The Telarch has chosen me to finish what Zil Magnus failed to accomplish. Finsterna's power over darkness grows ever greater and so must be ended. My plan, however, will not be the same as that of Zil Magnus."

"What plan is that?" asked Amaril with his hands on his hips.

"I will tell you when the time is right."

"*I will tell you when the time is right!*" Amaril mocked. Hatred oozed from the pores of his face. "I'm getting tired of your delay tactics! I am going to sleep!" In a huff, he lay down on the ground, facing away from the Companions.

"Are you the Seventh Archon?" asked Sindle.

"In a manner of speaking, yes," replied the Captain. "But I carry no Zarafat. No sword can destroy the Queen of Darkness."

Amaril turned over and glared. "I fail to see how you expect to succeed," he remarked.

"You will see in time."

"*You will see in time,*" Amaril jeered. His narrow eyes spewed contempt. "I hope you find a weapon strong enough to destroy her!" He rolled over and faced the other way again.

Suddenly, Sindle started gasping, and Keldon ran to his aid. "The pain just hit me again. It's worse than before."

Keldon looked at the Captain. "Can you help him?"

"I fear the wound in Sindle's side was caused by something more vicious than the sting of a mere creature from Spectara.

I'm beginning to think the Queen of Darkness herself is behind it."

"Is there no hope that he will get better?" asked Keldon.

"Sindle allowed Finsterna to infect him with fear and despair," said the Captain. "Such an infection cannot be easily cured."

"Hum your tune, Captain," Sindle requested. "That always seems to make it easier to bear."

The Captain began to hum. The deep, mellow tones, like Verdis ointment, relieved Sindle's pain. Healing warmth tingled through the icy cancer growing in his side, and soothed his troubled heart. His music also tamed the beast of hatred that was devouring Amaril's soul, and it calmed Keldon's worried mind in the way harp music subdues a zoa. Eventually, they all fell asleep.

When lumen-flow dawned, they set off again in the direction of Zanthis. They journeyed until mid-lumen-flow when, suddenly, Amaril caught sight of black objects circling above a formation ahead. "Thandoos!" he gasped with a look of horror. "Pray they do not see us."

"I thought they only feasted on dead things," Sindle remarked.

"That's true for the most part," replied Amaril, and then added in an eerie voice, "but they have also been known to kill if they are hungry enough." Suddenly the worst did happen. The thandoos caught sight of them and swarmed nearer until they circled overhead, casting dark and evil shadows across their faces.

"It is as I feared! They are hungry!" exclaimed Amaril in a panic. "Quick, we must get to one of the caves."

"Go on ahead," ordered the Captain. "I'll try to fend them off."

"Are you crazy?" Amaril screamed. "You'll be eaten alive."

"Do as I say!" exclaimed the Captain.

The Companions hurried toward a formation, hid in a cave, and watched with terror as thandoos descended on the Captain.

"Why wouldn't the fool listen?" Amaril asked, shivering.

"We can't let them devour him!" exclaimed Sindle. "We've got to do something!"

"You can do nothing to help him now," said Amaril. "Once they've tasted living flesh they will not stop until we all are eaten."

As they watched nervously, the Captain's song wafted into their ears across the desert breeze. "Oowissss... Oouummmm..." Though muffled, his voice echoed through their minds like a thunderclap, yet its sound was reassuring, not frightening. The moment the thandoos descended on the Captain, there was a sudden flash of white light!

"Look! They have become parjars!" exclaimed Sindle.

Amaril's eyes widened with disbelief. "Impossible!"

"A miracle," Keldon stated.

Soon the Captain joined them with the parjars.

"These look like the ones we rode from Ecru," said Amaril. "They must have become wild. How did you tame them?"

"By being in tune," said Sindle with amazement. Sindle again remembered how the fish had flopped into the boat when the Captain called them, but that seemed minor when compared to what the Captain had done with the thandoos. Sindle recalled how he had tried to imitate the Captain's voice. He had tried to call the fish but did not succeed. How did the Captain do such marvelous things? Sindle was baffled and mystified.

Soon Amaril and Keldon stepped into their parjars, and the Captain and Sindle shared one. They willed the creatures to carry them through the formations of Ameth toward Zanthis and Ecrusand. The parjars seemed to move more quickly than the Companions had remembered. The creatures whisked them away, and by mid-lumen-ebb Ameth's formations gave way again to fingers of yellow sand. In time, the outline of Ecrusand appeared on the horizon. Amaril, though weary, beamed with relief that he was nearly home. He anticipated the Patriarch springing up from his throne and welcoming them back with open arms. True, there would be sadness over the fate of the prophecy, but Zanthans were a tough people. They were used to tragedy, and giving up hope was rarely an option.

CHAPTER 27
THE EYE

The Companions of the Quest reached Ecru's gates a short time before low lumen-ebb only to find the city filled with deadly silence. Amaril's face twitched with anxiety. "We must get to the fire chamber," he said, his pale, thin lips barely moving. They willed their parjars to hasten through the streets. When they reached the tower of the eternal flame, they dismounted and hurried to the chamber. Sparks of horror flew from Amaril's eyes when he focused on the flame. All of it now burned deep black, and the Patriarch's throne was empty. At that moment, a servant ran toward them, wailing and sobbing. "Where's the Patriarch?" Amaril demanded.

"Dead!" he screamed. Amaril's eyes filled with horror as the servant continued. "Something in the flame killed him!"

Amaril jerked his head around and stared at the black fire.

"No one knows what happened to it," the servant went on. "After you left, it grew darker and darker. Your father watched it for lumens on end and became spellbound. No one could tear him away. Then, only a few lumens ago, it began to burn as it does now..." The servant broke down and wept.

"Tell me more," Amaril demanded.

"When the Patriarch looked into its center, a look of horror came over his face, and he dropped to the floor. Everyone in the chamber rushed to his aid, but his heart had stopped. Nothing could be done to help him. Then Lucius and several others also looked at the eye in the center of the flame."

"Lucius is dead too?"

"No. But he might just as well have died. He was driven mad by what he saw. Its power has taken over his mind."

"Find Lucius! I must speak with him!"

"Please, you must not," begged the servant. "Their madness is contagious. It has spread through Ecrusand and beyond to the desert clans. Since the flame began burning black, there has been only war and bloodshed. The clans are now claiming to be the true descendants of the holy men of Ameth. They are scheming to take Ecrusand. They say they have proof that we are not the true descendants of the holy men. They have already killed hundreds of our people. When we learned the insanity was contagious, we had to put the entire city under quarantine. I fear nothing can be done. Everyone's been infected, myself included. It's but a matter of time before all sanity is lost..." The servant started weeping again.

Fury flashed from Amaril's eyes, and he started toward the flame to challenge its evil strength. The servant screamed and ran after him. "No! Do not look! Please!"

Amaril yanked himself free. "I am now Patriarch and guardian of the flame. I shall destroy whatever it is that has taken it over."

"You should listen to your servant!" warned the Captain. "If you gaze into its center you, too, shall die."

The Captain walked over to the flame, and the servant screamed, "No! You will be destroyed!" The Captain paid him no mind but stared into its center. A shadow of darkness crept across his face, and he shut his eyes. "It is as I feared. It is no longer Lucia's right eye in the flame. It is the eye of Finsterna. She has gained control of Lucia's wisdom. Now nothing Finsterna purposes to do will be impossible."

Amaril fell to his knees and wept. Then he bolted to his feet and shouted. "Bring Lucius to me at once!"

"No," said the servant. "He will sway you with deceitful words. His insanity is contagious, I tell you!"

"Silence! Do as I say!"

As the servant left, his sobs echoed through the chamber.

The pupils in Amaril's eyes shriveled to a point. "I don't believe it *is* Finsterna's eye at the center," he fired at the Captain. "How could she gain control of the Holy Flame?"

The servant soon returned with Lucius. A strange aura surrounded Lucius's face, and his eyes were crazed. "Ah, Amaril," he droned. "How good to see you."

Amaril fidgeted. "How are you, Lucius?"

Lucius laughed softly. "I couldn't be better." The tone in his voice was odd. He walked over to the black flame, looked into it with wide eyes, and smiled. "Now that the prophecy has come to pass, all will be well."

"The prophecy?" Amaril almost swallowed his words.

"Don't listen to him!" shouted the servant. "He lies, I tell you!"

"The way beyond Arete Vitrea has been opened up. Your dear father has already gone there, and it's a matter of time before we shall join him. The way, my dear Amaril, is through this flame. Won't you look into it as the rest of us have done?"

"Don't believe him!" warned the Captain. "If you heed his words, your soul will perish!"

Amaril threw a sharp look at the Captain. "Why shouldn't I believe Lucius? He was my father's advisor. I've trusted his wisdom always. Why should I doubt it now?"

"There's one way to know for sure whether or not he's telling the truth," Sindle said. "Test him with the fires of Ameth."

"No!" trembled the servant. "He'll be burned alive!"

"Very well. Bring forth the wood," Amaril ordered.

The servant hesitated.

"Why do you wait? Do as I say!"

He left and soon returned with it.

"You needn't bind me," said Lucius. "I have nothing to fear since I speak only the truth."

"That is proof enough for me!" said Amaril. "He knows what Ameth's fires can do. No Zanthan in his right mind would wish to be destroyed in such a way."

"His deceit is working upon you," warned the servant.

Amaril's brow furrowed. "Very well, then! Place the wood around him. But do not bind him."

Lucius stood calmly in the midst of the wood as Amaril sifted the sulfur-colored powder from his bag into his hand. But Amaril hesitated to set it afire.

"Go ahead," said Lucius. "I fear nothing."

Amaril threw the powder onto the wood, and it burst into flames. Suddenly, Lucius screamed and leapt from the fire! His charred body fell upon the floor.

"Lucius!" cried Amaril. He knelt down and wept. Lucius's eyes were empty, and the crazed look had vanished.

"She no longer controls his thoughts," said the Captain. "The fires have purged his mind. He is delivered from her grasp."

Lucius spoke. "He tells the truth, Amaril. The prophecy... remember there will be the time of great darkness before the way will be opened up past Arete Vitrea? We did not want to believe such a time would have to come. Now it is here." Lucius closed his eyes and died.

Amaril shook him. "Lucius! Lucius!"

"He is gone," said the Captain.

Amaril wailed, his tears splattering upon the cobblestones.

"There is no time to lose," warned the Captain. "We now know Finsterna's power has reached through all Spectara. We must be on our way to Zil-Kenøth. Amaril, you may come with us, if you wish."

Amaril arose to his feet. "I, too, tried to put out of my mind the prophecy about the time of great darkness. Lucius's dying words are true. Nothing can be done here. The fulfillment of the prophecy now depends on the Captain. I'm coming along."

As they left the chamber, doom cast its shadow across their faces. Keldon wrung his hands. "I'm worried. I hope Biona is all right." Sindle then thought about Zoella and realized how much he loved her. Had she been able to survive Finsterna's evil? His heart throbbed with worry. The Companions soon were mounting their parjars again. Amaril's servant had followed to see them off. "Be on your guard," he warned. "The desert holds greater dangers than ever. Remember the tribespeople now kill on sight."

CHAPTER 28
THE PLAGUE

The Companions sailed across the deserts of Zanthis from the end of low lumen-ebb until high lumen-flow. All along the way were strewn bodies of tribespeople who had died in the war against the inhabitants of Ecrusand. Everywhere thandoos feasted on their decaying flesh. Sindle cringed at the sight and wondered if Helanthin's tribe, who had saved him and Keldon from dying in the desert, were among the dead. Pain began to flare up again in Sindle's side, and he now realized that his wound somehow could detect the presence of Finsterna's evil. Not only did the pain eat away at his body, but with each attack, his spirit seemed to sink deeper into a dark well of despair. In time it was apparent that slain Zanthans numbered in the thousands. Thandoos were starting to appear in swarms.

"I've never seen so many," said Amaril. "Where are they coming from?"

Just then a dark patch appeared on the horizon. It looked like a black hand creeping across the sand.

"Is it a sandstorm?" asked Keldon.

"No," answered Amaril. "More thandoos. I now know where they are coming from. They are coming from Viridia."

"How can that be?" exclaimed Keldon.

"They start out as wild zoas, remember?"

"There must be thousands," said the Captain. "We had best steer clear of them."

Keldon's eyes flashed with panic. "We must get to Viridia quickly. I fear something has happened to the zoaherders." Sindle again felt intense pain in his side. Low lumen-ebb had come, and they still had not rested. Fatigue was beginning to take its toll.

As they rode, the swarm of wild zoas moved in another direction and eventually vanished from sight. Then they sailed over the crest of a dune and saw the camp of a desert clan down below.

"If they see us, there will be trouble," warned Amaril. "We should bypass them."

"Listen!" whispered the Captain. "There is no sound in the camp."

"Odd," Amaril remarked. "Desert clans rarely leave their camps unattended."

Cautiously, they rode down only to find a horrible sight. Mangled bodies were strewn about. Then Sindle cried out, and the others focused on what he saw. He had found the corpse of Helanthin.

"I cannot bear to look," said Keldon, turning away. Intense pain again bolted through Sindle's side.

"I have seen this only once before," said Amaril. "They were attacked by wild zoas, and not too long ago by the looks of it." He dismounted his parjar to examine Helanthin's corpse. "This shouldn't have happened," he said. "The desert clans are experts at taming wild zoas. We had best leave before the beasts return."

They mounted their parjars and soon were sailing over the dunes again, but they hadn't gone far when they came upon another swarm of wild zoas. This time the travelers could see and hear their dark electricity in the near distance. Suddenly, the worst possible thing happened. The zoas caught sight of the travelers and started toward them.

"They're closing in!" shouted Amaril in a panic.

"Quick!" said the Captain. "Ride back to the camp. I will remain and try to draw them off."

They rode to the top of a dune and watched as the Captain dismounted his parjar. They could hear him calling, "Oowissss...Oowissss..." The Captain's comforting voice, full and rich, resonated through their minds as it had done so often before.

"Amazing," said Sindle, "he is taming them."

"Impossible," Amaril asserted. "If a Zanthan could not tame them, how can he?"

As the Captain stood in the midst of the swarm of wild zoas, they began sparkling with every color of the rainbow. Their horrible droning ceased and gave way to a harmonious symphony that filled the desert with music. Their changing patterns of colored light reflected upon the dull dunes below.

"I cannot believe my eyes," said Keldon. "They're as beautiful as the aurora we saw above Arete Vitrea."

They watched as the Captain pointed in the direction of Arete Vitrea.

"They seem to know what he is thinking," said Sindle. "Look!"

The zoas flew toward heaven in formation like a flock of geese and then headed in the direction of Arete Vitrea.

Soon the Captain returned to the Companions and they embraced him. "You did it, Captain," Sindle congratulated him. "You tamed them!"

"No Viridian harp or flute could have produced such glorious music," added Keldon. "Your powers are truly remarkable, even greater than my master Verlin's."

"The zoas are now filled with light and harmony," he explained. "I sent them on their way to the regions beyond Arete Vitrea. Otherwise they would have followed us to Viridia and interferred with our plans."

They again mounted their parjars and continued on their way. As they rode, they wondered about where the Captain had learned such remarkable powers. They had seen him destroy Finsterna's idol, transform thandoos into parjars, and change zoa devils into angels. Still it seemed that the Captain was not very different from them, for he, too, was a Shade, an inhabitant of Spectara. Amaril, most of all, desired to know the secret of the Captain's power. By low lumen-ebb, the Companions had again set camp, and Amaril took the opportunity to take the Captain aside. He spoke to the Captain in a low voice so that Keldon and Sindle could not hear. "How do you do such marvelous things? I must have such power."

"To possess wisdom is better," said the Captain. "Without wisdom, power is misguided and dangerous. Finsterna is proof of that."

Amaril took offense. "Surely I am not like Finsterna!" Keldon and Sindle jerked their heads around at the outburst. Amaril lowered his voice but still spoke with anger. "You forget I was born in Zanthis, land of wisdom. What wisdom could there be that I don't already possess?"

"You have some wisdom, yes, but your wisdom is the kind that seeks justice only. There is a wisdom higher still."

"You insult me," said Amaril. "What other wisdom could there be?"

"Why must Zanthans always think themselves right?" the Captain returned. "You would use your wisdom to punish untruth. If it were in your power to stop the wild zoas, would you not have stopped them with brutality? Sometimes the greater wisdom is that of understanding, compassion, and mercy."

"What kind of talk is that? You sound like our onion-headed philosopher over there!" Amaril said it loudly so that Keldon would hear.

"Pardon me?" remarked Keldon. "Do you need advice about Viridian philosophy?"

"Of course not," Amaril blurted in a scathing tone.

Keldon and Sindle began to listen in to their conversation.

"Nevertheless, your Viridian friend is right about one thing," the Captain added. "The way to destroy this power of evil that now grips Spectara is not through force. If that had been possible, Zil Magnus and his Archons would have succeeded in their time. I know Finsterna's dark power cannot be tamed by hate or retaliation. I felt the heat of her wrath within the idol. I saw her eye in the flame. I now know that rage and fury are her fuel. Otherwise she is powerless. The more that force is used to fight her, the more her power will increase. You cannot understand how great a feast the hatred of the inhabitants of Zanthis has supplied her. She sows seeds of hatred because that is the source of her power and life, if you can call it life. The zoas, too, were under her spell. They were unlike any wild zoa ever tamed.

They had Finsterna's mind, and she possessed theirs. The volcanoes of Pyrath, the idol, the eye of Lucia—all have fallen under her evil spell, and she will not cease working until darkness governs every inch of Spectara."

Amaril fixed suspicious eyes upon him. "I suppose then that you will try to destroy Finsterna through this ridiculous idea of understanding, mercy, and compassion?"

"That is my plan, yes. Of course, the risk is very great since I, like you, am a Shade. But the Telarch has also entrusted me with his power, for no other power in Spectara can now tame her. Still, there's a chance she could ignite my anger, and she will try with all her might to do so. If she succeeds, then she will be able to feed upon the Telarch's power forever. Then she can never be defeated."

Amaril's eyes became dark with suspicion, and deep lines became etched in his forehead. He could not understand why the Telarch would take so great a risk. Why could he not find an easier way to bring an end to Finsterna's reign of terror.

The Companions took time to bury the remains of Helanthin and his people before spending low lumen-ebb in what was left of Helanthin's camp. At the break of lumen-flow, they were off again. Soon, they arrived on the borders of Viridia only to find fingers of brown, dead grass that had lost their battle against invading desert sands. Keldon kept straining his neck, trying to see ahead. More of the brown grass stretched into the distance toward Viridia.

A look of panic flew from Keldon's face. "The grass has always had a hard time surviving on the borders," he said, trying to reassure himself that nothing really could be wrong in Viridia. At first, he had tried to think that everything he had been through thus far had only been a mirage. In time, however, they found the turquoise and emerald gravel path, but there was still no sign of green grass. Trepidation tightened its vice on his mind. Then he saw a flock of stray zoas migrating in the direction of Zanthis, and terror struck his heart. Something horrible had also happened in Viridia. As they traveled toward Chartra, they found no trace of zoaherders but stray zoas were everywhere.

Panic was flashing from Keldon's face. "I should try to save them. But without my harp, what can I do?"

"It's too late," said the Captain. "We must get to Chartra. Viridia has also fallen under Finsterna's spell."

The wound in Sindle's side throbbed. He thought about Zoella and feared the worst. When Keldon saw his beloved Viridia ravaged by death, he became frantic with worry over Biona. Tears welled up in his eyes, and he tried to restrain himself from breaking out into sobs. The Companions willed their parjars to hurry, and they sped down the road toward Chartra. The grass of Viridia now appeared almost the same color as the sands of Zanthis. It was after mid-lumen-flow when they came up over a rise and entered the vale of Chartra.

Keldon wailed at what he saw. The city resembled a broken wheel, and a dark pall covered it like smoke in the aftermath of a great forest fire. Keldon broke down and wept, and Sindle tried to fight tears.

"We must find Biona and Zoella!" cried Keldon.

When they entered Chartra's gates, a stench filled their nostrils. In the streets were scattered the bodies of the dead and the dying. Upon their skin were awful, black sores, and gray liquid oozed from the sores into the gutters. Keldon's face turned to stone. He willed his parjar toward the center of Chartra. "Something has happened to the Verdis Tree!" he exclaimed.

Thorns, thistles, and weeds now grew in the gardens that lined the streets, and dark soot had tarnished the once-sparkling buildings. When they passed the Zoaherding Academy, they saw more bodies lying on its steps, but the stench grew even worse as they approached the heart of the city.

Terror pulsated in Keldon's eyes. They came to the path beside the stream that flowed from the Verdis Tree and sailed down the path through the four walls. The stream was dried up, and ugly insects were breeding in its muddy bed. The three living walls that surrounded Verdis had shed their leaves and turned to briars like those at the cursed city of Har Bellak in Pyrath. As the Companions entered the clearing of Verdis, their eyes fell upon a most sickening sight. A snakelike heap of dying flesh writhed beneath the withered stump of the Verdis Tree as they fought to suck out the last remaining drops of healing salve. The people had shattered the pyramid and plucked off every leaf! Keldon's eyes glassed over with tears. He leapt from his parjar and ran toward the tree. The clamor of the greedy heap grated against his ears, and the stench of their rotting flesh turned his stomach.

Then he came to the sad realization that it was high lumen-flow, the time for Wittistide, and pain turned its dagger in his heart. He searched for the Queen, but neither she nor her attendants were anywhere to be found. Then he saw out of the corner of his eye a woman tending the sick. A flood of tears gushed from his eyes. It was Biona! "Biona! My dear, Biona!" He broke the sacred silence, but he did not care. What did it matter now? He ran toward her with Sindle and the others following close.

Biona lifted an ashen face, and her eyes, encircled with fatigue, lit up and gave way to a sudden flood of tears. "Keldon! My dear!" They met and embraced. "Oh, Keldon!" They both wept.

"Biona," he said, trying to gain control of his emotions, "this is Regius Pisces, but we call him the Captain."

"Good lumen," said Biona.

"And this is Amaril whom we met in Ecrusand of Zanthis, the son of the late Patriarch of that country. This is my wife, Biona."

"I am pleased to meet you both," said Biona. "Sindle, I'm delighted to see you again. Thank you for keeping Keldon safe."

"Truthfully, it has been the other way around," said Sindle. "I don't know what would have happened to me without him at my side. How is Zoella?" he asked her.

"She is fine, Sindle, but very tired. She's now at the palace caring for the Queen. We must go there. I have much to tell you."

As Keldon again embraced Biona, he could feel her bones. This was not the plump wife he had left behind. He looked into her face. In place of merry eyes were empty wells of grief and exhaustion. "My dear," he sobbed. "What has happened to our beloved land?"

"Oh, Keldon," she said, fighting tears. "It has been the most terrible thing imaginable. I don't know where to begin. The worse thing has been this plague."

"Who are these people? They're not all Viridians."

"Some of them are from Zil-Kenøth. It is they who brought the plague. Now it has spread through all Viridia. I have it, too, I fear." She pulled back the collar of her dress and revealed an ugly black sore that oozed with gray fluid.

Pain filled Keldon's eyes. "There must be some cure. Where is the Queen?"

Biona started weeping. "Our Queen is dying."

Shock and pain filled Keldon's eyes. "How can that be?"

"She used every last ounce of her power trying to heal the sick. But there was no cure for this plague. The victims did not respond to the Verdis salve. Still, she kept trying to save them. Now her strength is spent. About a week ago, they found her lying in her underground chamber. She had been trying to save the last drops of water from the fountain of Zoa Aeonum. But the fountain had dried up. With nothing to water the Verdis tree, it dried up, as well."

Tears formed in Keldon's eyes. "We must go to the Queen. I must give her news of our journey."

They started out across the brown grass toward the Eastern Gate.

"Zoella and others of the Vernesdan order have been praying for her," said Biona. "Zoella told me that her face has aged one-thousand lumnus-years. She is little more than a living mummy."

Keldon shuddered, and pain filled his eyes. "I can't believe such terrible things have happened in so short a time."

"I fear the end has come," said Biona. "I've forgotten how to hope."

"How are my zoas?" asked Keldon.

"My dear, Garn is dead, and the flock is lost," Biona replied.

Keldon broke down and cried.

"All of this is my fault and the fault of my people," said Sindle. "The Queen entrusted her pendant to me, and I lost it."

"Finsterna's darkness is to blame, not you," said the Captain,

"I'm sorry I have nothing to offer your friends to eat," Biona said, forcing a smile. "I know you must be hungry and weary from your journey."

They made their way down the streets to the palace. When they reached the palace gates, the guard, who had been told to expect them, let them pass. They walked down the path and up the steps to the court. The page had been given orders to take them directly to the Queen on their arrival. The page took them not to the throne room, but to the foyer of the Queen's bed chamber. To Keldon's surprise, Verlin met them at the door.

"Master!" he cried, embracing him. Tears rolled down Verlin's cheeks. "I suppose by now you know our Queen is dying," said Verlin in a hushed voice. "We do not know how to help her. We have tried everything. No one knows what else to do. Every lumen the order of Vernesdans pray for her. 'We don't know what to do,' they say. 'We pray, yet her life still ebbs.' I know it is for you and Sindle that she has waited. She has asked for you every hour since she fell ill. You and Sindle must speak to her."

Verlin led them into the Queen's bed chamber. The air was heavy and stale. Death perched upon the bed posts, waiting to carry away the last remnant of Viridia's soul.

When Keldon saw Veronica's face, he could not restrain his tears. The Queen's once-radiant skin had become a thin, translucent parchment that stretched tight over her bones and skull. Her cheeks were hollow, and her eyes, sunken. When she opened them, they were covered with a haze. "Has Keldon come? ...Keldon?" In her lungs was the rattle of death.

He tried to control himself. "Your Majesty... I am here."

She opened her eyes and fixed them on Keldon. "At last," she sighed. "Draw closer. I cannot see you."

He knelt beside her bed.

"I am dying."

"Please, Your Majesty," he said, sobbing. "You cannot leave us. Your people need you."

"Do not weep for me." The words fell slowly and with great difficulty from her lips. "I am...to blame for what...has happened here."

"No, Majesty. You are good. It is Finsterna who is to blame."

"I erred...when I gave Sindle the pendant. I let pity...prevail over wisdom. That has always been my...weakness."

"You did what you thought best. You had no way of knowing what would happen. We're to blame. We're the ones who lost the pendant."

"No. It was the Telarch's goodness...that allowed it to be lost. I should have known...that you were not ready to behold the Light beyond Arete Vitrea."

"Please, Your Majesty. Don't tell us these things."

"I must. I have tried for too long...to shield my people from the sight of evil. I thought...I could hide darkness from them. Now I know better...I have spent my last...bit of strength trying to keep Viridia pure."

Sindle walked over to her side. "Why has your power failed, O Queen?"

"The pendant...was my link to the power of him who dwells beyond Arete Vitrea. It contained...the power of life, and the wisdom of the left eye of my sister...Lucia. When I gave it to you, I thought, 'Surely...I can do without it for a time. The fountain of life is full. There is enough to last until they return.' Alas, I was wrong. There was not...enough to last. I did not expect the throngs to come from Zil-Kenøth with their diseases. I tried to heal them, but...to no avail. Still, I was determined...to make them well. I would cure them though it might take all my powers, yet I seemed helpless...against their plague. Before long, the fountain was dry, the Verdis Tree...had withered, and I was at the end of strength. I realized too late that it...was Finsterna's power I was trying to combat. Over the horrible disease that she...contrived, I had no power, just as I had no power to restore your father to life, Sindle."

"It's my fault," wept Sindle. "In my weakness I let Prince Neblas have the password that you told me not to divulge."

Amaril's eyes flared against Sindle. "You gave the password to Prince Neblas! You deserve death!"

"Please!" said Keldon. "The harm is done, and no amount of anger can change that!"

"Remember that we must be at peace with one another," encouraged the Captain, "or else we will fuel Finsterna's power. If we do that, we might not survive what lies ahead." The Captain then walked to the other side of the Queen's bed. "Have you lost all the wisdom of Lucia's left eye?"

"Yes."

"I knew this. Otherwise, you would have recognized me. Give me your hand."

The Queen lifted a hand, feeble, ashen, and eaten away by dark cankers. When the Captain took it, the despair at once melted from her eyes, and for a moment, her face became radiant and young.

"The Telarch waits for you in Lux Aeternum. He bids you come."

She nodded and closed her eyes.

"What has happened?" exclaimed Keldon. "Is she dead?"

"No," said the Captain. "She has only crossed the summit of Arete Vitrea."

Their tears flowed down their cheeks and spotted the green silk bed covers, now soiled and shredded.

Suddenly, Zoella entered. "I have heard that Keldon and Sindle have returned..." She then focused upon Sindle. "Thank goodness you are both safe." She hurried over to embrace them. When Sindle saw Zoella, his heart sank. She was very thin, and dark circles under her eyes revealed that she was sick and exhausted.

"Zoella," Sindle uttered. Though Sindle tried to restrain his emotions, tears welled in his eyes.

Biona went over and embraced her. "The Queen has passed away, my dear." As Zoella broke into bitter weeping, Sindle felt helpless. He wanted to share her sadness, to embrace her, and to comfort her, but he knew this was not his place. He merely stood by and watched as Biona, Keldon, and Verlin came to her aid.

"She is in Vernesda now," said Verlin. "I shall go and tell the attendant what has happened." He left the room.

"She did not deserve this fate," said Zoella. "What shall we do now?"

"It's a sad lumen for Viridia," Keldon lamented.

They stood around her bed and mourned for her. Outside in the courtyard, the death knell began to sound. It pealed forth not only the end of the Queen's life and reign, but the end of an age.

CHAPTER 29
THE DEATH BARGE

Viridia's anguished wails rose above the sound of feet shuffling across gravel. As the funeral procession of Queen Veronica crept amid dead and dying bodies, the pounding of the drum drove despair deeper into every soul. What little vegetation remained seemed to wither as the shadow of the Queen's burial pall passed over it. The pall was carried by the same four men with clean-shaven heads who had once carried Veronica on her throne for the Wittistide celebration. Sindle's eyes filled with tears as he compared this scene to that happier time. At exactly high lumen-flow, the procession passed through Chartra's four walls, through the Eastern Gate, and into the clearing where the Verdis Tree once grew. At length, the pallbearers halted beneath its withered stump where a fresh grave had been dug. All watched in silent grief as they lowered the Queen's body into the grave. When Keldon stepped forward to deliver the Queen's eulogy, the drummers ceased, and the mourners closed in.

"Fellow Viridians and friends." Keldon paused. Icy sorrow numbed his mind and froze the fountain of words. He began again. "Viridians and friends. On this lumen we grieve because our beloved Queen is dead. On this lumen, we grieve because we know pain and death are real. Under the rule of our beloved Queen, we believed no evil could touch us. Those were the lumens of Wittistide and Verdis when the wand, the fountain, and the pendant of Veronica assured life and happiness for all. To those lumens, we thought no end could come, but now our unchanging world has collapsed, and unending life and peace have given way to death and despair. Our Viridian paradise withers away before our eyes, and the body of our beloved Queen lies silent and still in the grave. Verdis is hewn down. The Queen's pendant is forever lost to oblivion. Veronica's wand is broken beyond repair. The fountain of life has become as the deserts of Zanthis. The solemn celebration of Wittistide has ceased, never to be observed again. The ring of harp and flute no more are heard in Viridia's fields, for our zoas have fled, and the zoaherding art dies with our dead artisans. Death haunts every street and casts its long shadow of sorrow over all our land."

Keldon walked over, broke off a dead branch from the stump of the Verdis tree, and planted it at the head of Veronica's grave. "This shall be for a sign of hope that new life shall spring forth from death. I plant this with hope that Verdis shall bud again. The Queen is not dead, but has journeyed to the regions of Lux Aeternum beyond Arete Vitrea where the celebration of Wittistide shall never cease. There in Vernesda's green and fertile land, she shall await her people. Still one thing remains that the evil plague has not and cannot destroy—love for our Queen and our fellow Viridians. In love's rich soil, hope shall flourish." Keldon scooped up a handful of dirt and cast it into the grave. One by one, the Queen's attendants and zoaherders did the same. Then Keldon's sad eyes met with Verlin's. His old master hobbled over to him. As they embraced and wept, Biona joined them.

Sindle watched as Zoella passed the Queen's grave and cast in her handful of soil. None of the evils that had struck Viridia had diminished her radiant beauty. He walked over to her, and she fell into his arms, sobbing. "I once believed nothing could disturb the peace I knew," she told him. "I was so near Vernesda, I could see it. Now all my dreams are shattered."

"Zoella, I have something I must tell you," Sindle said, looking into her eyes. "I dared not say it before because of your devotion to the Queen and the Vernesdan way. But now I must risk being honest." He paused for a moment. "I *love* you, Zoella. I love you with all my heart, and have loved you from the lumen on which we first met."

Zoella burst into tears and embraced Sindle. "Can what Keldon said be true? Is there hope where there is love? My feelings for you, Sindle, are the same. I, too, have loved you since that Wittistide when I first laid eyes on you."

A look of eagerness came over Sindle's face. "Zoella, you must come with us to Zil-Kenøth. The Captain goes there to defeat the power of Finsterna. There will be danger, but together we can face it."

Zoella smiled. "I have no reason to remain in Viridia now. My vows no longer bind me to the Vernesdan way. But please, say nothing of it yet to Biona or Keldon. Their grief for the Queen is too great."

Soon the crowd's wailing began again. As the crowd scattered, diggers shoveled soil into the grave. The Companions of the Quest, joined by Biona and Zoella, started back to the palace. "Can the prophecy I spoke be true?" Keldon asked the Captain as they walked.

"Yes," the Captain reassured him.

"Prophecies," Amaril remarked in a huff. "I've lost faith in them all."

"You've tried hard to make the prophecy of Helis come true, Amaril," said the Captain. "The time for fulfillment has not yet come."

Amaril's eyes sharpened with cynicism. "I doubt it will ever come. The situation seems much too hopeless now."

Sindle suddenly grabbed his side and fell to his knees.

"Sindle!" Zoella shouted, coming to his aid.

"The Captain knows what will help him," said Keldon. The Captain hummed gently, and they all walked in silence to the palace. Eventually the pain in Sindle's side subsided. Then the Captain became silent as the others talked. When they reached the palace, the Captain's brow was furrowed and his eyes deep with thought. "It's time, my dear friends, to say good-bye. I must go to Zil-Kenøth."

"You're not going alone!" stated Sindle.

"No. We *are* coming with you," added Amaril.

"Amaril is right," said Keldon. "None of us has a reason to remain here."

"The journey will be dangerous," said the Captain.

"We won't let you risk the dangers alone," said Sindle. "You may need our help."

"Yes," said Biona. "We are all with you, come what may."

"I have agreed to come too," said Zoella. "I am no longer bound by the Vernesdan way now that our beloved Queen is dead."

"You will face the darkness and danger more terrible than you have ever known," the Captain warned. "The time may come when you will want to turn back but will not be able to do so."

"We will help protect you," said Amaril. "The more of us there are to face the evil, the better."

"Very well," said the Captain. "We shall remain Companions of the Quest to the end. We shall face Finsterna's evil together."

Through the gates of what had now become a city of death, they struck out toward the sea of Marus Lazul. Along the way, throngs of refugees from Zil-Kenøth streamed toward Chartra. Sindle tried to recognize them, but they all seemed as zombies. Black sores had so covered their bodies and eaten away their features that they all looked very much the same. Some begged for food or for the magic ointment they had heard could be found in Viridia. The Companions finally had to detour from the main road to avoid the river of rotting flesh.

When they arrived at Marus Lazul, a nauseating stench filled their nostrils. The Sea of a Thousand Blues now resembled a pool of oil, and a brown, sulfuric fog hovered over it. Along the shore, carcasses of rotting fish mingled with sick and dying bodies. The Companions walked along the shore until they reached a ferry that had just landed. More Shades from Zil-Kenøth stampeded off like animals, not caring whom they trampled.

Sindle focused on one refugee who seemed pushier than the rest. The refugee saw Sindle and rushed toward him. "Please, mercy," he begged, groveling in the dirt. "I was a member of the royal family of Zil-Kenøth. Do you know of the cure in Viridia for our disease? Please help me find it."

His voice was familiar. Sindle stared into the Shade's face. Though diseased, Sindle recognized the bulldog features. It was Prince Neblas's uncle, Dargad, who had betrayed Sindle's grandfather. Dargad didn't recognize Sindle at first. Fear and anger were mixing a lethal cocktail in Sindle's stomach. Then anger welled up inside him and he exploded. "Who showed mercy when the Grand Inquisitor sacrificed my grandfather, Wizdor, to the Sea of Darkness? *Who showed mercy then?*"

With shock, Dargad stared at Sindle. Fear flashed across Dargad's face, and he tried to escape into the crowd. Sindle ran after him and grabbed him. "Spineless coward! Traitor! Murderer! You don't deserve mercy!" Sindle gritted his teeth as he screamed at him.

"W-W-What d-do you m-m-mean?"

"You did nothing to stop the Grand Inquisitor! You let Wizdor die!" Fire lashed from Sindle's eyes at Dargad who looked like a whipped dog.

"What could I have done? I was afraid."

"Coward!"

Dargad fell at Sindle's feet. "Please, Sindle. Don't hurt me."

"You're not worth the pain it would cause my fist. Stand up!"

He stood, but dared not look Sindle in the eye.

"Sindle. I am sorry. Please forgive me."

Sindle scowled at him.

"I admit I'm a weakling and a coward," he said, grovelling.

Sindle squinted angrily. "What has happened since my departure from Zil-Kenøth."

"It is too horrible to tell," replied Dargad, shaking his head.

"What of the other magistrates, the Temple Warden, the Starkeeper?"

Dargad hesitated.

"Answer me!"

"Sacrificed to the Sea. I thought surely you were as well," he gulped.

"Are you disappointed I wasn't?"

"No. I would never..."

Sindle's face turned hard as rock. "Tell me of the Trogzars."

"They are all-powerful. Nothing can stop them. The Grand Inquisitor waits every lumen for Prince Neblas to return. He waits to hear of his victory over the Hell of Light."

"You seem to have first-hand knowledge of the Grand Inquisitor's plans."

"Yes, well. He allowed me certain...privileges."

"I am not surprised."

"But I escaped. I could endure him no longer. That's why I'm here."

"So you've seen the light at last!" Sindle remarked sarcastically. "And your reason for leaving has nothing to do with finding the Verdis ointment to heal you of the plague?"

"So that's the name of the miracle cure! Now that you mention it, yes, it would be nice to have some."

"You're too late, Dargad. The Verdis Tree is dead, and there is no more medicine for you."

A shadow of terror crept across Dargad's face. "Surely you're wrong. There must be some left..."

"There is none," said Sindle with a tone of finality. Sindle turned and started back toward the barge, but Dargad followed. "Where are you going, Sindle?"

"Back to Zil-Kenøth."

"Are you out of your mind?" he said. "You won't get past the gates! You don't know the password."

Sindle lifted his eyebrow. "Password?"

"That's not the only thing. Only someone friendly to the Trogzar cause could get past the gates."

"Then do something courageous for once and help us," Sindle asked. "Unless, of course, you would rather die a coward."

Dargad stood on the shore as Sindle helped Zoella onto the ferry. "But what will happen to me if I go back?" Dargad trembled.

"You will die no matter what you decide, but at least you have a choice about how you will die. You can stay here in Viridia and die slowly of the plague, or you can come along and lend us aid. At least there's a chance your death will be quick and have some dignity."

The Captain untied the ropes to set sail and was about to push the ferry away. Suddenly, to their great surprise, Dargad leapt aboard.

"Does this mean you'll help us?" asked Sindle.

"Yes," said Dargad. A faint smile crept across his face.

"I admit, I never thought you'd come," said Sindle. "Thank you."

As they crept across the dark waters of Marus Lazul, the Captain hummed a slow and sad tune. Eventually, everyone except Sindle, Dargad, and the Captain fell into a much needed sleep. Sindle would have done the same, but Dargad kept probing him. Why were they going back to Zil-Kenøth? What could be gained by it? Who were the people that traveled with him?

"It is better that you not know for now," Sindle replied. "If they catch us, you might be forced to talk, and that would be fatal for everyone."

Soon Sindle's fatigue became so great he could no longer keep his eyes open. He leaned back, and drifted off. As he slept, he dreamed again of the death barges carrying their slaves. This time, he dreamed that he and the Companions of the Quest were being carried to Finsterna's volcanic island in the heart of the Sea of Darkness. From it spewed her dark fire, and she ranted and raved against the Light. He woke up with a scream, startling the others.

"What's wrong?" asked Zoella, putting her arm around his shoulders.

"Just a bad dream," he replied. Part of the dream had been about the Captain. He tried to remember the details, but he couldn't.

CHAPTER 30
DEEP WINTER

As the ferry approached the shores of Violinda in early lumen-flow, the Companions of the Quest awoke to a throng of refugees from Zil-Kenøth who were fighting to get aboard the next available ferry. The refugees waved and flung their arms about wildly as they shouted for help. On the shoreline lay bodies of the dying and the dead. It was obvious some had been trampled by the mob only moments before.

"The murderous dogs!" Amaril snarled. "They care for nothing but their own hides. Do they think they can escape?" Amaril shouted at them. "Go back! There's no help for you in Viridia! Your filth has spread through every land in Spectara. Go back to where you belong."

The crowd shook angry fists at him and shouted curses.

"You shouldn't have done that," said Dargad. "We'll be lucky now if we get past them alive."

As the barge approached, the refugees rushed into the water toward them.

"They're after the barge," said Dargad. "Bail out. We'll have to swim ashore."

Dargad jumped overboard, and the others followed. The icy water chilled them to the bone, tearing the breath from their lungs. When they got to shore, they watched as the crowd scrambled to the barge. Water splashed and bubbled as the stronger among them drowned the weaker.

"There will be no going back across Marus Lazul now," said Dargad.

Keldon was shivering. "It's freezing. How will we ever get warm?"

"We'll have to get dry clothes from the dead bodies," said Dargad, approaching a corpse. "Help me get these off."

"Must we do this?" Keldon lamented.

"We have no choice," said Dargad. "It is this or freeze."

"Here," said Dargad to Zoella. "Wrap this around you."

Keldon started to wrap a garment around Biona, but then hesitated. "What if the plague has contaminated the clothing?"

"Freeze to death now, or die of the plague later, take your choice," remarked Amaril with a tone of sarcasm.

"I've been infected anyway," said Biona. Keldon wrapped the garment around her and found one for himself. Sindle and Zoella huddled together, trying to get warm. "A good idea," said the Captain. "Stay as close together as possible, and keep moving."

They began their trek over steel grey dunes of sand into the vale of Violinda. Deep winter had now settled upon the land of autumn. Ice-coated trees clattered in the wind. Bitter cold gnawed their ears and noses, numbed their limbs, and drained the color from their skin until they had turned a dismal shade of gray. "It's just as well," remarked Dargad. "At least now you will all pass as citizens of Zil-Kenøth."

"Is it colder there?" Keldon asked through clattering teeth.

"Much colder," replied Dargad. "And there hasn't been fuel to keep warm for weeks."

"This is a miserable land," said Amaril. "I would prefer the deserts of Zanthis any time."

"I'm inclined to agree with you for once," said Keldon. "At least there we were warm."

"It's always been cold in Zil-Kenøth," said Sindle. "I guess I had forgotten how it was."

"It became worse after you left," said Dargad, "and it seems to grow colder with each passing lumen."

"It must be Finsterna's doing," said the Captain. "Her dark fire doesn't burn like other fire. It's a fire that freezes, though the damage it does is just as bad."

"Now we know a little of what my grandfather must feel," remarked Sindle.

"What do you plan to do to Finsterna, Captain?" Amaril probed. "Now that you've seen the damage she can do, do you still think you will need no weapon?"

"Any ordinary weapon used against her would only make her grow stronger," he replied. "Of that you can be sure."

When the Companions reached the cliffs that overlooked the city of Zil, they huddled together and tried to decipher a way in.

"The roads are heavily guarded," cautioned Dargad, "but I think I can get us through. As far as I know, I'm still in the Grand Inquisitor's favor. I have a plan, so listen. Sindle, Keldon, Amaril, and the Captain will pretend to be Trogzar agents who have returned with their prisoners, Biona and Zoella. Biona and Zoella, you must pretend that you are escapees from the death camp. You must pretend as though you were among those to be sacrificed to Finsterna. Put up a struggle when you see the guards so that they'll think you are really prisoners. Since I know the password, I think I can get you through the blockade."

"Do you expect me to lie?" exclaimed Amaril. "I am a Zanthan. I must uphold the truth, even upon pain of death!"

"Would you endanger the rest of us by telling the truth as you call it?" asked Keldon. "Which is worse, death or a little lie?"

"Don't try to make me compromise, Viridian."

"Then maybe you should turn back," said Keldon. "Otherwise, you may put us all in jeopardy."

"All we ask of you is to be silent," said Dargad. "I'll lie for you."

"I can't condone that," said Amaril.

"Then what would you condone?" asked Keldon with a tone of anger. "Would you tell the truth to Trogzar liars? You would be compromising with worse liars than our friend Neblas here."

"There are no *degrees* of right and wrong when it comes to untruth," said Amaril. "I have no tolerance for liars of any kind, be they friend or foe. Captain? What do you say?"

"If it comes to the point that you can't in good conscience go in, then you must do as Keldon suggests and turn back. To destroy truth is evil, yes. But to destroy life is just as evil."

"We cannot save both," remarked Amaril.

"The very thing I hope to do is to save both," said the Captain. "That's the reason I am going to Zil-Kenøth. But it will not be easy."

"Very well," said Amaril. "I'll pledge to remain silent upon pain of death. I'll give you my word now. It shall not be broken."

"Thank goodness," muttered Dargad, rolling his eyes. "Biona, Zoella, start acting like our prisoners now. There may be spies. If anyone suspects we're impostors, we'll all be sacrificed to Finsterna."

Biona and Zoella did as Dargad asked, and the men, acting as though they were guards, surrounded them. When they arrived at the city gates, Biona and Zoella struggled. The men, except for Amaril, pretended to restrain them. Dargad approached the guards, held up his left hand, and pointed his little finger toward the ground. "Cogert Neblas nost pat fluglar," he droned.

Suspicion flared in the guards eyes. "What? You have not heard the new password? Cogert Neblas nost *hat* fluglar! NEBLAS HAS CONQUERED!"

"Wonderful, I'm glad to hear it," replied Dargad. He tried to hide his nervousness. "We've been tracking these women for several lumens. They were to be sacrificed to Finsterna, but they managed to escape. They must be brought back for sacrifice. It is the Grand Inquisitor's wish. So, Prince Neblas completed his mission, I take it?"

"Indeed. He has returned with Asdin," said the guard. "His victory over the Hell of Light is being celebrated this lumen-ebb at the Temple site."

"How fortunate for us that we've returned in time for so momentous an event," remarked Dargad. "I'm sure these runaways will serve as suitable sacrifices to our Great Mother on this grand occasion."

The guards seemed pleased with Dargad's words and allowed them to pass. Dargad led the others down the streets until they were well out of the guards' sight. Then, when no one was watching, they ducked into a back street.

"That was close," said Dargad, panting.

"We've arrived in the nick of time," said the Captain. "I must confront Neblas in the sight of the people of Zil-Kenøth."

"But the guards said Neblas has brought the Star back," said Sindle. "Now that Asdin is again in Zil-Kenøth, Finsterna will fear to strike."

"You forget that she now possesses the wisdom of the right eye of Lucia," the Captain countered. "Not only that, but she has drunk of the waters of the fountain of life through the power of Veronica's pendant. She won't fear Asdin now in the least. I'm also sure she knows you are here. But she will not be able to sense my presence because of the darkness in her heart."

Suddenly, they heard the marching of a Trogzar squadron and huddled fearfully against the walls of a building until it passed.

"It's much too dangerous here," said Dargad.

"Could we go to our lodgings in Stargazer Street?" asked Sindle.

"Not there of all places!" answered Dargad. "All abandoned buildings have become compounds for plague victims. We can only hope they have not yet discovered mine is empty. I don't think they yet suspect I tried to leave Zil-Kenøth."

As Dargad led the group to the safety of his home, wheels turned in Sindle's mind. The thought of plague victims in his home, the last sacred shrine to his past, infuriated and sickened him. When the Companions reached Dargad's house, they entered through a back way. Dargad rushed through the house, drawing all the curtains. Then he returned to the others.

"I know you must be hungry," he said to them. "Please sit around the table. I'll see if I can find something to eat."

He left the room and soon returned with a few slices of stale bread and a pitcher of weak tea. "I'm sorry. This is all I have. There hasn't been adequate food in Zil for months." They shared the bread and tea, and all but the Captain devoured their portions quickly. "Aren't you going to eat yours?" Sindle asked him.

"I'll share mine with you and the others. You will need the nourishment more than I."

"A little tea may help warm you up," said Biona.

"Thank you, but the time has come for me to negotiate with the Trogzars. I'm not sure how they will accept me."

"Confront them with their lies, then dissolve them as you did Finsterna's idol!" Amaril barked.

"When will you confront them?" asked Sindle.

"During their celebration of Neblas's return this lumen-ebb. You and the others must remain here. I don't want to put you in further danger."

"We *will* go with you," said Amaril. "If they try anything, we will protect you."

"It might not be as easy as you think," returned the Captain. "They may decide to sacrifice me to Finsterna."

"Then you must not go," said Keldon. "Not if there's a chance something like that might happen to you."

"Keldon's right," said Sindle. "I know these people. They will listen to you as they listened to Wizdor! No, Captain. If there's a chance you might not come back alive, we won't let you go."

"But I must go. Otherwise Spectara will cease to be. Finsterna must be stopped. The Trogzars must be made to understand that their hate is fueling her power. They must be made to face the evil they have caused."

"Good!" shouted Amaril. "We're with you, Captain."

"If you go with me, you must be ready for the worst."

"We have no reason to fear them," said Amaril. "We've seen your power. We know you can stop them."

"The Trogzars are not made of stone like Finsterna's idol, and they are not like wild zoas. They have a choice to follow light or to embrace darkness."

"I'm sure when they see that you are not cruel, but kind," said Keldon, "they will listen to reason. I believe you can convince them."

"I hope you're right," said the Captain. "But these people have listened to the voice of the Sea for a very long time. Some may be beyond the reach of reason just as the caves under Pyrath were beyond the reach of our words."

Amaril frowned at Keldon. "Words, words, words," he said impatiently. "The solution is simple. If they listen to reason, fine. If not, then they should be destroyed! That's the only way."

The Captain rose from his chair. "The time grows short. Come with me if you wish, but make me a promise. Let me handle the Trogzars. Promise whatever happens that you will not interfere."

"I give my word," said Amaril. "The matter is in your hands."

The Captain looked at each of them, and they nodded.

They proceeded through the dim streets of Zil to the celebration. To keep them from being suspected by Trogzars, Dargad suggested they not go as a group, so they broke up and arrived at the Temple site at different intervals. The icy wind penetrated to their bones, and soon all feeling had left their flesh.

When they reached the Temple site, Trogzars had already gathered. They chanted strange words and played Ophis horns. They then began to chant the sacred words of the High Guardian. "Ophis cogert Trogzar crugar! Latrat pogsnif shalarun soogar!" Sindle's blood curdled when he heard it.

"Join in," whispered Dargad. "We don't want to draw attention to ourselves."

Amaril glared at him, thinking that death would be better than to join in! Had he not made his vow of silence, he would have screamed with outrage. No one except Dargad joined in. The rest stood behind the crowd, trying to stay out of sight.

Soon, the Grand Inquisitor arrived and mounted the rubble where the temple had stood. Sindle's hatred for him burned. Maybe now he and Neblas would get what they deserved.

"People of Zil-Kenøth and fellow Trogzars," cried the Grand Inquisitor. His face, once handsome, now appeared twisted with evil. "The Holy Task is complete. The great eternal lumen-ebb approaches. Prince Neblas is victorious!"

The crowd cheered!

"Neblas has conquered the ruler of the Hell of Light!"

The cheers rose again!

"In doing so, he has vanquished the Hell of Light forever! Now our Mother, the Queen of Darkness, shall reign over Spectara forever."

The roar of the crowd sickened Sindle and the others. The hole in his side was throbbing with pain.

The Grand Inquisitor extended his hand, and Prince Neblas mounted the rubble of the Temple with the Sacred Star. He stood beside the Grand Inquisitor and lifted Asdin over his head. "The Hell of Light is no more!" he proclaimed. "Long live Finsterna, our Mother!"

"Long live Finsterna, our Mother!" the crowd repeated.

The strong voice of evil overpowered the Companions of the Quest as they watched. Even Amaril had come near to breaking his vow of silence when suddenly the clear voice of the Captain pierced the air. "The Queen of Darkness has deceived Prince Neblas and your Grand Inquisitor!"

A hush fell over the crowd and shock filled every eye. The Captain leapt up onto the rubble and stood at a distance away from Neblas and the Grand Inquisitor as they glared at him!

Amaril smiled, but Dargad's mouth hung open in shock.

"Finsterna, Queen of the eternal lumen-ebb, is the worst deceiver of all! The end of the reign of light has not come, but the end of her reign of darkness has!" He turned to Prince Neblas. "Have you forgotten what happened? The Telarch who reigns in Lux Aeternum showed you no harm. Try to remember what really happened to you there."

Twin flames of anger burned in Neblas's eyes. "You again," he hissed. He panicked and screamed at the crowd. "Don't believe him! He lies!"

The Captain's eyes burned. "You have become so much a part of her you can't remember what truth is. Try to remember. Try."

"Curse you, fool!" screamed Prince Neblas. "Curse you!"

The Captain remained calm, but Amaril fidgeted. Why didn't he teach the rogue a lesson? Why did he hesitate?

"You wish to destroy me," said the Captain, "as you tried to destroy the Telarch. Why do you hate the light so?"

"You shall be destroyed," said Prince Neblas in a rage.

"Bind him!" shouted the Grand Inquisitor.

Neblas's eyes flared with fury as the Grand Inquisitor stumbled over the rubble to the Captain and slapped him across the face. "You will take back the false words that you spoke before these people! Take them back or you shall perish!"

The Captain fixed a steady gaze at him. The Grand Inquisitor slapped him again. "Take them back! I order you!"

The Captain said nothing.

"You who pretend to speak for the Hell of Light! Who are you to dare challenge the Holy Task?" He signaled for Prince Neblas. "Bring the shield against the Hell of Light! Bring Asdin! There is still work for it to do!"

Neblas climbed the rubble with the Star and whispered to the Grand Inquisitor. "Who he is, and who he claims to be, are two different things, my Lord. He claims to be the Emissary of Light, our ancient foe! But he is scum."

"The Emissary of Light?" the Grand Inquisitor said, laughing. He stared the Captain in the eye. "Is this true? Do you claim to be the Emissary of Light?"

The Captain did not reply.

"Answer, fool!!"

Again he said nothing. "You are an enemy of our Great Mother. What further need have we to question you? You must die. There is no other way."

Amaril started forward, but Sindle caught him by the arm. "No," he whispered. "You must not interfere. Remember your promise."

Amaril's eyes boiled, and he whispered. "He'll destroy them yet. Just wait and see." Then he realized he had broken his vow of silence, and shock bolted through his face.

"Let the points of the Star stab his head!" shouted the Grand Inquisitor.

Prince Neblas lifted Asdin above the Captain's head and with the viciousness of a deadly snake, struck the Captain on the head. The Captain fell to his knees as Asdin pierced his skull.

"Now the fool looks vaguely like the Telarch who used to dwell in Lux Aeternum," Prince Neblas chuckled to the Grand Inquisitor. "Don't you think?"

"I have an idea," said the Inquisitor. "Pretend he is the evil ruler of the Hell of Light. Act out here what you did when you vanquished the one beyond Arete Vitrea. It will give the crowd a thrill." The Grand Inquisitor shouted to the people. "Behold! The Telarch of Light!" he shouted. "Look how weak he has become!"

"What is wrong with him?" said Sindle. "Why doesn't he defend himself?"

"Shhh!" cautioned Dargad. "You are putting us in danger."

"What do you wish me to do with him?" the Grand Inquisitor asked.

"Sacrifice him to Finsterna!" rang a voice from the crowd.

The crowd cheered at the suggestion.

"Of course he will be sacrificed! The Telarch of Light must die so that the darkness will reign forever!"

The crowd roared, and the Captain fell to the ground.

"Get up, fool!" hissed Prince Neblas. He spoke to the Captain so that not even the Grand Inquisitor could hear. "Did you really think you could come here and slobber your nonsense about kindness and good will? You have caused nothing but pain in Spectara."

The Captain remained silent and merely looked at him.

"Must you keep staring at me with those eyes? I am sick of seeing them."

Just then, Prince Neblas pulled out a sword from his sheath and held it to the sky. Sindle recognized the sword as the very one he had wielded on that fateful day of his grandfather's demise in the Sea of Darkness. "Behold Trogzars, the Zarafat of Zil Magnus!" Prince Neblas shouted.

He held it up to the Captain's right eye, but the Captain did not flinch.

"What shall I do with it?" Prince Neblas asked the crowd.

A chant started up. "Blind him, blind him, blind him!" It grew louder and louder.

Amaril, Sindle, and Keldon watched with shock, while Biona and Zoella turned their heads. Amaril gnawed his tongue as Prince Neblas drove the sword into the Captain's right eye.

At that moment, Amaril broke his vow of silence a second time. "It is just as they did to Lucia, our Queen," he whispered to Sindle. "They are killing the truth again."

A Trogzar watched Amaril. "Why do you not chant? Are you also a servant of the Light?" Amaril did not know what to say.

"Join in, you must," Dargad whispered to him. "He does not hear very well," Dargad told the Trogzar. "Don't pay attention to him." Amaril, fearing for his life, started chanting with the crowd, breaking his vow of silence a third time. The Trogzar seemed satisfied.

Prince Neblas then drove the sword into the Captain's left eye. The Captain held his eyes in pain! "You who claim to be the Emissary of Light!" Prince Neblas shouted. "Now you shall never see light again! You shall serve Finsterna, Queen of Darkness!"

"Now," said the Grand Inquisitor, quieting the crowd, "what more suitable sacrifice could be offered to the Sea of Darkness than one who has said in public that he is the Emissary of Light?" He spat on the Captain. "Fool! Did you think you could hinder the coming of the age of darkness, the lumen-ebb of our liberation? To the Sea with him!" the Grand Inquisitor ordered.

Sindle and the others felt their hopes sink into the abyss. As the servants obeyed the Inquisitor, the sacrifice of Wizdor flashed again through Sindle's mind. Tears of anger welled in his eyes. With Prince Neblas and the Grand Inquisitor in the lead, the Trogzars carried the Captain toward the Sea.

"We've got to get back to safety," said Keldon. "It was as the Captain feared. They didn't listen to reason."

"Have you no backbone?" said Amaril. "We must try to save him. We can't let them go through with it."

"Try if you will," said Keldon. "It would give me pleasure to see you break your oath in front of the Captain."

"How dare you say that!" shouted Amaril.

"Please," said Biona with a scolding tone. "We must not argue. We must stand together."

Just then Sindle felt the darkness in his side engulfing him. This time there was no Captain to hum the tune and ease the pain. He clung to Zoella who helped him along. "Sindle, my dear," she cried, "I wish I could ease your suffering."

As they looked on from the distance, they could hear the crowd chanting as it moved toward the Sea, "Ophis cogert Trogzar crugar! Latrat pogsnif shalarun soogar!" The Sea heaved and undulated. Its dark mouth opened wide to receive its morsel. The awful sound of sucking and growls of hunger filled the streets.

The Grand Inquisitor raised his hands against the churning black gulf.

"And now, O Finsterna, O Great Queen of Darkness, the greatest of all sacrifices we offer Thee! Accept this wicked Emissary of Light, and be Thou forever appeased!" He gave the signal and they hurled the Captain into the Sea. Biona and Zoella shielded their eyes and wept.

"It's the end!" cried Sindle, "the end of the Captain, and the end of Spectara!"

"It may be the end for you," said Dargad. "But I'm thinking about joining the Trogzars again. I want to live as long as I can."

"I would gladly die first," shouted Amaril.

"Stop this foolish squabbling," sobbed Biona. "We've got to get back to Dargad's house before we're discovered?"

"Biona's right," said Zoella. "We've got to escape this horrible land."

"Is there any chance of that?" Sindle asked. "Could we go back to Viridia?"

"Back to the plague?" remarked Amaril with a sneer.

"That sounds better than staying in Zil-Kenøth," said Dargad.

"How will you get across Marus Lazul without a ferry?" asked Amaril in a scathing voice.

"We could make a raft from the trees of Violinda," Keldon suggested.

"I have tools," said Dargad.

"We can draw up plans," Keldon chimed in. "We'll have to make it in secret, of course. Otherwise the refugees may steal it from us."

They started back toward Dargad's house to devise their desperate plan. Only Amaril realized they were grasping at straws. "You are fools," he said. "Face the truth. The age of darkness is here to stay. Eventually the Trogzars will take over Viridia and Zanthis too."

"To the devil with your talk of truth," said Keldon. "All we want to do is to live as long as we can."

"If you can call *this* living?" Amaril barked. Sindle keeled over in pain. "Now there *he* goes again," Amaril huffed.

"We'll have to smuggle the tools out of Zil-Kenøth," said Dargad. "Convincing the guards won't be easy."

"How did the plague victims get out?" asked Biona.

"The Trogzars fear the plague and they know it is contagious," replied Dargad. "That's how I got out. This means Biona and Sindle and I could get out, since we all have it. But the rest of you will not pass the examination."

"What do we do then?" asked Amaril. "Wait until we all get the disease?"

"That may be what it takes," said Dargad.

"You are all insane!" growled Amaril. "Catch a deadly disease so you can escape and save your lives? What utter nonsense!"

"There is always hope of a cure," said Keldon.

"How can you believe that now?" replied Amaril. "If the Queen of Viridia could not help, who can?"

Upon arriving at Dargad's house, they entered through a back way and sat around his table. Dargad began drawing up plans for the raft.

"If ever we needed the Captain, it's now," said Sindle. "He would know how to build one."

They stared at Sindle. They had tried not to think about what had happened to the Captain. Just then, Biona broke down and wept. Then the rest, even Amaril, joined in.

"He was a good man," said Biona. "It's a pity they wouldn't listen to him."

"We tried to warn him not to go," added Keldon. "Why wouldn't he listen?

"You should not cry for him," said Amaril. "He died bravely with the truth on his lips. If only he had used his power to destroy the Trogzars."

"He loved life too much to destroy any creature," said Keldon. "He did not want to destroy the Trogzars, as bad as they are."

"Now he is dead," said Amaril. "What good is that?"

"Amaril is right," said Zoella. "We *are* fools. Our plan to escape is useless. We won't escape the Trogzars and this plague, no matter how hard we try."

"Then what shall we do?" said Dargad. "Sit here and die?" Despair filled the room. They sat speechless, faced with the terror of waiting for the end. They began to face up to the fact that they could do nothing to turn back the approaching age of darkness.

CHAPTER 31
REFLECTIONS

The Companions had been asleep for some time when Sindle started groaning and gasping for air. Keldon awoke first. "Is it the pain in your side?" he asked.

"Yes," replied Sindle. "I didn't think it could get any worse, but it has." said Sindle.

"I wish the Captain could hum his tune for you," remarked Keldon. Suddenly, Sindle screamed out in pain, awakening the others.

"What is wrong with him?" Amaril gripped. "Can we not have a moment's peace?"

Zoella arose and walked over to where he lay. "Is there anything we can do for you, Sindle?" He did not answer, but grimmaced and held his side.

"Some hot tea might help," Dargad suggested. "I'll go warm up what the Captain did not drink."

Sindle kept gasping for air.

"Let me see the wound," said Zoella. She examined it. "I'll try a Vernesdan prayer."

Dargad returned. "Here's the tea and bread the Captain left us."

"I don't know what good it will do," said Sindle, panting. "I'll die soon whether I drink it or not. Let's share it. I'm sure the Captain would wish us to do that. Get some more cups, Dargad."

He left and soon returned with the cups. They poured tea into each one and divided up the slice of bread the Captain did not eat.

"I propose a toast to the Captain's memory," said Amaril. "Let us not forget his courage."

"To the Captain's memory!" they replied, raising their cups. Then they drank.

"How odd," Keldon remarked. "This is more delicious than coolum. It can't be the same we had earlier."

"But it *is* the same," Dargad replied. "I don't understand how."

"The bread is sweeter, too. Sweeter than the wafers of Karash," remarked Amaril. "How is that possible?"

"It's all very strange," Dargad remarked.

Sindle, who had just drunk and eaten, felt of his side. "The coldness," he said pulling up his shirt. "It's gone! I can't believe it! There's no more pain! It's gone, I tell you!" He jumped up from the table, laughing and shouting.

"Let me see," said Zoella.

Sindle pulled back his shirt again, and Zoella examined him. The black wound had entirely disappeared. "Only Verdis ointment could have done this, Sindle. Could the Captain have something to do with it?"

"The Captain is dead, or have you forgotten," Amaril retorted. "How could this be his doing?"

"See for yourself," said Zoella.

Amaril looked at Sindle's side. "Our eyes must be deceiving us."

Tears streamed down Sindle's face. "Believe it or not, Amaril, the sore is gone, and I'm free of pain!"

Biona suddenly jumped up. "The sores on my neck have vanished too! Keldon, look!"

He ran over to her, and his eyes lit up.

Dargad examined his skin. "Mine are also gone! I'm cured! I'm cured!" he exclaimed as he touched the healthy skin of his arms and shoulders where sores once oozed.

"The Captain must have done something to the bread and tea," said Sindle. "How else could these things have happened?"

"Go ahead. Celebrate," said Amaril. "But remember that Trogzars are still about. How will you get past the guards now that you have been healed of the plague?"

"Must you always be so gloomy?" asked Keldon.

Just then, the room lit up, and a strange ball of light flickered and sparkled in the air. They backed away, watching it suspiciously.

"What is it?" asked Amaril, standing ready to defend himself.

Keldon squinted. "It resembles a zoa."

"It couldn't be," remarked Biona.

"Look, it is changing!" said Sindle.

The glowing sphere of light unfolded into the seven colors of the rainbow and then took on the shape of a person.

"Who are you?" Sindle asked.

A voice spoke. "Do you not recognize me?"

Gradually, the face became clearer.

Sindle couldn't believe his eyes. "Grandfather?" He felt in his pocket for the stone, but it was missing. "Grandfather! Is it really you?" Sindle rushed over, embraced, and kissed him.

Dargad's face filled with fear when he saw Wizdor, and he started to leave the room.

"Halt there, Dargad," he said. Dargad stopped dead in his tracks and waited to hear words of chastisement. "Come here," Wizdor commanded.

Dargad walked over and fell at his feet. "Please, Wizdor, forgive me."

"I no longer remember deeds of darkness very well," said Wizdor. "Those deeds are becoming ever dimmer as the light of goodness grows ever brighter."

"You must not see much of me then," said Dargad.

"On the contrary," said Wizdor. "I see a spark of goodness—if only you could manage to fan it into a flame."

Tears welled up in Dargad's eyes.

"Wizdor, what's happened to you?" asked Sindle. "Your clothes—your face—everything about you has changed."

"I am no longer a Shade," he replied. "I have become a Reflection. We all in time must put away these garments of the shadow world and don the new robes of Lux Aeternum. I once wore robes of bondage and darkness. I now wear robes of freedom and light. The scintilla of my soul is no longer confined in Finsterna's cold, dark prison. The Captain has set me free.

Others sacrificed to Finsterna have been released from her grasp also. They are dwelling with the Telarch in Lux Aeternum. I can see them from where I stand even now."

"But how can that be? asked Sindle. "You are still here with us, and we can't see the others."

"I have been allowed to appear to you from the world beyond," said Wizdor. "In time, you will see the others too."

"I don't see how that is possible," Sindle remarked.

"The Captain tried to explain to you about the region beyond Spectara where all things are one, but you didn't understand. I suppose you really can't until it happens to you. Didn't you ever figure out who the Captain really was?"

They gave each other a puzzled look.

"The Seventh Archon?" Sindle commented. "The Emissary of Light."

"You're right, of course," said Wizdor. ""He took the place of Zil Magnus, since Zil never went in to help the other Archons defeat the power of Finsterna. But he was more than an Archon, and more than an Emissary of Light. Not only was he a Shade like us, but he also was and is the Telarch of Light himself who came into Spectara disguised as a Shade to reconnect the inhabitants of Spectara with the Light that shines beyond Arete Vitrea."

"Impossible," Amaril stated. "How can the Telarch become a Shade without contaminating his Light with darkness?"

"The Telarch can do anything he wishes," stated Wizdor, "even become a Shade without diminishing his light. The Captain was a Shade, yes, but he also was and is the Telarch who reigns in Lux Aeternum. Now he has brought the Light that shines beyond Arete Vitrea to the very heart of darkness. I know it is true. I saw it all!"

"But the Trogzars sacrificed him to Finsterna," Keldon remarked. "How could he have survived?"

"He both did not, and did, survive."

"What kind of double talk is that?" asked Amaril.

"He did not survive, and yes, he did survive. He did die. When they blinded the Captain and threw him into the Sea, he wandered through the mazes of darkness that led to Finsterna's abode. She tried with all her power to freeze the spark within him, but he would not let her do it until he could confront her face to face. When he finally reached her domain, she was enraged.

'Fool,' she said. 'Why have you come?'

'To restore and recreate Spectara,' he answered.

'You do not like my improvements?' she asked.

'I have come for the keys to Arete Vitrea,' said he. 'They do not belong to you. Hand them over.'

'Trifle with me not,' she warned. 'Who do you think you are?

'The Seventh Archon,' he told her. 'Who else could have entered this place?'

She accused him of lying. 'You are not Zil Magnus.'

'True, I am not,' he replied.

'Then who are you?' she demanded to know.

Then he told her. 'I am he who dwells beyond Arete Vitrea.'

'The Telarch of Light?' she answered, and then laughed at him.

'How else could I have entered your abode of darkness without being frozen? If you know, tell me.'

She had no reply. Then it dawned on her that he really was the Telarch.

'So you *are* who you say,' she said. 'Have you come to torment me? Were not the other Archons enough? Have you come to inflict more pain after my centuries of agony? Fool! Now that I am free, I suppose you think you can restrain me again. I won't let you! Now I shall have my long-awaited revenge.'

'If revenge is what you really want,' he said, 'then take it.'

His willingness to let her so easily have her revenge made her all the more furious. Like a spider, she wrapped her web of freezing darkness around him and injected him with her venom.

'So you thought you could sneak into my realm disguised as a Shade, did you?' she ranted. 'What utter stupidity! A mere Shade has no power over me. I am the Queen of Shades.'

She injected him again with her venom until he could no longer move.

'Look at you now, weakling!' she scoffed. 'You are no match for me. How do you expect to harm me?'

The Captain writhed with anguish, and Finsterna knew the pain she was causing him.

'Ha!' she said with delight. 'Is your suffering too great to bear?'

'It is great,' he said. 'But the pain I bear is not only my own. It is your pain and the pain of all Spectara I feel as well. Do you not understand that in destroying me, you will also destroy yourself?'

The Captain's words drove her mad. 'I would gladly do that to destroy you,' she howled. Then she injected her final dose of venom, and he died," said Wizdor. "But in doing this, Finsterna also died."

"I don't understand," Amaril remarked. "Why did the Captain have to die to destroy her?"

"Finsterna had turned into a vampire. She fed upon destruction—not only the destruction that she caused, but the destruction others caused, as well. Because of this, the Telarch of Light was faced with a dilemma. If he were to destroy Finsterna through force, he would feed her power all the more. The greater the power he might try to use, the greater *her* power would become. That is why he had to die. In his death was a kind of power she did not understand, a power she could not fathom. In destroying the Captain, she destroyed the very host she fed on. Without the Light to feed on, the parasite of darkness could no longer thrive. The host died, true, but when he died, the parasite also died."

"So the Telarch didn't destroy her," said Keldon. "She destroyed herself?"

"Yes. His shadow form was like the worm, and Finsterna, like the greedy fish that went for it. When she took the bait, she was caught upon the hook of Light hidden beneath the bait."

"So Veronica was not the Fish-Faced Queen, Finsterna was!" exclaimed Sindle. "And the Captain caught her just as he did the fish on Marus Lazul!" He rolled with laughter.

"Yes, my dear Sindle," Wizdor replied. "I'm sorry my old fables about Veronica misled you. Now we really know who 'Old Fish-Face' was, don't we? Remember, too, that the Captain's true name was Regius Pisces. Do you not know what that means?"

"No," replied Sindle.

"It means *Fisher King* of all things! Now isn't that interesting?"

Amaril, still doubting, walked over to the window and drew back the curtains. "Tell us. If the Light has come into Spectara, then why does this darkness remain?"

"The darkness isn't evil in itself. The Telarch had a plan for darkness just as he did for light. That's why he made Spectara. He wanted its inhabitants to choose freely between light and darkness. He did not want to force anyone to choose light, for such a choice would have had no meaning."

Amaril peered out of the window. "Listen to the Trogzars shouting." He cracked open the front door.

"Why are they so excited?" Sindle asked

"Shhh, listen," Amaril returned. "They're saying that all the buildings of frozen light are melting."

The Companions looked at the walls of Dargad's house. What the Trogzars were saying was true! Liquid light was dripping from the walls and collecting into puddles on the floor.

"They're melting because Finsterna's power has been destroyed," said Wizdor. "She no longer controls darkness. Her power to freeze light has been exhausted forever."

"Listen to them!" said Amaril, continuing to watch. "Why are they so happy?"

"They don't know Finsterna's reign has come to an end," remarked Wizdor. "The Trogzars always opposed light-freezing. They think that the melting of the buildings is a sign of Finsterna's triumph, not a sign of her defeat."

"Extraordinary," exclaimed Keldon.

As they watched from the door, they heard a Trogzar running through the streets, proclaiming, "Asdin is melting! The age of darkness has come! Long live Finsterna!"

"You're right," Sindle said to Wizdor. "They believe she's still alive. But can what they say about Asdin be true? I thought that the Star would never melt."

"The melting of the Star means that the Telarch of Light has penetrated the very heart of darkness. What they say *is* true."

"This reminds me of the dream I had on the shores of Marus Lazul," Sindle told Wizdor. "Servants of the Fish-Faced Queen were taking you on a death barge to her volcanic island to serve as one of her slaves. Prince Neblas asked her what she intended to do with the Star. 'Bring it forth,' she said, 'and I shall dissolve it.' I had no idea the Star would really melt."

"Shhh! Someone is coming!" warned Amaril. "He's headed this way."

Dargad trembled. "Shut the door!"

Suddenly, Wizdor changed back into a ball of light. "Wizdor, what's happening to you?" exclaimed Sindle.

"My time is up. I can no longer remain here."

"No! Please don't go!" Without a further word, the ball of light faded and disappeared. Then a horrible thought struck Sindle. He recalled the withering image of his grandfather in Queen Veronica's fountain. Could this be another of Finsterna's deceptions? Could she still be alive? Zoella took Sindle by the hand and tried to comfort him. At just that moment, someone knocked at the door, and their hearts raced. "Don't answer it," whispered Keldon.

The knock came again. "There's no use hiding," said Amaril. "They know we're here."

"Quiet!" Keldon whispered.

"Maybe it's not a Trogzar," said Dargad. "They don't make a habit of knocking. They usually break in without warning."

"Who else could it be?" asked Keldon.

The knock came a third time, and they heard low whistling. Their eyes widened. "That's not just any tune," said Sindle, his face lighting up. "It's the Captain! Don't just stand there, open the door and let him in!"

Dargad opened it and peeked outside. "It is the Captain!" he shouted. He pulled open the door and jerked the Captain inside.

"You are alive!" exclaimed Sindle.

"Yes," he said.

"I can't believe it."

"Could it be an apparition?" Amaril surmised with a look of distrust.

"Look closely at him," whispered Keldon. "Does he look like an apparition?" Biona and Zoella had walked up to him, had each taken one of his hands, and were feeling of him to be sure they were not dreaming.

"Captain, we have seen Wizdor," Sindle informed him. "He was just here, but his appearance was unusual."

"He is a Reflection now," said the Captain.

"But Captain, you're still a Shade."

"True."

Sudden shock bolted across Amaril's face. It seemed something was wrong with the Captain's eyes. "You are blind," he observed.

"Yes," said the Captain. "But the Light cannot be destroyed so easily. I now see by the eyes of the one who dwells beyond Arete Vitrea."

"What about your own eyes?" asked Keldon.

"Finsterna's dark fire now burns in them. It had to be this way. Otherwise, the Light would not have absorbed the powers of darkness that had corrupted the peoples of Spectara."

"Are you saying Finsterna is now part of you?" asked Amaril.

"Her rage could not be stopped. It could only be contained. Now it will burn forever, but it will be contained always within my blinded eyes. They have absorbed her power."

"You let her contaminate you with her evil?" asked Amaril.

"I have not been contaminated," answered the Captain. "The fullness of Light is still in me."

"But how can you let her be part of you without being swayed by her evil?"

"The Telarch of Light made the darkness when he made Spectara. He therefore can endure the hell of darkness Finsterna created."

"But why does the Telarch have to do that?" asked Amaril. "Does he enjoy torturing himself?"

"It was the only way to fulfill the Zanthan prophecy—to open the way through Arete Vitrea to the people of the three lands. The people of Spectara had allowed her power of darkness to become a part of them."

Amaril frowned. "Not Zanthis, surely. It was not under her spell. At least not until the very end."

"You are wrong, Amaril. Zanthis, too, has been infected for many lumnus-years."

"Zanthis was the Land of Truth!"

"During the time of Lucia, yes, but it has been under the spell of Finsterna since the wars of the Queens."

"What?"

"Your people responded with hatred against the Pyrathans and their Queen. What the Zanthans did not realize was that this hatred was both spawned by her and nourished her. Had Lucia lived, she would have shown you the error of your ways. Through the centuries, Finsterna has fed upon the hatred she bred within Zanthis and other places. Although the Zanthans clung to the ideal of truth, this one lie blinded them, contaminating and perverting their wisdom. That was the lie that hatred and even the destruction of other people are right if they are done in the name of truth and justice. Did you know that the Pyrathans tried to settle again in Pyrath after Finsterna's power was quelled?"

"I've heard it was so," said Amaril.

"The Zanthans refused to allow the Pyrathans to resettle there."

"Our ancestors were right not to let that evil lot return, especially after what they had done."

"The decision was understandable but unwise. It meant the people of Pyrath had to settle by the Sea of Darkness where they would have to listen to the voice of Finsterna through the centuries. You must realize it was Zanthis who drove Pyrath into the land of lies."

"I'm glad Viridia was not affected by Finsterna's spell," Keldon stated.

"Viridia was affected, too," stated the Captain. "But it took a different form there. Viridia was as tolerant as Zanthis was intolerant. Viridia accepted too easily the evils that multiplied in Zil-Kenøth. More than once, Viridia had the chance to direct the Kenøthian people in the ways of truth and peace, but Viridia chose to remain detached. She was afraid her stable way of life might be upset, and afraid of how the citizens of Zil-Kenøth might react. So she held her tongue. She stood by while the fruit of evil in Zil-Kenøth ripened over the centuries. So you see, the only way that the path through Arete Vitrea could be opened up was for the Telarch himself to absorb her darkness. Now that he has done so, it will be possible to absorb the darkness from everyone in Spectara as well."

"And when will this happen?" asked Sindle. "Earlier, we heard the Trogzars running through the streets shouting that Finsterna had triumphed. They think she still lives."

"It will take time to convince them. Some will never believe, because they, like Finsterna, are too far gone. Others will lose their fascination with the darkness once they discover it has lost its power. Then some will turn to the Light."

"But why don't you go and prove to them that you have destroyed the power of darkness forever?" asked Amaril.

"You and the others have seen it. That is enough. You must tell them. There is much to be done in Zanthis, Amaril. The sacred fire must be rekindled so that it shall forever burn crimson, blue, and gold."

"Then shall we journey beyond Arete Vitrea?"

"I thought Wizdor told you. The Light that dwells beyond Arete Vitrea is now here among you. There is no need to journey there now."

"And what of the future of Viridia," asked Keldon.

"You and Biona must return. Now that the curse of Finsterna is ended, the plague will lose its power to destroy. Even now, Keldon, the branch of the Verdis tree that you planted has begun to bud again. You and Biona must return to tell the Viridians why it is happening."

"And Zoella will know how to teach people the Vernesdan way," remarked Keldon.

"There will be no need now to teach the people the Vernesdan way," said the Captain. "Now that Finsterna has been defeated, the old ways will no longer be profitable. Besides, I think that Zoella and Sindle have something else in mind."

Sindle looked at Zoella and smiled. "Shall I tell them, Zoella?" She nodded. "Zoella and I are to be married."

Biona and Keldon looked shocked and surprised.

"We discussed it secretly," Sindle told them. "But we agreed that we could not marry as long as Spectara lay in the grip of tragedy. Now that Finsterna has been defeated by the Captain, there's nothing left to stop us." Sindle and Zoella embraced and kissed.

A light went on in Biona's eyes. "This is the most wonderful news I've heard in a long time." She began weeping for joy. "What a happy lumen-flow this is. Imagine it, Keldon. Now Sindle will be our kin!"

"Excellent," smiled Keldon. "This is truly a lumen-flow of new beginnings!"

"I wonder, Biona," interrupted Amaril. "Do you and Zoella have other sisters?"

"Amaril!" Biona scolded, laughing. "I *am* sorry, but no. We are only two. But come with us to Viridia." They chuckled. "After all, there are other followers of the Vernesdan way whose vows have been annulled. Isn't that right, Zoella?"

She nodded.

"I'm ready now," smiled Amaril. "When shall we go?"

Everyone laughed.

"What do you think, Captain?" said Biona. "Won't Sindle and Zoella make a lovely pair?"

"Yes. But they must not remain in Zil-Kenøth. They must journey to Violinda and make a new world. More refugees will be coming there and victims of the plague will be returning from Viridia. There the Companions of the Quest will grow in numbers, and the land of dusk will become a land of dawn."

"But what about the Trogzars?" asked Sindle. "Who will convince them of the error of their ways?"

Dargad spoke up. "They do trust me, you know. I may do some good."

"I'm sure you shall," said the Captain. "But be shrewd. Most will not believe that the Seventh Archon lives until they learn Finsterna is no more. Many will journey to the heart of darkness in search of her. Those who give up and return may listen to your words. But those who do not will be lost to the mazes of darkness forever. Like Prince Neblas and the Grand Inquisitor, they will travel to the regions beyond hope and not want to return. Even now, Neblas and the Grand Inquisitor have made a terrible choice. They have tried to offer themselves as a sacrifices to Finsterna, not realizing that she has ceased to exist. Out of gratitude for what they think she has done, they have used the Zarafat of Zil Magnus to pierce their hearts!"

Sindle remembered the words Wizdor had spoken to the Grand Inquisitor on that terrible lumen when Wizdor was sacrificed to the Sea of Darkness. "By your sword, too, shall your heart be pierced!" The words had echoed through Sindle's head many times. Now, at last, the words Wizdor spoke had come to pass.

"And what will you do, Captain?" asked Amaril.

"The time has come for my departure," said the Captain, changing into a reflection. "I must return to Lux Aeternum to welcome all who will be transformed from Shades into Reflections. When your work in Spectara is finished, you will join me there." His body became robed in iridescent colors, and his face radiated light. But in his eyes the horrible dark fire of Finsterna's wrath still burned. Keldon suddenly remembered the vision he had in the Groves of Ameth and realized it was now coming true.

Then the Captain changed into a sphere of light. In the center of the sphere was a black sword, the sword of Finsterna's darkness. It had pierced the Captain's soul but had not been able to destroy it. When Sindle saw the sphere with the dark sword at the center, he at once recognized it to be the symbol the Trogzars had set up in front of Wizdor's lodgings on that lumen-ebb after Prince Neblas had stolen the Sacred Star. The ball of light soon faded and vanished. "Remember that the Telarch who dwells in Lux Aeternum has absorbed the darkness of Spectara so that he may overcome it," they heard the Captain say. "Now it is your task to be emissaries of Light." Suddenly, the wind blew the door open and a warm breeze filled the room.

"We had best leave this place," said Dargad. "The frozen light is melting so quickly the house might collapse."

They ventured into the street. Everywhere, puddles of liquid light evaporated into a dense, bright fog.

"It reminds me of lumen-flow in Chartra," said Biona, taking a deep breath. "What an excellent occasion for a wedding."

Everyone laughed.

"Look!" said Sindle, pointing in the direction of Spectara. "A rainbow!"

Smiles appeared on their faces. Amaril remembered the rainbow bridge he had seen vanish at the feet of the Crystal Mountains. "Could it be that the prophecies of Zanthis are being fulfilled at last? Is the way past Arete Vitrea truly opening up for the people of the three lands?"

"It must be true," said Sindle. "The Captain has brought Lux Aeternum to our shadow world. He has joined Spectara to his one Light. Long live the Captain."

"Long live the Captain," they all replied.

THE END